INGRID BORGES

Resilient

A story about courage and friendship

Ingrid Borges

Credits

Author: Ingrid Borges
Edition: Yasmín Rodríguez

Book Cover illustration: thenetmencorp.com
Ms. Borges' portrait: Jaime Franco, photographer

This is a book of fiction. Names, characters, places, and incidents
are either the product of the author's imagination or are used
fictitiously. Any resemblance to actual persons, living or dead,
business establishments, events, or locales is entirely
coincidental.

Library of Congress Control Number: 2012915412
ISBN-13: 978-0985740405

DEDICATION

I used to tell stories to my one and only beloved son. He told me many times to write them down. This is for him; he has always been my number one inspiration.

CONTENTS

	Acknowledgments	1
1	Introduction	3
2	How It All Began	13
3	Change	23
4	Remodeling Inside-out	41
5	The New Man	51
6	The Best Birthday Gift	61
7	The Day After	73
8	Business Travel	93
9	The Caribbean	109
10	Surrender in Paradise	135
11	Back Home	151
12	New Beginnings	173
13	The Engagement Party	189
14	The Weddings	207
15	The Big Move	229
16	The Franchises	241
17	The In-laws	251
18	Babies	273
19	Five Years Later	281
20	A Change of Destiny	303
21	Life Goes On	317
22	Moving On	329
23	Resilience	345
	About the author	355

ACKNOWLEDGMENTS

I had wanted to write a novel for a long time.
What finally inspired me to follow that goal was a
gentleman writer I met some time ago while traveling in
an airplane. He told me the secret to writing a book is to
sit in front of the keyboard for two hours a day, no
matter what. I did it, and he was right.
I'm sorry I never got his name.

I also would like to acknowledge the valuable advice I
received from my good friend Frank Suárez. A writer
himself, he steered me in the right direction when I
needed to decide whether to self-publish or not.

I want to say "thank you" to my editor and friend,
Yasmín Rodríguez. I used to admire her vitality,
wittiness and spark when I saw her giving presentations
many years ago. Destiny pushes and pulls at me the
most when I'm traveling, since I found Yasmín in
another airport after years of not seeing each other.
We got to talk and I discovered she was in the
copywriting and editing business. I knew right then and
there she was the team player I had been searching for.
She became the driving force that got me to finally
publish the novel I wrote a few years ago.

Finally, I want to thank my 99 year-old mother.
From her, I learned resilience.
She taught me when things go wrong, you may cry for a
day or two, but then the show must go on.

 # 1 INTRODUCTION

"You want us to sell the London flat? But it is the absolute worst time to sell!"

Diana was fuming.

The brownstones' backyard was the perfect setting for the party. The balmy, humid breeze marked another splendid cool summer evening in Manhattan. Yet Marie Terre's face was transformed by worry. It was very difficult for her to accept this was the farewell party for her kids to go away to College. Brenda kept on wringing her hands, her worries and embarrassment written all over her.

Diana said. "That flat is the only property we still own in England. Only a year ago the real estate market was booming, but now it's a seller's nightmare." Then, with reproach, she looked at Brenda. "Why did you make investments without consulting with me first?"

Brenda looked away. "The investments were suggested by a broker at the bank where I work."

Marie Terre understood what Brenda was going through, and in solidarity she said she would be willing to sell also. Diana was outnumbered. It made her so upset that, unexpectedly, she called her attorneys and had them start drawing up the papers.

This was a touchy subject. The flat had become a symbol of their friendship. It was the act of buying that property that bound them together in the first place, back in the eighties when they all worked for the same bank in London.

Diana had always been the financial genius. Always one step ahead of the trends and the social ins and outs, she had made a name for herself at the bank. This, against her family's wishes, who wanted her to capitalize on her royal lineage instead of her brains. She was sure of herself, and always knew what she wanted. Like when she decided to meet Marie Terre, the nice petite that made the same long commute on the bus after work. She just went over to her and presented herself.

Marie Terre, in the other hand, had been an emotional pillar for her piers, her family, and her closest friends. A daughter of Cuban immigrants, she had been raised to be a kind creature, grateful for all the little things that made her life complete. However, underneath her kindness there was an iron will, and an unwavering goal to do what's right. She had been very pleased to make Diana's acquaintance. She just loved meeting people and having a good time.

Brenda, the insecure one, had such a poor self-image and attitude that when they first met her, a friendship was not even considered. But what she lacked in self-confidence, she more than made up with intelligence, candor, and a admirable desire to better herself.

The three co-workers started an unlikely friendship because they bought that flat together, and for two decades afterwards had been inseparable.

George observed their long faces from the other side of the room, with sympathy. He knew that look on his wife's face. He walked over to them. "Settle whatever is going on in private, and remember this is a celebration, not a funeral. Why don't you go to the library and start counting your blessings?"

Diana was still too upset to comply.

"Brenda, why don't you tell us all, including my dear George, the reason you want to sell the flat? I just want to have his input on the subject. Afterwards I promise, George, I will go into the library."

Brenda could not hide her guilt. "I have lost most of my savings in the stock market, and I need the money to send Teresa to a boarding school in the UK or a finishing school somewhere in Europe. Teresa has gotten out of hand; sometimes she is even slimy. My daughter is so beautiful, many of the tenants in our apartment building in Puerto Rico have told me about cool cars with young teenage boys that cruise the building to get a glance at her.

Even the security guard told me he heard Teresa tell four different boys that she loved only them and they were the only ones in her life. He told me because he is worried if any of the other boys find out what she's doing, it could turn out to be a very dangerous situation, especially among Latin men.

Teresa is havoc to live with. If I say yes she says no, she does not respect my rules. I can't ask her father for moral support, because he just wants her to live with him in the Dominican Republic. He keeps on telling her that she should not live so far away from him. Every time he hears her complaining about me, he suggest she could live with him.

This is why I need to find a very prestigious finishing school that would impress him so much he could not refuse to let her go."

Marie Terre confirmed what Brenda had just said. "One day my own son Philip told me he thinks Teresa needs to get her act together. She is too much of a flirt, and it is damaging her reputation, but what she does not realize is that it could easily get her in big problems with some guys."

George told Brenda: "I would love to help you, but I have most of my assets tied up with a new venture. And I had not counted on paying for Philip's tuition, room, and board until a year from now."

Diana was very sorry. "And against my own will, George has also kept my family in the lifestyle they have always ambitioned. Just recently he had to bail my brother Harry out of some financial difficulties. With his financial support his family developed a small village with lovely houses for his brothers and their families, but that is also another burden in our finances."

George interrupted Diana. "I will talk with my financial comptroller, and see how they could include Teresa's finishing school into the budget." He walked away to let the friends talk in private.

The three friends looked at each other, and slowly made their way into the house as Diana had promised.

There was a lot to talk about, and as they got comfortable in the well-known surroundings of Diana's library, they remembered how it all came to be.

2 HOW IT ALL BEGAN

That Friday night at the pub Diana and Marie Terre were having a great time when they noticed Brenda; she was a bank teller that made the same commute they did. The young woman had too much to drink. Brenda was big: about 100 kilos with red pimples all over her face. She had a perm so bad, you could see some bald spots in the front of her head. Her natural red hair was showing under the blond hair dye that had turned orange from too many badly administered chemicals. She practically had no chin, and it looked even worse because of her large hook nose and the thick eyeglasses hanging from it. Her green eyes were bloodshot from too much alcohol. She seemed like an easy prey.

She walked over to them. "Hi, I am Brenda; we work for the same bank". Diana and Marie Terre both said hi, but did not start a conversation with her. The situation was uncomfortable, so Brenda just said "Cheery Oh!" and walked to the other side of the pub.

Diana and Marie Terre did not think of themselves as snobs, but their reaction was very snobbish.

As usual, Marie Terre talked first. "It would be nice if we could let her know she needs to control her alcohol drinking."

"And her diet." Diana replied. They both looked sad and changed the subject.

The Monday after this encounter Marie Terre and Diana saw Brenda in the train, but she was shying away from them. They felt guilty for the way they treated her at the pub.

Mary Terre turned to Diana. "She works for the same bank we do, and now that she is not drinking I think we should talk to her". Reluctantly, without saying a word Diana said yes by shaking her head. They walked over to Brenda.

"Hi Brenda, I'm Marie Terre. Sorry we did not get to meet you the other night. Where are you from, and how long have you been working for the bank?"

With a shy grin, Brenda started to talk. She let them know she came from a very small village where parents made their kids eat potpies practically every day; food was their way of showing their love for the children. Once she started to talk to Diana and Marie Terre she couldn't stop.

As a small child she had been sent to boarding schools that had no heating system. When the children got up in the mornings it was so cold she and her classmates had to scrape the ice from inside the windows. This always made her think of her childhood as cold and lacking affection. She complained so much about this boarding school that her parents sent her to another one that had a fireplace. The fireplace was very high up so the children would not burn themselves. She recalled the children would get close to the wall where the fireplace was, and would bring their arms up to get some heat from the fire, but to her it seemed like the cold was inside her bones. She would fall asleep crying because of the cold. These memories made her long for warmth. One of her dreams was to visit sunny Spain, where she knew people went on vacation during the winter to warm up.

Both Diana and Marie Terre were astounded by the openness and sincerity this total stranger showed them. This was certainly a humbling experience.

That afternoon an American lady walked in the bank and wanted to talk with someone from Investment Banking. Diana attended her at her desk. With a worried expression in her face and in her tone of voice, Mrs. Morgan explained her situation.

"I have inherited a flat from my uncle. The flat is located about two and a half blocks away from this bank. I went to see it just now and it is in deplorable conditions. I took a real estate agent with me; she says the flat needs to be fixed before she can make the place marketable. However, I can't stay in the UK until that happens! My husband and children need me in the USA as soon as possible. Also, I would not even know how to begin fixing the place up. The real estate agent told me that in today's market, if I fix the flat, I could get about 150,000 pounds for it because of its size and location. In the states I have accounts in one of your branches, and the people form Investment Banking usually know investors ready to jump on a good investment. I am willing to let it go for 100,000 pounds as is. But it would have to be a cash transaction. That way I can transfer the money to the USA before I leave."

Diana though about it. "At this precise moment I do not know of anyone that would like to invest in the purchasing of a flat, but early tomorrow morning I will contact some investors as well as the Mortgage department, explain the situation, and see what they suggest." It was already 5:30pm and Diana did not want to miss the 6:00pm train, so she told Mrs. Morgan she would call her back the next morning.

Diana barely made it to the train station on time. Marie Terre questioned her lateness, and got Mrs. Morgan's story.

"It would be nice if we could buy the place ourselves, and this American lady is so desperate that we could probably get the flat for much less than one hundred thousand pounds. The only problem is that the mortgage department takes about a month to qualify us, plus the fact that we haven't been a full year working with the bank and most mortgages require at least one year at your present job".

Marie Terre knew a lot about the bank's internal policies. "As bank employees one of our benefits is to get a personal loan for 25K pounds each. I could start the paperwork early tomorrow next morning and it would take less than a day or two to get the money. The beauty of it is they only take out 400 pounds a month off your paycheck. But even if we did get the loan the fact of the matter is that we still need another 50K."

You could almost see Diana's wheels turning. "Let's speculate that Mrs. Morgan would accept 75K pounds for the flat; we would only need another twenty five thousand pounds."

That's when they saw Brenda half asleep in a corner seat. Diana's investment education started to work real fast. She told Marie Terre that Mrs. Morgan sounded so desperate she may take the 75K pounds if she could get it in a few days. "Maybe Brenda would be willing to get in the deal with us."

Marie Terre hesitated. "We don't know her that well, and buying a flat is a serious matter."

Without taking her eyes off of Brenda, Diana added: "In business school the first thing they teach you is to work with OPM: Other People's Money. Now we are speculating, so let's see what happens."

They both decided this was the opportunity of a lifetime and they really needed to try to make it work out some way or another. They walked over to Brenda and invited her to the pub.

Brenda was totally surprised but delighted to have the two lovely ladies from work invite her to the pub. However, she was suspicious. She knew she was fat, ugly, and shy, which is why no one in college would be her friend. The only way she was able to get a man in bed was if they were both drunk. This had made her a very lonely and sad person.

She tried to improve her looks by dying her hair blond. Then she had red roots, and it started to look orange. She also had several bold spots because of the bad perm, which made her look worse than she did with her straight red hair.

She graduated Magna Cum Laude, but the only job she could find was as a bank teller. Her productivity was so outstanding that same morning she had been informed that, starting the next Monday, she was to be promoted to head teller supervising all of the others. She got a promotion and two of her co-workers were inviting her to the pub the same day. Brenda decided this was a good omen: her life would never be sad, dull and lonely again.

When Brenda arrived at the pub her new friends were already there. The ladies explained what the plans were. Brenda was one hundred percent interested in the project.

That night they could not sleep. Each one of them kept on thinking about their reasons for wanting to buy this flat. Marie Terre never thought about buying a flat with friends. She figured that when somebody proposed, she and her new fiancé would look together for a place to live. She was used to consulting her parents before making mayor decisions, and this was a very big commitment that made her feel like calling them right away. She liked being Diana's friend and having her approval. It felt childish to even consider asking her parents for their advice. Instead, she concentrated on how her life would change if they got the flat near the office; she would have three additional hours per day to do other things such as exercise, go to the theater, or just sleep an additional hour in the morning. Thinking about these things convinced her: this was the correct thing to do.

Brenda was very excited to be included in the purchase of the flat. Her heart swelled with positive thoughts and there was a lot of courage in her spirit. She believed these ladies where sincere and candid. To think of them as her friends filled her with warm feelings that lifted her spirit. It felt like her life was going for a big and wonderful adventure at last.

More than anything in the world Diana wanted to make it on her own. The purchase of the flat would represent a big profit within a year or two. By placing their money in one pot and helping each other out now, eventually they would each have sufficient equity for a down payment on their own individual flats. This would take years to accomplish if they were to try and do it individually.

Before Mrs. Morgan arrived at the bank the next morning, all three friends had applied for the personal loan. They took their lunch break early and went to see the flat; it was a 12-minute walk from the bank. As soon as they walked in the musty smell overwhelmed them. It was dark, dirty and cluttered with antique furniture. They inspected the one large bedroom and a smaller one that must have been used as maid's quarters in the past. The kitchen was very large and separated from the dining and living rooms. The bathroom had an antique claw tub and before that door there was another one that led to what could have been a laundry room. However, right now it was an airy room with a concrete floor. The large bedroom has a small balcony with mosaic floors, and most of them were missing. It overlooked a small garden with overgrown trees in need of tender loving care. The living room had a big stone fireplace and built-in wooden cabinets that were piled with clutter, books and old figurines. Marie Terre started to sneeze from all the dust.

Diana looked at her two friends and started to whisper. "The flat has great bones to it and it's all about location. With a little work it will be a lovely place to live in."

They shook their heads in agreement.

Diana made Mrs. Morgan an offer for seventy five thousand pounds and all three of them crossed their fingers. Mrs. Morgan stared at them with disbelief. Before she could say a word, Diana pointed out her options.

"You can go to the Mortgage department and see if someone there can find a client that wants to pay cash for the flat. You could wait for someone to get a mortgage; the standard procedure takes about a month. Or, you could place an ad in the newspaper and request a cash sale of the flat. With us you will get your money in cash and you do not have to pay commission to a real estate broker".

Mrs. Morgan's first impulse was to get up and leave, but out of politeness explained that she needed some time to think about the offer and consult with her family. That evening she called her husband in the USA. He had not been to work because one of the children needed to have her tonsils removed and he needed his wife back in the states before the operation. Trying to be calm and collected he asked her to start thinking about the situation.

"I am running out of vacation days at work, and if you add the amount of money I will not be making, or the cost of a nurse for the baby after the operation, it doesn't make sense. Even another trip to the UK, adding hotel, taxis, phone calls, and food expenses are costs we cannot afford. More important is the speculation of finding another buyer. These ladies are the only ones that made a serious offer, but it's up to you. If it were up to me, I would take the money and run back home."

Within two days Mrs. Morgan was on her way to the USA with a transfer into her savings account of more than seventy five thousand US dollars. Everyone was happy.

3 CHANGE

The entire week was full of excitement. Diana made them all a budget. They had been paying over 600 pounds each for the flat they had in the outskirts of London, plus an average of 12 pounds a day for the commuting. Now they would be paying 400 each for their personal loans, about 50 pounds each for building maintenance, and another 50 pounds each for utilities. This would give each of them a savings of more than 390 pounds per month. Diana explained that if they agreed, she could take the savings and invest them in order to make a profit.

What made them the happiest was they could sleep until 8:00a.m. if they wanted to. Marie Terre suggested they could save even more money if they had breakfast and lunch at the house. She volunteered to cook the meals. Brenda volunteered to do the laundry.

Diana did not want to volunteer cleaning up because the

task seemed too overwhelming. "First we need to move to this place and make it feel like home." That weekend they packed their clothes. None of them had any furniture. Their commute to London was filled with laughter, giggles and fun.

They took two taxis from the train station to the flat, one full of luggage. George, the building superintendent, came running to help them with the bags. He was a tall, muscular, handsome man with dark blue eyes and dirty blond hair. He was very happy to see two lovely young women move into this old, dilapidated, smelly building. He did not even notice Brenda.

George came from a hard working family whose only ambition was putting food on the table. They had lots of family reunions, when money was available. But George wanted more. He wanted to make something of himself. He enrolled in night school and became a carpenter, a plumber, an electrician, and was working all the part time jobs he could find.

George came running to the taxi, where there were about nine or ten pieces of luggage. "Hi! I am George, the superintendent of the building. It would be my pleasure to help the ladies carry their bags to the flat." All three ladies accepted his help.

Diana had the keys to the front door of the flat, and as she opened it a grotesque foul smell impregnated the hallway. Immediately, George said: "Allow me to open the windows to clear the air." He tried several times, but they were sealed together. "I will be back with a screwdriver and a hammer to unseal the windows."

The ladies waited for George outside of the door, and as they stared inside they could see at the end of the living room the massive amount of dark red drapery covering some French windows that went from the high ceiling to the floor. George came back to the flat with his tools and tried several times to open the windows to no avail, so he opened the door that went to the little terrace in the back. He walked back to the ladies and explained: "If you spend the night here with all this dust you could all get ill. The flat needs to be ventilated and it's going to take me some time to get the windows open." The ladies agreed but started to look at each other questioning where they could stay for the night. George was very intuitive and when he noticed this, his generous country boy's soul took over.

"I remodeled a flat on the fourth floor of this building for a couple of North Americans, and it has the same dimensions as this one. The US people left the UK two days ago. They usually come back every other month and I am in charge of cleaning and fixing the flat whenever they get back. I can let you stay in that flat only if you promise to leave everything in its place and clean it up leaving a good shine."

The ladies could not believe their good luck! Humbly, they followed George to the fourth floor. To their amazement the apartment was very bright and contemporary. The fabulous ceiling-to-floor French windows had no drapes. The mosaic in the little balcony had been reconditioned. The dining area had a very contemporary, simple but classic dining room set with eight chairs. The two couches in front of the fireplace could also be used as beds

The door that went to the bedrooms and the kitchen had been eliminated as well as the wall that went to the kitchen. It was a wide-open space with a lovely counter and four stools. All the appliances were brand new and they even had a dishwasher and a wine cooler. The counters were in some kind of stone that they later found out was granite.

Half of the old kitchen had been converted into a walk in closet for the small bedroom and the other half for a laundry room, with washer and dryer. The small bedroom had an American full-size bed, two end tables, and a large mirror that made the room look twice its size. A lovely office was built in to the space where the small closet had been. The bathroom was like nothing they had ever seen before. All the walls were covered in some kind of Travertine Marble. The faucets were to die for.

The door that went to what could have been a laundry room in the past had been eliminated. The large bedroom now had a walk in closet in its place as well as another lovely bathroom with the most impressive vanity and storage area. George explained the entire flat had a new air conditioning and heating system, with the central unit in a corner of the small terrace in the back. When the ladies went to see it they noticed a lovely French bistro set. This flat was exactly what they wanted theirs to look like.

George was proud to say that he had done practically all the work himself. He explained that the owners had a U.S.

architect design the remodeling of the flat. The design was easy to read because it had pictures of how the place was supposed to look like. The cost was over one hundred thousand pounds. The ladies looked at each other, with an expression that read: "Where will we get so much money!"

Diana and Marie Terre thanked George for his kindness. Brenda did not say a word, because George had only looked and talked to her friends and not at all to her.

As soon as they closed the door behind George, the ladies started to jump up and down with excitement. The possibilities of making their flat look as splendid as this one was thrilling, even if they did not know how they were to get the money to pay for it.

The ladies had requested two days off from work to settle into their new flat. As soon as they opened their eyes in the lovely remodeled flat where they were staying, they knew how much they wanted theirs to look just like this one. Looking at their surroundings let them realize the amount of work needed on their own. After having an exquisite breakfast they went back into their flat. Immediately Marie Terre started sneezing, her eyes were crying, her nose was running, and a rash developed on her face, hands, and arms.

If the circumstances were not so real, anyone looking from the outside would easily say that Marie Terre was trying to get out of doing her share of work. But it got so bad she called the dermatologist for an urgent appointment. Brenda offered to go with her. Diana said she would talk with George for some advice on how to get started. She wanted to dump most of the furniture so they would have some space to move around.

Dr. Bernard's office was full of patients. Marie Terre had to wait until he saw all the other patients before it was her turn. She and Brenda were the last two people left in the office. The doctor seemed much more interested in Brenda than in her. He gave Marie Terre a prescription, and told her she had a dust allergy. Then he went over to Brenda.

"I can prescribe a regiment of shampoos and facial creams that will get rid of your acne, and your hair will grow back healthy if you follow my instructions. However, I highly recommended that you cut your hair off as short as possible in order to eliminate most of the chemically damaged hair. I am also going to give you a diet to follow. It is very important that you consume more fruits and vegetables and less sweets and processed food". Brenda became Dr. Bernard's patient on the spot. She and Marie Terre went to the drug store to get their prescriptions filled.

In the meantime, Diana had asked George were she could dump the old furniture. He explained the night school he went to for his electrician's, carpenter's, and plumber's license was only a few blocks away. The school had upholstering classes for antique furniture and the students were frequently looking for old furniture to practice with.

"I can take you there myself if you would like. My car is not much – I have an old Fiat I use to carry materials around.

But it will take us there and back. You can make arrangements with the school to have the furniture picked up. Does today at lunchtime work for you?"

"What kind of a public school is it? Is it only for mayor jobs like carpentry and such?

"It is a public high school during the day and a crafts school during the evening. It offers computer courses, sewing, upholstery, carpentry, plumbing, electrical, and installation of mosaics, among others."

"Done. We will go there at noon then."

During his lunch break George took Diana to the school and left her in front of the building while he went to look for a parking space. Diana walked right in. At the Director's office she requested to talk with someone in charge of the night school. She was sent to talk with Mrs. Brady in Human Resources. Mrs. Brady took one look at Diana and immediately started a conversation where, to Diana's amazement, she asked more questions about Diana's career and preparation than explained the schools offerings. Eventually she noticed Diana's questioning look.

"The night school is looking for a director with good organizational and motivational skills. Our teachers are used to the classroom and the school wants more real life experiences for the students. I am going to explain with an example. One of the teachers bought an old Luis IV chair built in 1830 for 50 pounds. She invested another 100 pounds in fabric, re-upholstered it, and then sold the chair for 3,000 pounds to an antique collector.

The students need to get involved in the community, know where they can find these treasures and their worth. They need to visit antique shops and look at the quality of the upholstery, the fabric, and the craftsmanship. The students need to know what their work will be worth in the marketplace. They also need to know their customers and the needs of the UK market. There is lots of money to be made by knowing how to fix up all the old flats in London.

The director's position only pays twenty pounds an hour and the shift is from 6p.m. to 9p.m. from Monday to Friday and from 9a.m. to 3p.m. on Saturdays. One of the fringe benefits is that the students may help the director and the teachers with their own handyman work as part of their training, and we would love to have you."

Diana was astounded, but carefully listened to all she had been told and started to see the possibilities and advantages of the position. She figured that as director she could enroll Marie Terre and Brenda in different courses and have their furniture fixed, sell it, and use that money to fix the flat. She accepted the position as night school director, confident in her ability to convince her roommates. Mrs. Brady was happy to fill her in on all the details. She would start working that same night. Diana was excited about this new venture and what it could mean for her and her friends.

George came inside the building looking for her: he needed

to get back to work. He spotted her leaving one of the offices. She was so happy that when she approached him she hugged and kissed him on both cheeks.

"Thank you so much for bringing me here! Work can be so much fun! Would you please take me to nearby antique shops?"

After feeling her kisses, his face turned very red and he felt a tingling sensation in his stomach. He could not speak clearly, however much he tried, and with a trembling voice said: "I have to get back to work".

After observing George's reactions she felt very flattered. This made her notice him more then she had done so previously. She studied his handsome face, the strong muscular body and his friendly dark blue eyes. Slowly her knees got weak and her hands started to perspire. She said to herself: "This is crazy". She decided her demeanor needed to be composed and proper.

"I am so sorry, please let's get back to the flat".

Neither of them spoke during the four-block ride. When they arrived to the building, Diana was the first to speak.

"I am going to take a taxi to an antique shop. Is there any one in particular you could recommend?"

George felt dumbfounded; he did not want to let her out of

his sight. He wanted to be near her for the rest of his life. But she was a lady and he was a building superintendent. So in a sad tone of voice he said: "No I don't".

During the taxi ride Diana recollected the incident with George. It became evident to her that she was attracted to him. But she had to remind herself how much her parents had struggled to get her presented in society, and yes, she was a lady. She actually did not feel at ease with high society people, they reminded her of the stress her parents had every time they were invited to some event. They could not afford to get new expensive clothes and they could not be seen in department store articles or, God forbid, to be seen in the same clothes they had used last summer. The tension was projected to all the family members. These memories made her tense and she wanted to be as far away from that world as possible, but falling for a commoner was not her ideal future either.

It was almost 6p.m. when Marie Terre and Brenda arrived at the flat. They had no energy to start cleaning up, so they went to the fourth floor flat and were going to take a nap when Diana ran in and started explaining.

"There is a fortune to be made in antique furniture! It is a totally unknown world for us, but we need to start reading and learning more on what the needs of the big city are. I have to run now because I am working as the new director of the night school. I will fill you in with all the details when I get back home after 9p.m."

She was out the door with a great big smile on her lips.

Marie Terre and Brenda looked at each other totally confused, but Diana was out the door before they could ask any questions, of which they had many.

Diana was exhausted and hungry when she arrived at 9:15p.m. The three of them were starving; they all went to the corner deli for sandwiches. Diana finally started explaining the possibilities of fixing old furniture and selling it.

"The profits from these sales will provide the money we need to remodel the flat, just like the one on the fourth floor."

Marie Terre said: "Here go the three hours we were saving from the commuting." Then she gave Diana a big smile. "I will enroll in the upholstery courses."

Brenda's body language let the others know that she did not like the idea very much, but then she said: "Well, this is not going to last forever, so I agree to sign up for the mosaic course."

The next morning Marie Terre took an allergy pill and put on the mask prescribed by the doctor before she entered the flat they had purchased. The first thing they did was to inspect the furniture. Marie Terre saw something she wanted.

"We need the hall stand for ourselves. This tall piece of

furniture with the mirror is fantastic for us to look at and inspect ourselves before we leave the flat and to see what we look like when we arrive. We also need the pegs for our hats and coats and the rack for the umbrellas is great. We can even use the compartment as storage for our boots."

They all agreed. Brenda liked the chiffonier with its high and narrow chest of drawers. Diana said they could probably get lots of money for the sociable; the S shaped sofa designed to seat two persons partially facing each other. The love seats would also sell well. Marie Terre wanted to keep the couch in front of the French windows. Diana inspected it and looked it up in some manuals she had.

"This is a Knoll Barcelona Couch, created by Ludwig Mies van der Rohe for his 1929 Pavilion, at the International Exhibition in Barcelona. The Barcelona pure composition came to optimize modern architecture. Each piece is a tribute to the traditional craftsmanship and meticulous attention to details. In this case the buffed frame and the individual leather squares are carefully welded together." Diana screamed: "We could get as much as nine thousand pound, for this couch alone, and it does not even need to be upholstered!"

Marie Terre started to laugh. "I guess we will not be keeping this one!"

With this information they switched into high gear. All three ladies began to distribute figurines and old books neatly into labeled boxes. Everything they touched was considered a precious possibility. Even the Lorgnette - a pair of eyeglasses or opera glasses with a handle, was treated with special care.

They were taking down the heavy old drapes covering the French window when they saw George working in the overgrown back yard. Marie Terrie waved at him and he waved back. Diana's heart felt a tug when she saw him from behind the window.

Brenda went to the back porch to inspect the mosaic on the floor: more than half of the tiles were missing. George overheard her make a comment about the missing tiles. He could not help himself and shouted from the yard.

"The wind and rain have blown several tiles to the back yard. I didn't know to which flat they belonged so I saved them. I have a bucket full of old tiles. I can bring them upstairs for you to inspect."

Brenda became cheerful and said: "That is fantastic! I can start cleaning the tiles and working with them as if it were a puzzle."

George tried to focus on his conversation with Brenda but was looking at Diana from the corner of his eye.

Diana and Marie Terrie were each standing on a different chair at separate corners of the large window overlooking the back yard. They were removing the old velvet window drapes when George knocked on the door with a bucket full of small tiles. Brenda opened the door and invited him in. As soon as Diana saw him she started to tremble, lost her balance and grabbed on to the dirty, dingy, full of dust, rotten drapes. George saw this and ran to her rescue, grabbing her in mid-air. When he felt her arms around his neck, her heart pounding and her lovely blue eyes, he also lost his balance and both of them fell to the floor. Everyone in the room started laughing: the scene was hilarious. George and Diana stayed embraced a little longer than necessary. They too were laughing but their laughter was more nervous.

Marie Terrie told the group she would get some refreshments. They were all in a festive mood but in need of a break, and the drapes had been taken down faster than anticipated. George wanted to leave but they insisted he stay. During their conversation George mentioned: "The American owners of the flat will not be back to the UK for about another month and a half. You are welcome to use the flat during that time." Marie Terrie asked permission to use the cook wear and the exercise training videos. She promised to take care of everything and leave it as if it had never been touched at all. George did not know what to say, so he agreed.

At 5:45pm all three ladies walked to the night school and got very much involved in their own activities. After their classes they went for a light dinner. They all agreed that more than work, these courses felt like therapy. Time just flew when they were learning these manual skills. Diana was learning a lot about the market and the cost of antiques and remodeling. Brenda said that for the next semester she wanted to get into a course in remodeling old flats. Diana mentioned that George had already done several courses in the school and had also mentioned that he would also like to do the remodeling course. Brenda and Marie Terrie noticed a change of tone in Diana's voice when she mentioned George's name, but opted to ignore it.

Marie Terrie said: "I was thinking about our meals! I would like to get some groceries and start using the slow cooker in the flat. We could save lots of money if we eat our breakfast, lunch, and dinner there. But the biggest advantage would be that I could cook healthy meals, mostly non-fattening. We can also use the exercise videos to exercise before we get to work in the mornings. I know Diana does not need to lose any weight, but you can tell she grew up doing lots of outdoor sports and exercise."

Diana thought about it for a moment. "I agree. Exercise makes me feel better and less tired, and I also know very well the advantages of home-cooked meals. In fact, I think it is very noble of you to offer such an wonderful thing."

Shyly, Brenda said: "I have never been into exercise, but I am grateful to be included, so I agree even if I do not like the idea. I have noticed that since I started this project with the two of you, I can finally button the skirt of my oversize uniform. Actually, I need a new uniform since this one is stained, and losing its color, and it's too tight on me. But, it was a size twenty-two and I did not want to purchase a size twenty-four, so this new approach to life seems like another good idea."

Marie Terre said: "Do not ever agree to anything you do not like." But she was pleased.

Ever since Marie Terrie could remember she had struggled with an extra five, sometimes ten kilos. She loved the idea of having a support group for the exercise and the meals. Staying away from the cafeteria could also steer her away from temptations. They could all eat organic, whole-wheat cereal with skim milk and one half of a banana for breakfast. She would leave a crock cooking in the morning with chicken and vegetables, and another one with white rice. She would also make a big salad and they could eat that for lunch and dinner.

She started to make a list of the different kind of meals she could prepare in the mornings that she could leave in the slow cooker and have ready for lunch. The walk to and from work during lunch would also help in the battle against fat. The next day at 7am she turned on the video with exercise music. The music gave them sufficient time to get out of bed and start warming up to do the exercises. Afterwards Marie Terrie happily fixed breakfast from leftovers, and told everyone her plans to provide only wholesome meals from now on. Since neither Brenda nor Diana wanted to do any cooking, they totally agreed.

Brenda was starting to feel some withdrawal symptoms. Ever since she was in college she had taken two or three drinks of scotch before going to bed at night. She also missed her morning Danish and her mid-day chocolate bars. But having friends compensated for her cravings and she was happy to notice her jeans were not so tight, and in general she felt better. It was also the first time in her life that she was not being bullied into going on a diet: this was a nice kind of control. She looked at the change in her food as part of moving to the city and sharing with friends.

She could not sneak any food or alcohol to her room at night because she shared the big room with Marie Terre. They had flipped a coin to see who would get the small room and have total privacy. Diana got the small room all for herself, and Marie Terre and Brenda got to share the large room.

The ladies decided to make an inventory of all their antiques. They took pictures of everything they thought might be of value. They made a list of the antique shops and divided them among each other. They needed to find out how much their articles were worth and who would be willing to purchase them.

At every antique shop they noticed articles that were similar to what they already had. They wrote down the prices and asked the person in charge of the store for a little bit of the articles' history.

At five thirty in the afternoon they met at the school. They were very tired but optimistic with their findings. If they could sell the articles on their own they could make sufficient money to remodel the flat and maybe even take a vacation. But, that would take some doing and the process was longer. They developed a strategy: Plan A was to place articles in a newspaper and try to sell the bigger items on their own. Plan B was to try and sell the articles to the antique shops. Plan C was to take the articles to an auction. Plan D was to get a table at the Sunday flea market and try to sell the articles there.

It seemed to be a sensible plan. They could not wait to get started.

4 REMODELING INSIDE-OUT

George had not seen Diana at all the day before. Even though he knew the feelings he had for her were pure and lovely, he also knew that he should not and could not pursue them. He just wanted to see her even if it was from a distance. So he decided to offer his services to remodel their flat. He would use the same floor plan he had used on the fourth floor flat and he even prepared a budget. He was charging them much less than he had charged the Americans, because he had to give them a price they could not resist.

He would use the students at the school to help him out, and he would supervise all the work. As part of the student curriculum they had to do an internship that required them to do real live projects, and he knew how that worked, and how they always welcomed projects that were close to the school building. The only problem with this plan was the students could only work from 6p.m. to 9p.m. It would take them a long time to finish the project and the ladies would not have a place to live when the Americans arrived. But he was sure they could figure something out when the time came.

George looked at himself in the mirror as he practiced his presentation for the ladies, and how he was going to explain the plan and the budget. When he felt confident on what to say and how to say it, he took a shower and put on his best pair of trousers and shirt. He climbed the stairs to the fourth floor flat and knocked on the ladies door. Marie Terrie invited George in.

Diana was sitting at a table writing out the sales ad for the antiques that were to be published on Sunday's newspaper. When she saw him, that tingling feeling attacked her stomach again, and she felt the sweat in the palms of her hands. She acted somewhat indifferent to his presence, but stared at him from the corner of her eye. "What an amazingly handsome male specimen. I could just stare at him all day long" she though.

George looked only at Marie Terre. "I have a business proposal for the three of you."

In a friendly gesture Marie Terre walked George toward the table. "Please have a seat and let us see what you have." Brenda walked over and sat at the table next to Diana. George opened the plans he had made for the fourth floor flat and explained his proposal and the budget he had prepared.

"We need to start as soon as possible because the flat will have to be practically gutted. To save money, I am going to have the wood floors polished and I am only replacing the sections that are worn out or broken. We will be using the solid wood kitchen cabinets. I will paint them and add glass doors, trims, and new handles to make them look contemporary. All of this takes time and I know you want to live in your own flat as soon as possible." He had prepared a hand-written, basic contract.

Brenda told George the flat was filled with antique treasures. Again George came to the rescue. He offered to make some space in the building's basement.

"It is full of old stuff that renters have left behind and needs to be trashed or disposed of."

All three ladies looked at each other with great expectation and agreed to whatever George was talking about. They wanted to take a look at the trash in the basement.

To get to the basement one had to go outside of the building, and on the side you could see some steps that led to the two doors. One door lead to George's small flat and the other door opened to a horrible looking, one hundred year old very big heater. The space was cluttered up with several old trunks, boxes with people's names on them, and about four claw tubs. After careful inspection of the place they decided that they could pile the stuff up and make room for their own boxes.

Before going back upstairs Marie Terre asked George: "Have you done any work on your own flat?" George smiled. "Yes I have. Would you like to see it?" She looked over at Brenda and Diana, and their wide smile and bright eyes demonstrated they also felt curious to see his flat.

As a gentleman, George opened the door to his basement flat and let the ladies in. To their surprise, it was immaculate. The kitchen was small but clean and useful. The French bistro set made the place cheerful and homey, and matched the end tables as well as the coffee table. The old but recently upholstered love seat and two armchairs were charming. He had painted a mural on the back and sidewalls. The mural had Roman columns with hanging vines. The sidewall was actually the back part of a closet.

"I converted part of the space into a bedroom by making a closet as a divider wall. This opening will lead you to the bedroom and the front side of the closet. Please walk in." The room was simple but elegant. He had two different end tables at each side of the bed, painted in dark mahogany. A lovely antique lamp was placed on top of the right corner end table. A heavy red blanket covered the bed and he had four pillows with white pillowcases. On the wall opposite the bed was a very large, old desk with a computer on top and a stack of well-organized papers. It was a masculine environment done with lots of taste.

"May I offer you something to drink?"

All three ladies refused at the same time. They realized it had been an intrusion on their part to agree to see his flat in the first place, so they apologized. He was very understanding and assured them it was natural curiosity.

Diana looked at him. "The three of us need to sit down with this proposal, figure out our numbers, and get back to you."

"I understand. Let me know what you decide."

"We will, and thank you for your help."

As soon as they walked back into their borrowed flat and sat around the table Diana explained: "The budget I had prepared for us included savings of 400 pounds each by moving to the city. I had planned on using this money for investment purposes, but if it's alright with the two of you we can give this money to George so he starts purchasing the materials necessary for the remodel."

Marie Terre thought about it. "Yes, he seems to be a very decent person, so let's do it tonight."

Brenda was not totally convinced. "Don't you think we need to consult with our pillows first?"

"There is not very much to consult. We are living on borrowed time in this flat, and our own place needs to be ready before the Americans come back. I think Marie Terre is correct: we need to give George the 1200 pounds for him to start buying the necessary materials tonight. The price he is giving us is a lot lower than the going rates, plus I like the quality of his work. This flat is outstanding and even his own small basement flat is an admirable place."

Marie Terre added: "Plus he seems to be a decent and

honest, hard working man. And my pillow never talks to me." She winked.

Diana told her: "You just said the words that were going through my own mind."

Outnumbered, Brenda agreed.

The ladies prepared the payment, and added a few comments to George's contract before bringing it to the basement flat. George opened the door and let them in. Marie Terre handed him the 1200 pounds. "We signed the contract you prepared and added a few comments. You need to sign it also and tomorrow I will make copies for all of us to keep."

George was elated. "Thank you very much! I know you will be very happy with the results and with the cost. I will save all the receipts for your Tax purposes."

Behind her, Brenda was hiding a bottle of red wine and Diana had four wine goblets. As soon as George signed the contract, Brenda poured the wine and they toasted to a great remodel.

It was the first Saturday of December; a month had gone by since the ladies had moved to the City. The flat was still in demolition. The men could only work from 6 to 9pm. It was taking longer than expected. The ladies were in need of a break. They had been working all day at the bank, going to the night school every week day plus Saturdays, and on Sunday they worked at the flea market selling what was left over from the antiques.

Brenda was in a fantastic mood because in one month she had lost eleven kilos without even trying. She had gotten rid of her size 22 uniforms and fitted into a size 20 that was in better condition.

"Marie Terre, your routine is working. I'll admit at the beginning I did not want to get up at seven in the morning to do 35 minutes of aerobic exercise, take a shower, and eat non-fat meals."

Marie Terre smiled. "Don't forget the daytime shakes, and the fruit snacks. The ten-minute walk to work also helps, as well as walking to and from the flat at lunchtime and to the night school. I feel the difference too."

"I was very opposed to the night school, but now I find it entertaining. It even takes my mind away from food, and anyway I am always too tired to eat. I can't believe for so many years I tried to get rid of my fat with nerve-killing diets and now the fat is simply melting away. It seems a miracle."

Marie Terre agreed. "Talking about miracles, it seems as if it was yesterday that your hair had been practically shaved off after your visit to the dermatologist. I believe the haircut makes you look interesting and bold, and to top it off, your complexion also looks good. I know you are following the doctor's instructions without skipping a day. Congratulations!"

Brenda thanked her. "The good news is that I have already started to feel some tiny hairs growing on my head. I hope the procedures scheduled for tomorrow are not too painful. Early in the morning I am scheduled to have braces placed on my front teeth and a couple of hours later I am going to have laser surgery for my eyes in order to get rid of my heavy eyeglasses."

Marie Terre was so proud. "You were lucky to have the doctors fit you in on the same day. With our busy schedule it is best to have both things done the same day. I will be at your side during both procedures. Then I will nurse you back into proper health."

Tears filled Brenda's eyes as she thanked her friends for their advice on what to do to improve her looks and for helping her during the process.

There was a knock at the door, and when Brenda opened it she saw George standing in the hallway, looking very frazzled.

"I just received a phone call from the USA. The owners of the flat will be arriving next week. But you don't have to worry. I thought about this, and all three of you are welcome to stay at my flat. Two of you may sleep on my bed. Marie Terre is petite, so she can fit on the love seat, and I will sleep on the floor."

Diana, sitting at the dining room table, was listening to everything George said. As soon as he finished she blurted out a very loud "No", but Marie Terre thanked George and told him they would let him know. This was a decision they had to make between all three of them. George walked away with a disappointed look on his face.

As soon as Marie Terre closed the door behind George, Diana explained: "We made about 80,000 pounds from selling the antiques, so we can afford to stay at a hotel."

Marie Terre interrupted: "May I remind you that we still need about twenty thousand more to complete the remodeling, and we have no more antiques to sell?"

This was out of character for Diana. She was the one always saving the money and coming up with ways to make more of it. Marie Terre continued: "We have all seen how clean and charming George's flat is, and he has always been more than helpful. On top of that we do not want to offend him by undervaluing his hospitality, plus it would be fun to stay with George. I can't understand why you don't want to stay at his place." Jokingly, she asked: "Unless you are afraid of falling for him?"

Diana snapped at her. "Don't be ridiculous."

Mary Terre looked at her with suspicion. "Just a joke! But please think about it. I need to leave with Brenda to the clinic. If it makes you happy, do some research in the newspaper and see if you can find a flat that we could afford on a monthly rental."

After having Brenda's front braces installed, she and Marie Terre went to the third floor of the clinic for Brenda's laser eye surgery. The doctor and nurses were very soothing. They explained the entire procedure would only take a few minutes. The doctor gave her some instructions to follow, and in what seemed like seconds he said it had all been very successful. He told Brenda: "If you would please, sit up, look at the clock on the wall, and tell us what time it is."

Brenda could not answer because she started to cry. The worried doctor and nurse tried to console her. When she could finally talk, she said: "For the first time in my life I can see better without my glasses than with them on."

The doctor gave her more instructions. "You need to rest for twenty-four hours and tomorrow you should see even better than today. Please wear sunglasses at all times for the first week."

Brenda could not stop her tears. It was like her emotional floodgates had been opened wide. She was happy, but more that that, she felt so relieved knowing nobody would call her ugly names like four-eyes, cow, or all the other horrible things she had been called by the bullies in school. Again she remembered the day that her two new friends approached her and asked her to join them in the adventure of buying a flat in the city. She knew then, as she was experiencing now, that it was the beginning of a wonderful life

5 THE NEW MAN

A large investment company was throwing a fancy cocktail party to present new investment strategies. Most of the "who is who" in London would be there. Diana had to attend the party because it was job related, but she did not want to go alone. She had begged Marie Terre to go to the cocktail party with her, but Marie Terre had offered to stay with Brenda during her recuperation just in case she needed help.

As soon as Brenda and Marie Terre arrived at the flat, Diana wanted to know all about Brenda's health. Brenda gave Diana a hug.

"Thank you for caring and being such good friends. I feel emotionally drained but happy. The procedures are over, and all I want to do now is go to sleep. In fact I feel so well physically, I told Marie Terre to go with you to your cocktail party, because if she stays here she will be very bored and lonely."

Marie Terre looked at Brenda. "You do look fine to me, and it would be fun to do something different after the hard work we have all endured. Well, Diana my dear friend, I will accompany you to the fabulous cocktail party! Now the problem is deciding what to wear."

Diana rushed to where Marie Terre kept her wardrobe, pulled out a lovely spaghetti-strap little black dress, and without a word gave it to her. Marie Terre put it on, and the dress made her look slim, but with attractive female curves. She had lost about two kilos but still had another eight to go.

Diana looked her over. "It is a keeper. Now that the wardrobe problem is solved, we need to hurry if we want to get out if here in time!"

The two friends started to run madly around the flat. They took showers and then helped one another by drying each other's hair and putting on their makeup. They looked lovely. The running around and the wild laughter made them glow, showcasing their youth and beauty.

Once they arrived to the lavish party, people started greeting Diana. She was well known among the rich and famous; she just breezed her way among them. She gave out her business card to many of her parent's friends to let them know she was now working in investment banking. This was a great opportunity to build up her portfolio. In fact, she knew the bank had hired her because of her family name and contacts, and she was not about to let them down.

Marie Terre was all wide-eyed and fascinated with the beautiful people and the surroundings. She was impressed with the big, unusual flower arrangements. She just adored the wine, the shrimp, the salmon and all the other foods; she had no idea what they were, but she ate them with gusto. As a child, her parents had often taken her to museums and cathedrals. She had been trained to admire the arts and everything that is delightful to the senses. She put this skill into practice as she inspected her surroundings.

Out in a corner she saw an extremely attractive man. He must have been a little over six feet tall. She noticed his light blue eyes, brown hair, and his expensive suit, which fit him so perfectly it was obviously tailor made. She even noticed his pinkie ring, which she imagined must be his family crest; this was the kind of man she really liked.

William noticed how she was staring at him; he stared back. When she realized it, she gave him her brightest smile. He felt the air escape from his lungs in a rush. That smile was a magnet pulling him in her direction, but he could not get away from the person he was talking with. In fact, this person had introduced him to a billionaire businessman he had been trying to get in touch with. He finally talked with the billionaire and they exchanged business cards. He made a note to himself: as soon as this goal was accomplished he would meet the young lady with the magnetic smile.

William went searching for the young lady, but other people kept coming up to greet him and he had to make small talk, even though his eyes roamed all over the place looking for her. He was dating a woman much more attractive. She was tall, with a perfect figure and a face to be seen in any magazine cover. Yet this petite, round faced woman with the big smile lit him up. He couldn't care less about meeting more prospective clients. His main goal at that moment was to meet her.

When he finally spotted her inspecting the rose garden, he paused and had a good look from afar. There were other people in the garden, but he only saw her. He could not help himself from comparing her with the roses. He thought: "Her complexion is as soft a rose petal, and her cheeks are as pink as a pink rose and her full lips resemble a red rose".

He was immersed in these crazy romantic thoughts when she noticed him staring at her. They made eye contact for what seemed like an eternity because, in their universe, the world stood still. After a few seconds she acknowledged his presence with that smile; he felt his heart had skipped a beat and he smiled right back at her. And as if a gigantic magnet pulled his entire body toward this lovely female flower, he walked straight up to her. "Hi, I am William! And your lovely name is...?" He felt positive that any woman would automatically respond to any of his methods of introduction.

However, whenever Marie Terre got nervous she talked too much, or not at all. When William approached her she could not respond. Not a word came out of her mouth. She wanted to impress him so much she needed to figure out how she should act. She started remembering all the things her mother had taught her. Things like: women should not flirt with men; men should come after them and not the other way around; you must act ladylike at all times; do not talk too much; let him give you all the information first; ask questions about his career, but you must act mysterious and as if you are not interested.

Trying hard to follow all these instructions, she did not tell him her name, and instead started talking nonsense.

"Aren't these flowers beautiful? I love how they smell! I just can't believe how many colors they have! Can you imagine how much work goes into these gardens?" And she went on, and on, and on. She thought she had flirted with him to begin with, and now she just could not stop talking. The entire situation made her blush with shame.

He had never seen anything like it: she was like an open book. It was so obvious she liked him and had no idea what to do about it! She was blushing; this gave her porcelain complexion an angel-like glow. She seemed pure, honest and so real. He thought she was adorable and wanted to take her into his arms and kiss her, but she also gave off all the "hands off" signals, which made her even more desirable. He felt like he had met an angel and he needed to treat her with kindness and be gentle, or she would disappear. On the other hand he also felt as if the big bang had just occurred: his entire existence had collided with this lovely unknown world and nothing else mattered but them.

The magic was broken when Diana approached them.

"Greetings, William. I see you have met my friend Marie Terre precisely when we need to leave."

William felt as if a big bucket of cold water had been poured over his head. He became a little sarcastic.

"Well Diana, it's nice to see you too. I was trying to find out how I can call back: I believe you said her name is Marie Terre? I would like to see her again."

With ice in her voice Diana said: "Goodbye, William."

He could not believe what had just happened. He knew Diana, and Marie Terre had given him all the normal signs of attraction.

"Maybe it's just best I did not get her phone number. I am working on several investment projects, and I definitely do not need more female distraction."

As soon as Marie Terre and Diana got into the taxi to leave, Diana started to explain why she had acted so impulsively.

"William is a very famous playboy. He comes from old money that had been drying up just like my own family's money is at this point. However, when he was eighteen years old his parents died in a car accident. A tourist bus collided with their car and they died instantly. He was given custody of his younger brothers and received five million pounds from the bus's insurance company.

William is the oldest of three brothers. He took the money and invested in cattle, doubling the family's cheese business. Within a year he sold the company to a big USA conglomerate, making a tremendous amount of profit. The following year he and his second brother went to Harvard. Two years later the third brother followed in their footsteps. All three brothers have their MBA's. William specialized in Mergers and Acquisitions; he has become a money-bagger.

The other two brothers work for him and they are married. William, on the other hand, is thirty-years-old and dates several models from five different continents, all of which have been on the cover of major magazines, very tall and anorexic. One model tried to commit suicide when he dumped her; it was all over the news. He is considered one of the most desirable bachelors on this side of the Atlantic."

She did not tell Marie Terre that when she saw them talking she could see how Marie Terre's face glowed, and William was mesmerized watching her. She did not want to see her sweet friend get her heart broken by this womanizer, so she decided to intervene before anything happened. She looked at Marie Terre's' face in order to get some kind of acknowledgement for what she had just said, but what she got was the back of Marie Terre's neck. She kept on staring out the taxi's window, and looked as if her thoughts were somewhere else.

Marie Terre realized this party was just a glimpse of a world that was totally unknown to her, and she also knew that Diana was watching over her as a good friend even though she did not like her "mother hen" attitude. She listened carefully to everything Diana explained, and she got the picture of a grief-stricken, responsible teenager, a fabulous leader, and a hard working caregiver for his brothers. She did not even care about the models. Her heart filled with admiration and warmed up to him. She was smitten.

All she wanted to do was remember William's face when he walked up to her, smelling so clean, new, and refreshing. Many times she had wondered what her perfect man would look like. In her teens she had liked handsome movie stars, but they were distant and unknown. On the other hand, William was the picture of an ideal man, and she had met him in the flesh. She wanted to relish the moment by keeping her memories intact, so she turned her back on Diana and stared out the taxi window until they arrived at the flat.

Finally it was Sunday, and they could rest and not even think about going to the flea market to sell antiques. It had been lots of fun, and they had learned plenty from other antique dealers who volunteered information on the value of their merchandise. For example, when a client wanted to bargain with them they were taught how low they could go so as not to upset the other merchants. Many of them made funny jokes at their expense, but helped them out when possible.

Diana got the classifieds from the Sunday newspaper and started calling different flats for rent.

Marie Terre decided to cook something special and warm. At her aunt's house in Puerto Rico she had learned how to cook "asopao". As soon as the big pot of Puerto Rican style chicken soup was ready, she served three bowls and placed them on the table to cool down. When Brenda walked into the dining room Marie Terre offered to help her walk to the table.

"I am doing fine, and it's just as the doctor said: I can see better today than I saw yesterday."

Diana was in a bad mood. "I have called over a dozen flats for rent that are not too far from work, but most of them want a one-year lease. They do not rent on a monthly basis. The ones that do monthly rentals are very small and way out of our budget."

Brenda had been thinking about this. "If you want to spend the money that is up to you. I am going to stay at George's flat."

Marie Terre stared at Diana. "Do you have anything against George?"

Diana became very defensive. "Of course not."

Mary Terre told her: "We are all in this together, and if we were to vote I would definitely insist on staying with George and save over three thousand pounds".

Diana finally looked up at her friends. "I will give in with one condition; we are to purchase three folding cots for us to sleep on and place them in his parlor. George is to sleep in his own bed. He deserves his own privacy. Even though he does not want to charge us rent, in exchange for his hospitably we are to cook and clean for him and as a gift we will get him his own electric table saw, because his hands are full of blisters from using the hand saw."

Brenda and Marie Terre had not noticed this and they glanced at each other with a bewildered look.

Marie Terre said: "That is very sweet of you and as far as I am concerned, it's a done deal."

Brenda approached her two friends. "I second the motion."

All three friends started laughing as they were hugging each other. This was one of those little things that Marie Terre has got them used to.

The chicken soup was delicious. They were eating and talking about how wonderful it tasted when Diana interrupted.

"Brenda and I, and some other bank employees have planned a surprise party for your birthday next Friday. I am sorry to ruin the surprise, but if we are going to be staying at George's place the proper thing would be to invite him."

Marie Terre had guessed they would be doing something for her 22nd birthday, but she started to giggle like a teenager when she was told it was a surprise party. They all started laughing, and then Brenda and Diana tickled Marie Terre's and messed her hair, with joyfulness and without a worry in the world. They were happy. Just three good friends with a brilliant future ahead of them.

6 THE BEST BIRTHDAY GIFT

William was an extremely occupied man. Working hard and making money were his biggest satisfactions after his parent's sudden death. He had adored his mother, and his father was a good friend that talked with him about practically everything. In just one second he lost all that. He became attached to his brothers, but the horrible fear of another major loss made him stay distant to others. He was terrified of going through that immense pain again; he figured he was better off not getting close to anyone.

He dated lots of fashion models because they were good for his business. He had met several clients because they had seen him somewhere with this or that model. He also got lots of free publicity, but it was all part of his business plan. Most of the models he dated did not talk very much and when they did, it was to let him know how starved they were and all the different kind of foods they could not eat. It was also good for the models' career to be seen with him. It was a quid pro quo; this was how he justified his behavior.

All throughout the week after the party he kept thinking about Marie Terre's lovely, magnetic smile that kept on pulling him. It was Friday, and he had no plans for the weekend, so he made a snap judgment and decided to go to the bank where Diana worked and persuade her to give him Marie Terre's phone number. He just had to see her again. He realized it was almost five in the afternoon when he called his chauffeur to meet him in front of his building. Traffic was horrendous.

"With this traffic we will never get there on time. Take a side street. No, take that other side street."

From the look his chauffeur gave him, he knew his behavior was erratic. He had to tell himself to calm down. This was out of character for him. When they were a block away from the bank he noticed a group of people walking in a festive mode toward a nearby restaurant. And there she was, with her magnetic smile pulling him toward her. The group was composed of men and women, but Marie Terre did not seem to be with any man in particular. He instructed his chauffeur to turn the Mercedes Bens around the next block and to drop him off at the restaurant the group had entered.

Most bank executives had their business lunches at this exquisite restaurant. Diana also brought most of her business clients for lunch here. The owner offered special treatment to all bank employees because they were his most frequent customers. For this special occasion he had prepared a big table in the back with a finger buffet at one side, and another long table surrounded by chairs with a big birthday cake in the center that said "Happy Birthday Marie Terre". He knew the bank was very discrete about their private parties. They did not like for outsiders to see them partying or consuming alcoholic beverages, so he set up two large, heavy, burgundy drape panels separating the party and keeping it private from the other tables in the restaurant.

Because of the heavy traffic, many bank officers stopped by the bar for a drink or two, and to wait for the streets to get less congested. About seven or eight bank officers walked in and could hear people laughing at the back of the room. One of them went toward the drapes and out of curiosity peaked in to see who was having a party. When he saw it was Marie Terre's birthday he called the other bank officers sitting at the bar and said: "It's Marie Terre's birthday party!" Most of Marie Terre's colleagues at the bank liked her very much because she helped them out and was very sweet. The party got louder and bigger by the minute. They lit a candle on the cake and started to sing Happy Birthday.

When William walked into the restaurant the owner recognized him and immediately offered him a table, but he politely refused and looked around until he heard the noise from the party. He realized he had not been invited, so he decided to have a drink at the bar and think about his next move. He started to feel more relaxed when he heard the Happy Birthday song; he picked up his drink and slowly walked toward the drapes.

Marie Terre was as happy as can be. The group asked her to make a wish when she blew out the candle. She closed her eyes and wished to see William again. When she opened her eyes, there he was, smiling and walking toward her. Most members of the group recognized him at once and were in shock to see him walking toward Marie Terre, the cute, petite, Cuban immigrant.

William wanted to take her in his arms and run away with her, but he realized that he had no right to even be there in the first place. When he was finally in front of her he put his hands on each of her shoulders, pulled her towards him, and with his eyes closed kissed her gently and slowly on the forehead, then said Happy Birthday. There was total silence. The group was staring at them, and the situation was odd to say the least.

William was a man of the world and knew how to get in or out of any kind of situation. He said: "Champaign for all! It's on me. We most make a toast for the birthday girl!"

The owner came running to William and asked him if he would like to see the Champaign list. William said: "We are to have the '75 Louis Roederer Cristal for everyone, and lots of strawberries."

The owner got in motion immediately, sending one of his waiters to the market for more strawberries while he went for the best Champagne in the house.

Diana had ordered a finger buffet of mostly sandwiches and chicken wings. William told the owner to add some shrimp, lobster, and caviar, and he was to pay for the entire party.

The owner was delighted! He danced into the kitchen and, in what sounded suspiciously like singing, he told his chef about the new order. "This is the reason I give my bank clients special treatment. They are special!"

The guests were delighted, and Marie Terre was in a dream state, but Diana was furious. She went over to William and asked him how he knew about the party. William lied.

"I stopped by for a drink at the bar, when on my way to the water closet I peeked into the party and recognized you, so I walked in. But I know you did not invite me; that's why I offered the Champagne. I do not want to be treated as an outsider, and I really hoped you would not mind my intrusion."

She did not have much to say after his explanation, and everyone was so pleased with how things had turned out, especially Marie Terre, that she decided to back off.

George noticed how worried Diana looked so he sat at her side and asked her if something was wrong. He looked so handsome. He had a leather jacket on, and underneath it a black turtleneck that made the lovely color of his eyes and hair stand out, making him look more desirable than ever. She stared at him and, with hopelessness in her voice, explained: "William is a tycoon, and I am very worried for Marie Terre. I can't see why he is so interested in her. I don't want my dear friend to get her heart broken over this impossible man".

The champagne corks started popping, and when all the guests were holding their wine glasses Diana said: "I want to make a toast for Marie Terre".

Everybody raised his or her champagne flutes. "To the kindest person I have ever met, may your life be filled with happiness and health."

Brenda added: "To Marie Terre, the best friend a person could ever have."

All the guests took turns offering their own toast. In a matter of minutes William was getting to know Marie Terre much better by the comments provided by each guest.

"To the most helpful person." "For your cooperation when asked for help." "For your uplifting attitude." "For your willingness to listen." "For your high level of responsibility." "For your cleverness." "For being there for us." "For your kindness." "For being so sweet."

It went on and on. Finally, everyone had offered a toast except for William. The guests all turned to him with expectation. At once he lifted up his glass and said: "To Marie Terre, for lighting up a room with her smile". The crowd agreed with a big yes, and some applauded. They were ready to start the party all over again. Guests started drinking champagne and eating the new food that William ordered.

A waiter came over to the table to cut the cake and serve it in small plates. The guests started to get into their own little groups; some around the food, and others just eating strawberries and talking.

Diana got very tense when she noticed William walking in Marie Terre's direction. George could tell Diana's intentions of barging in.

"She is a big girl, let her decide what should or should not happen."

Diana thought about this. "I realize that at some point in our lives we all get our hearts broken. I don't want this for my dear friend, but it seems there is nothing I can do to stop it. I already explained to Marie Terre about William's reputation, and it is true, she is a big girl. She needs to take responsibility for herself."

It was completely out of character for William to go around chasing women. In fact, most women called him, and volunteered their phone numbers without him asking. The toasts offered by the guests confirmed his impressions about Marie Terre: she was a nice girl. He also realized that his display of attention when he crashed this party was somewhat overwhelming, and she could misinterpret. He kept on telling himself to stay and act calmly, as if this were a pure coincidence. He was going to thank her and her guests for letting him share her birthday celebration.

He walked over to her and said what he had planned, but it sounded rehearsed and it came out wrong. He remembered when they met she had done most of the talking. He wanted her to take the conversation over, but it seemed as if she was expecting him to say more. The one thing he needed to know at this point was if she had a man in her life and if so, where and who was he. He did not want to be obvious about it, so he asked her a silly question: "Is there somebody you would have liked to have here that didn't come?"

Marie Terre was at a loss for words. Her knees were shaking, and she knew for sure she would fall over if she got up from her chair. Her hands were perspiring and now she was mute. For sure he would think she was also stupid. But she had to answer his question.

She drank the entire content of champagne in her glass, and this gave her some courage. After thinking about it for a few seconds, she started to mumble.

"Birthday parties always remind me of mom and dad. If they saw how good this one turned out to be, they would be so happy for me! I'm very proud of them. They have worked very hard all their lives to be able to give my brother and I a good college education."

William was even more impressed with her. He had never met anyone that was this real, warm, and tender, but with a delicious shimmer, a Latin spark that acutely penetrated into his soul. She provoked an intoxicating blaze of passion in his body, while his spirit felt uplifted from just listening to her.

When Marie Terre realized how intense he was observing her, she remembered what Diana had told her about his parent's tragedy. It made her sad to be talking about her parents when he had lost his.

He sensed she knew about his parent's untimely death and that made her look sad. In order to change her sad look he started sharing information about his brothers. He had a beautiful two-year-old niece Lisa, and vibrant one-year-old twin nephews, one called William and the other Edward. His conversation was full of enthusiasm, explaining how much fun it was to see them grow and the amazing things they do.

Giving Marie Terre all these explanations made him realize that he was not as cold or as distant as he wanted others to believe. It was so refreshing to share his family experiences with her and know she wouldn't think less of him for being so fascinated with his niece and nephews. He had not felt this human since before his parent's death. It was a spiritual, warm, relaxing feeling. To get where he was, he had filled his life with barriers and staging appearances in order to attract customers and women. With Marie Terre, he felt free of these barriers that had been choking him for so long.

After they both got over their initial awkwardness, the conversation started to flow as smooth as honey. They talked about little things and also about world events, they agreed and disagreed, the conversation ranging from interesting to funny and back. They made jokes about silly things and then laughed as if they were the most hilarious jokes they had ever heard. Their spirits had recognized each other, and it was divine.

The guests started to leave but none dared interrupt Marie Terre and Williams' delightful conversation. Someone said that it would be rude to break the aura around them. They thanked Diana for inviting them, and asked her to also thank the birthday girl and the fabulous Mr. Burgess.

Diana, George and Brenda felt a predicament. Diana refused to leave them alone. But George and Brenda kept on insisting that it was none of her business. Diana finally interrupted the couple.

"It's time to leave."

Marie Terre gave William a tender look. "I should leave also. Thank you for a wonderful chat, and for all your splendid gifts of champagne and food for my guests."

"Please allow me to take you all to your places. My car can accommodate us easily."

Diana was quicker than anyone else. "No need to. We live within walking distance."

William did not object. He had already made plans with Marie Terre for the next day. They were going to the country. He waved for his bill, and as soon as it was settled he got up to help Marie Terre out of her chair. He kept on talking with Marie Terre as they exited the restaurant and, much to Diana's dismay, walked with them all the way to their building.

As soon as they arrived in front of the building where their flat was, Marie Terre kissed William on the cheek with candor, as most Caribbean people do. He felt the others watching, so he didn't kiss her back but he grabbed her shoulders and very slowly let his hands slid caressingly from her shoulders to her hands. He was feeling every inch of her arms and then gently he took her hands in his and brought them to his lips. Marie Terre was frozen on the spot.

Before he turned to leave they all thanked him for making the party spectacular. William acknowledged their gratitude and walked back to his car. A small drizzle started to fall; the wet rain and cool night had never felt so enchanting.

As soon as they walked into the small basement flat, they all started talking at once. They could not believe that any two people could talk so much, and what was so interesting anyway?

"Not another word. It was a lovely night. I thank you all for a very special birthday party. I want to cherish it forever. Please, not another word."

Marie Terre was in the ninth cloud and did not want the others to bring her down with any reality crap. The others became silent; her authoritarian voice demanded respect. The sweet, polite Marie Terre got what she asked for. In total silence they all made up their cots and went to bed. George was the only one to say "Good night".

William could not sleep. He kept on thinking about Marie Terre. Everything about her made him feel just plain happy. He tried to remember when was the last time he felt so full of joy, like he was feeling now. He had made many business deals that made him feel proud. When his brothers got married and then had the children he felt glad for them. This feeling of total bliss was new to him. It could not be love because he had only seen her twice in his life. Before he could figure these feelings out he finally fell asleep.

INGRID BORGES

7 THE DAY AFTER

Brenda was desperate to ask Marie Terre about William, but Marie Terre would not look or talk to anyone. She got up from bed, took a long bath, put on her best jeans and a lovely lavender sweeter. She fixed herself up as best she could and stared in the mirror for about five minutes. Everyone just sat on the cots, waiting for her to fix breakfast or say something. When they heard a knock at the door, she smiled and said to the others that she would be gone all day. She did not even fix up her cot.

With a big smile Marie Terre opened the door for William and again kissed him on the cheek. He had red roses for her, which she took and hastily put aside, then rushed him to the sports car he had parked in front of the building. He realized she did not want him to see the others or the basement flat. All was understood. He was just glad to see her.

Nobody in the basement flat was in the mood to cook breakfast. Brenda was the first one to say something.

"What do you think about getting some breakfast at the corner deli?"

George said it was fine with him. The walk to the deli eased some of the tension. Again it was Brenda the first one to speak.

"I wish someone could fill me in on what's happening."
Diana filled Brenda in on what she knew about William
and how worried she was about this situation.

George kept on insisting on Marie Terre's freedom. "Marie
Terre needs to live her own life and none of us should get
involved."

Brenda added: "I am very happy for Marie Terre; if any one
deserves a man with William's charm it's her."

Diana was very upset. "Just because I am outnumbered
does not mean you are correct about the 'oh so charming'
William!" She was very sarcastic and obviously worried.
"You have no idea how Mr. charming operates, and I don't
want to see Marie Terre get hurt."

George looked at Diana. "Your logic is stereotyping a
certain kind of man, and that will limit your objectiveness
not only with men in general, but with potential clients. I
am sorry if what I am saying does not agree with your
opinions, but the fact is most of the wonderful things that
happen in this world is because someone decided to think
outside the stereotypes."

For almost a minute Diana stared at George's handsome
face and said nothing. She thought to herself: "My God, he
is so right! This man is far wiser than that of most of my
so-called educated College friends."

"You are right, George. I am usually not so quick to jump
to conclusions. Thank you for shedding some light on this
subject."

The food arrived and George kept on staring at Diana, trying to figure out if she was upset or if she had actually seen the situation as they saw it. She looked up at him and gave him a reassuring smile that made his heart skip a couple of beats.

As soon as Marie Terre and William were together in the car their conversation started to flow like magic. William wanted everything to be just right.

"For lunch we could go to several restaurants, but first I need to know what kind of food you can't eat."

After thinking about it for a few seconds, she said: "I don't know of any kind of food that I can't eat!" They both started laughing, and kept on giggling throughout the conversation.

William was elated. "First I want to take you to see a special garden that recently won a competition, since I know you like to admire flowers. I believe we will like this one."

As they walked in she noticed the garden had an elegant selection of flowers and a tree of great beauty at its center. Without thinking about it she stopped to smell some very large, white, fragrant flowers. When Marie Terre turned to thank George for bringing her to this lovely place, she caught him staring at her and blushed.

He thought she was lovelier than the loveliest of flowers. The way he felt when he was with her was amazing. He just wanted the whole day to be perfect.

"I would like to take you to a very quaint but chic restaurant that I hope you like just as much as I do."

"What kind of food do they serve?"

"Why, the kind of food you can eat!"

They laughed all the way back to the car.

It seemed as if William and Marie Terre had known each other for an eternity. During their lunch he used his own fork to feed her.

"This food is so exquisite! I did not know this existed. What is it called?"

He was full of tenderness when he helped her out. "These little snails are called escargots, and over here we have raw oysters with lemon. You remind me of my niece Lisa. I love to feed her and watch all the funny faces she makes." The sweetness of her smile let him know she liked being compared to Lisa.

It was the food that reminded her she had promised her parents to visit them the day after her birthday, making her jump up from her chair.

"Oh my God, I am so late! This is totally out of character for me! Please forgive me, but I told my parents that I would take the morning train to their house, have dinner with them, and return to the city on Sunday! My parents are going to be very worried if I don't show up."

William was fascinated with it all: the abrupt interruption, her nervousness, the redness of her face that denoted how embarrassed she was, and most of all how she did not want her parents worried about her. He just wanted to make her feel better.

"Now that you mention it, I had told my brothers that on Sunday I would spend some time with the children. I can take you to your parents house and still make it to my brother's place in time."

Marie Terre was extremely embarrassed for her forgetfulness and for making William drive out of his way, but most of all she felt terrible for having to break such an enchanting moment.

"If you really don't mind and if it's not too much of an inconvenience, I would really appreciate it. You may drop me off at a bus station near the freeway and I can make it to my parents' home from there."

Her fingers were crossed behind her back as she hoped he would not want to meet her parents. She knew they would first interrogate him as if he were a common criminal, and then let him know she was a princess, and tell him they expect him to treat her as one. It would be awful. It would also put her in a spot, because her parents were not expecting him.

William could see the predicament in her face, so he decided to say nothing and drive on. He wanted to be in her company as much as possible, and the long drive would allow for that.

During the drive to her parents' house they were entertained playing with each other's fingers and singing old love songs. The four-hour drive vanished without notice. William insisted on leaving her in front of her parents' house, and there was no way she could resist him.

As soon as he stopped the car, he took a close look at the surroundings. He liked the small townhouse with colorful flowers her mother planted in small porcelain pots on each side of the steps; it had a Spanish flavor to it. As a courtesy, Marie Terre asked William if he would like to come inside, but again she crossed her fingers behind her back hopping he would say no. He was wishing she would ask because he wanted to know more about her. Meeting the parents was never a cool idea, but he was thirsty for information, he wanted to see the house where she grew up, and spend some more time with her. He just did not want to be far away from her.

Marie Terre and William were still standing on the sidewalk when her mother opened the front door of the townhouse and came running to hug and kiss her several times on both cheeks. It was cold outside so her mother pulled them both to the front hall. Her father heard his daughter's voice and immediately came out running and saying "Happy Birthday 'Princesa'" or princess, in Spanish. He put his arms around her, kissed her on the head, and hugged her tight.

William had never seen such a display of affection from someone's parents before. The brother came to the door and also kissed and hugged her, saying "Happy birthday, sis!" The family then stared at William expecting an explanation. In a shy tone of voice Marie Terre introduced the Gonzalez family to "Mr. William Burgess, a friend that kindly drove her to their house". The family's greeting was warm and inviting, and William felt instantly welcomed.

He liked everything about the family and the friendly surroundings.

Marie Terre's father, brother and William sat in the front parlor, since it was too cold to sit in the back patio. The decoration was simple but tasteful. The furniture consisted of a love seat, two wing chairs, two end tables with a lamp on each one, and a coffee table in the middle with books and a small flower arrangement on top. On the large wall there was a big abstract painting that he later found out the entire family had painted together after visiting a contemporary art museum. The brilliant fire coming from the fireplace warmed the entire living room.

The ladies served them rum and coke with a twist of lemon. Marie Terre's father told William "the drink is called Cuba Libre in Spanish, which means free Cuba, and that is the biggest irony of all because Cuba has not been free since Fidel Castro took the island over." William already knew this information, but he listened with interest and was authentically amused with the conversation. They also had fried green bananas as hors d'oeuvres, which William consumed in excess to demonstrate how much he liked being in these people's company.

Mr. Mike Gonzalez was intrigued about him but was diplomatic and made small talk, asking about the traffic and how long did it take them to get here by car. He was a hard-working man that was very proud of his family. Freely, he volunteered information about his princess, and how she was the perfect daughter even though she could be stubborn. He was a friendly man that liked to make up jokes about himself and his surroundings. He started to like William and felt comfortable making funny jokes about Marie Terre when she was a baby. William liked them so much that he volunteered several funny incidents with his own niece and nephews.

Ralph Gonzalez had heard his father's jokes so often that they were not even a bit funny anymore. He had noticed the expensive sports car parked in front of the townhouse, and he wanted to find out what kind of work William did that allowed him to afford that kind of car. So, he asked him. William explained that he had an MBA and worked with investments. He did not want to seem different and say he owned several companies. Ralph, a freshman in college, wanted to find out more on how he got into investments, but they were called to dinner.

Marie Terre had helped her mother set the table. She was still placing the wine glasses when her mother invited the family over, explaining to the new guest she had cooked her daughter's everyday simple but favorite meal: ground beef with spices called "picadillo", white rice, black beans, and yellow fried bananas. Lillian had also baked a homemade cake for her daughter's birthday.

The food was delicious; William thought this could easily become his favorite food too. After dinner they sang Happy Birthday first in English and then in Spanish, and when the singing was over they took turns kissing and hugging and presenting their gifts. The first gift was from her mother; the box had a big pink bow on top. Inside was a hand-knit, delicate, simple red sweater. Thanking her involved more hugs and kisses. Her father gave her a small box with a little car charm for her bracelet. He had been giving her a charm for each one of her birthdays. Again, more hugs and kisses. Her brother gave her a book on decoration; he said she needed it to help her decorate her new flat in the city. All the demonstrations of love in this family were a complete new experience for William. His family was caring, but proper and distant, and there was not much touching at all. William felt bad he didn't have a gift for her. He figured as soon as he got back to the city he would get her something special.

The phone rang and it was Diana, asking to speak with Marie Terre. Marie Terre walked over to the kitchen to speak in private. She listened to Diana. "I am so very glad to find you at your parent's home. How did you get rid of William?"

Marie Terre was upset with Diana for asking this, and it showed in her voice. "I didn't, he is with us. We are celebrating my birthday. I'll see you on Monday. Good-bye."

On the other side of the line, Diana was shocked. She had met the Gonzalez family, and knew just how proud they were. It terrified her to think of what would happen when William did what he always did; shatter their hopes and dreams.

It was almost midnight, and William knew he had to leave. He had more than abused this loving family's hospitality, but he did not want to. Mrs. Gonzalez offered him her son's bedroom, saying Ralph could sleep in a room they had in the basement. He was very grateful but insisted that he had to leave. Marie Terre's heart was beating so loud that she honestly believed others could hear it. She was very worried about him driving back to the city so late at night and for so many hours. He assured every one he would be fine.

Marie Terre walked him to his car. The weather was freezing outside and he did not want her catching a cold, so he insisted she get back into the house, but kept on holding her hands with such force as if he would never let go. Finally he kissed her on the forehead and pushed himself to get back, telling her to run back into the house.

He turned the car on and waved at her. He hoped the drive back to the city would help him clear his thoughts. He felt warm and happy inside. But then he worried about how this delicate flower would fit into his life. He had told himself that he would never marry, and Marie Terre was definitely the marrying type. She was not the kind of woman you could just have some fun with, and she was not the type of person that would fit into his crazy life style. He realized he was getting way ahead of what had happened. They had not even kissed properly. He just needed to take inventory of the events of the day, remember how pleasant everything was, and leave it at that.

The Gonzalez family was waiting for Marie Terre to walk back into the house. She was dreading the interrogation she was about to go through.

Her father was the first one to talk. "What a gentleman".

Her brother then said: "What a pleasant surprise. I like him, and he has a dream of a car. I can't even imagine how much that car is worth."

Before Lillian could say a word or ask any further questions the phone rang. A phone ringing at this time of the night always made them nervous. As soon as Mike answered, a smile came to his face and he started speaking in Spanish, then he handed the phone to Lillian. It was aunt Carmen, Lillian's sister calling from San Juan, Puerto Rico. She wanted to wish Marie Terre a Happy Birthday, but she always got mixed up with the different time zones. After talking in Spanish with her sister, Lillian handed the phone to Marie Terre.

Her aunt wished her happiness, health, and lots of blessings, and then handed the phone over to Marie Terre's cousin Claudia. Claudia was all bubbly, and invited her for a spa in February of the coming year. She would not stop talking about the spa. "It is in Punta Cana, a town in the Dominican Republic. It's only 35 minutes from Puerto Rico by airplane. It will be lots of fun, and we get to spend some time together, lose some kilos, and get beautiful in the process! It would be a cool vacation and it only costs one thousand dollars per week."

Marie Terre explained she would love to go, but she had purchased a flat in London that needed fixing up, so the money was tight. Then Ralph took over the phone and also said hi to Titi Carmen, as they all called her, and to his cousin Claudia. When they finally hung up the phone, every one was so tired they said good night with a small kiss to the cheek, and went to their own rooms. Marie Terre was happy that the telephone call had saved her from her family's interrogation. She had been literally "saved by the bell". She had not slept well the night before and today had been a long day. She was worried about William driving for so many hours all by himself, but she was so tired that she fell asleep instantly.

Before preparing breakfast, Lillian went to her daughter's room and gently woke her up. As a woman, and as a mother, she wanted to offer her daughter the proper advice about dating men. Marie Terre had heard this many times before. "Only one out of a thousand that is not a virgin will marry the proper man." "The reason a bride dresses in white on her wedding day is because she is a virgin." Then she would go on to mention all the girls she knew that had been deflowered by men they had been engaged to, and had been left alone because they had been too easy to get into bed with.

Marie Terre figured that her mother thought she lived in the Victorian age. Then she remembered her high school sweetheart Peter. He was only one year older then her, they had been going out on and off for two years, and she went with him to his senior prom. He had been begging her to make love with him and that night she finally gave in. It had been physically and emotionally painful. That summer he became distant, and then he went to college and never called her again. When she went to college she found out he had married. Her virginity had been lost on a one-night stand. Her mother continued: "After you get married, then you need to be passionate and loving in bed. This will keep your husband from running away." It all sounded so last-century, but it did penetrate her thoughts.

During breakfast the family asked all kinds of questions about William. She kept on insisting they were only friends. "I just met him." But they all looked at her with a smile on their face as if they knew something she did not. On the ride to the train station her father teased her about William. "Just friends, and he drives almost five hours to your parents' home? I wish I had friends like that!" Marie Terre just gave him her "I have all the patience in the world" look. Before she boarded the train he wished her all kinds of blessings.

On Sunday, William had lunch with his brothers and played with the children. One of his brothers made a starling comment. "You seem less worried than usual. It's a miracle you have not insisted on talking about business."

William paid no attention to him and from his brother's house called his jeweler. He gave the jeweler the following instructions: "I need for you to find a gift for a lady. It should be something petite, precious, and remarkable. And I need it today." The jeweler said he had several pieces of jewelry he could select from. Then William called the train station to find out at what time the train from Marie Terre's hometown would arrive.

William arrived at the train station half an hour ahead of Marie Terre's train. The thrill of seeing her again gave him an adrenalin rush. He could close his eyes and see her big smile. And just as he expected as soon as Marie Terre walked out of the train and she saw him smiling, she lit up. He could not take it anymore and ran to her side kissing her on the lips in front of others to see. Marie Terre thought she was going to faint. She remembered all the things her mother had just told her and gently pushed him away.

William was hurt. "I realize that I acted impulsively. Maybe you don't feel the same way I do."

"You just took me by surprise. I was not expecting that kind of behavior from you."

"You are right, this is way out of character from me." He led her to his car and once they were inside he pulled out the gift he had for her. Her embarrassment showed all over.

"You did not need to give me a gift. Paying for the buffet at my birthday party was more than generous." He ignored her and asked her to open up the gift. As soon as she had unwrapped the box and opened the lid her eyes opened wide. "This is the precise piece of jewelry I have wanted ever since I turned eighteen years of age!" For the longest time she just stared at the small pendant heart clustered with small diamonds that had a gold chain attached to it, made by Cartier. "Whenever I went shopping and had a moment to spare, I would look inside the jewelry store window where it was displayed, and look at it for as long as time permitted." Then she looked at him: "How could you have ever guessed that I would like this so much?"

She started doubting her own perceptions. She wanted to make sense of all that was happening. She questioned herself. Could this man be for real, or was she just seeing the things she wanted to see in him? It could all be a figment of her imagination. Ever since Peter had left her, she had not been intimate with any of her dates. She had been alone for a long time. Was her loneliness making tricks on her mind? Was she making up this fairy tale? In silence, she stared at the pendant.

From the expression on her face and from what she said, William knew she liked the chain with the little heart, and he also knew it was not too much for the first gift. She closed the box with the gift in it, handed it over to him and said it was too much, she could not accept it. At that precise moment he realized they came from different backgrounds. He knew it was not "too much". He was so disappointed. She did not respond to his kiss, she even pushed him back, and now she returned the gift. He was so confused by her behavior he did not feel like talking, to her or anyone.

She immersed in her own thoughts. She remembered the times Diana had warned her about him. She felt in doubt about everything. She needed time to think about what was happening and learn more about this man. The man who made her feel like running away with him to the end of the world. But she kept on hearing her mother's voice. "The woman that gets to marry the man she wants will keep a mysterious distance with him, and never kisses in public."

William interrupted the silence and asked her if she would like to have a nightcap at his place. She wanted to be with him, but needed time to gather her thoughts and find out what she was getting into. She was afraid of this unknown world and fear froze her. It took her a long time to answer. "Thank you very much for the invitation, but please give me a rain check because tonight I am tired. I want to go straight to my own flat."

When they were in front of the flat he insisted she take the gift. It was a small gesture for her birthday. Without looking him in the eye, she reminded him he paid for the party at the restaurant, and that was more than what she usually accepted from a friend.

"Thank you again for all your generosity." She gave him a quick peck on the cheek and walked out of the car, leaving the gift behind.

William was also tired. He had not slept well the night before, and he was not expecting this attitude from her. He liked the spontaneous, caring woman he had met, not this cautious, guarded person. He knew something was wrong, but he didn't have the foggiest idea what it was and tonight he was not in the mood to find out. When they were in front of her flat she kissed him on the cheek and before he could kiss her back, she ran to the flat and disappeared from his sight. He could not believe what had happened. He had been a perfect gentleman and this is how he was treated? On the drive to his place he decided he needed to sleep and forget the entire situation.

Marie Terre tippy-toed into the flat. She did not want to talk with anyone. She took a long, warm shower and silently got into her cot. Brenda was expecting information on how things had developed with William, her family, and what had happened, but Marie Terre just said "Good night".

Brenda overheard Marie Terre sobbing. She went over to Marie Terre's cot and in silence, without asking any questions, started stroking her hair. This was consoling but it made her cry even more. Diana got out of her cot and wanted an explanation. George got out of his bed and told them he would make tea for everyone.

They were all drinking tea when finally Marie Terre stopped crying and started talking. She explained in detail everything that had happened. They all agreed that it sounded great. She realized she agreed with them. She had started to think she was hallucinating or that her perception was distorted in some way. Then she started to explain how her mother's advice and all the warnings she received from Diana made her think that in some way she was misinterpreting his behavior. She did not know what was happening to her.

"I am going to try my best to explain. I have always believed in my own instincts, but whenever I see William my entire body starts reacting in such a way that I feel totally out of control. Because of this, I feel uncertain, and then I become scared. I am sure my behavior tonight has ruined whatever chances I could possibly have of developing something with William. He must think I am a total moron, or just recognize the fact that I am not a classy lady like the ones he is used to going out with."

George said she should continue to trust her own instincts; he looked at Diana when he said this. Marie Terre looked at all of them with tears in her eyes. "My instincts are to run away with him without thinking about the consequences." Every one in the room stared at each other, and they all knew the love bug had bitten Marie Terre real hard.

Her friends started to hug and console her. Deep inside, Diana was relieved that it ended so soon. George was not so sure. "If William is really interested he will not let this incident keep him away, and eventually he will call you again."

"Thank you for that glimmer of hope. I want to thank you all for being here for me, and please accept my apology for my behavior. I am so grateful to have such good friends I can lean on at a moment like this; I love you and trust you all." That being said, Brenda suggested they all go to sleep because they needed to go to work in a couple of hours. Marie Terre fell asleep as soon as her head touched the pillow.

8 BUSINESS TRAVEL

William was totally confused with Marie Terre's behavior. Regretfully, he did not have time to think about the situation. As soon as he walked into his office, his assistant Mrs. Camille Bronson informed him the franchise they had in Sao Pablo, Brazil was in trouble.

"The franchise's owner called a few minutes ago to let us know all his employees had resigned, in a strike to try to force a corporation take-over. Apparently, the employees found out the corporate employees receive better benefits than the franchise employees. The franchise's owner says he can't keep up the reservations operation without them, and he can't afford to give the employees the same benefits the corporation gives theirs. He sounded desperate when he said he needs our help right now."

William instructed her to call one of his brothers and tell him to go to Sao Paulo with an expert that knows about reservations. Also, call the owner and have him recruit English-speakers for the reservations department. They should start offering trainings the day after they arrive.

Camille looked at him with pity. "There is more bad news. Argentina's franchise's owner called to let us know the police closed down the Buenos Aires' office. He says the previous owner sold him the business, but he is considered a foreigner. Argentine law specifies that at least fifty-one percent of any company must belong to a natural Argentine." Before she could continue, William gave instructions to have his other brother travel to Argentina and settle this matter with the counselors they secure in Buenos Aires.

William stared at his assistant with a look that said "What else?" With a barely noticeable smile she also reminded him that his airline ticket for Australia was on top of his desk, next to his work schedule. Also included were his two tickets for the theater. One of Australia's most famous and beautiful models would be his dinner and theater companion during his stay. Camille had spent hours on the telephone trying to get William's return flight reservations. It had been difficult, but she did get him a flight arriving back to the UK on December 24, so he could spend Christmas day with his niece and nephews. He preferred using a commercial airline rather than his private jet for these long business trips.

As a wise and experienced corporate detective, Camille took it upon herself to obtain additional information on subjects she figured William would like to know a little more about. She had gotten used to procuring information she knew he would need before he even asked her to do so. Today, she followed him to his desk.

"Some very wealthy businessman from Japan mailed you a letter, letting you know they are interested in investing money in shopping malls in the USA and they would like to meet with you. They want to hire you for your expertise and knowledge of the business world on both hemispheres. As soon as I read the letter I knew you would need some background information on these Japanese people." As an old married couple, he lifted his hand to take hold of the papers with the report she had prepared without saying a word. As he studied the information provided he looked up at her with a big grin on his expression.

"Very well done Camille, as usual. Now I need you to find out what malls are for sale if any, where and why, and where are new malls needed. As soon as you have gathered this information send it to me via fax to Australia. I need this information as soon as possible. I will call you from the airport to get a summary of what you have found. That will give me time to study the information during the flight and I will call the Japanese when I get to Australia."

Camille also packed his traveling clothes. He had a big closet in his office with a wardrobe for any and every occasion. As soon as he arrived from a business trip she would have his clothes sent to the laundry and all she had to do was prepare the luggage with the proper attire. She would even place notes on top of the plastic bags so he knew what he was to wear for each engagement or meeting.

Doing business with the Japanese was not an easy task. It took lots of time and energy, but the profits were very rewarding. He would have gone to hell and back to get these clients, but they had called him. He gave himself a pat on the back and felt good about himself. From his previous experience of working with the Japanese, he knew they were very proper, hard working, and expected the same from anyone they did business with. He would prepare for his meeting by focusing not only on their wants but also on their real needs. Finding out this information was an art William had acquired after performing many negotiations. He was looking forward to working with these clients, even though they represented a special challenge.

Marie Terre tried to keep occupied and not think about William, but his attractive face, and the amusing way in which he stared at her kept popping up in her mind every so often. She knew he deserved an apology or at least some kind of explanation for her behavior. It was torture to keep on feeling the way she did and not do anything about it. In her mind she tossed ideas from one end to the other. She kept going over the words she wanted to use to try to explain and make sense of what had happened. But deep down inside nothing made sense any more. She just wanted to talk with William, and that was all that mattered. After hours of internal emotional debate, she got the courage to look up Williams' office phone number and called him.

Mrs. Bronson was an expert getting rid of the many women that tried to stalk Mr. Burgess. When Marie Terre called, she sounded just like a stalker. Camille explained he had left the UK on a business trip and did not know when he would be back. Marie Terre left her name and office phone number. Out of courtesy Mrs. Bronson wrote the information down, but did not give it priority.

On the airplane, William was studying the information Mrs. Bronson had provided. He tried to concentrate on the reports. However, he kept on seeing Marie Terre's face and how sad she looked when she returned the gift he gave her, the one she positively liked so much. He needed to find out what was wrong; he knew she was spontaneous and a joy to be with. He never expected her to act the way she did. He wanted to call her right at that moment, but he told himself he would call her as soon as he arrived in Australia. When he started looking for her telephone number he could not believe he never asked her for it. Astonishment overcame him.

How could he have been so insensible? When he picked her up at the train station all he could think of was taking her to his place and making love to her. How could he have overlooked such a big detail like asking her for her telephone number? He knew he was sharp in business and with women, but Marie Terre was so different she had something that made him clumsy. In his mind he saw her magnetic smile. Remembering every detail about her made him light-headed.

For months, the corporations that were now merging in Australia had been preparing for the celebrations. Mr. William Burgess was famous for his hostile takeovers of major corporations, but this one was a friendly and very profitable merger. The preparations included the media and of course one of Australia's top models, who would be seen with him during his entire stay. As soon as he got there he called the bank were Marie Terre worked, but because of the time difference, it was closed. He tried the next day but the international lines were busy. His tight schedule was fastidious, and provided practically no time for personal telephone calls. One thing led to another, and a week had gone by without having spoken to Marie Terre.

Mrs. Lillian Gonzalez was very worried about her daughter and called her at the bank. William's face was all over the newspapers and on TV, next to one of the most beautiful women in Australia. Again Marie Terre assured her mother that he was just a friend. She would never let her mother know her heart was aching. Her mother knew better though, and she begged her daughter to let her know if she had been intimate with him. This sounded so Victorian to Marie Terre that she started laughing and reassured her mother that she had not gone to bed with him. Lillian was very relieved, and so was Marie Terre. It would have been devastating for her if she had. She realized now what Diana had been trying to save her from, and she felt grateful.

Lillian tried to fix most problems with a nice vacation. "My darling, you should accept your cousin Claudia's invitation to go to the spa in the Dominican Republic. I will pay for it - it's going to be my Christmas gift for you." Marie Terre's spirit was at its lowest. All she could say was "I will think about it".

William's scheduling problems kept getting worse. After traveling for two hours on his flight back to the UK, the pilot turned the aircraft back to Australia. Something was malfunctioning with the airplane. The passengers were informed that the flight would be delayed for about five hours. He called his office and Mrs. Bronson informed him he needed to call his brothers urgently. Both of them were in Argentina, and they had not been able to find local investors so the operation was closed.

Both brothers were very upset and they told him their families were more important; they had to be with their own children for Christmas. He was single and he should leave for Argentina and handle this situation himself. William got the message loud and clear; he agreed to go to Argentina.

With grief he changed his airline ticket to Argentina. Again he tried calling Marie Terre at the bank, but was informed she was with a customer. Before he could give his name, the speakers at the airport were calling his flight, and so he hung up. He decided to have a good look at the present state of affairs. He needed to consider what life really meant for him. He had become a slave of his own wealth. He thought about Mr. Gonzalez, good-humored and content. That guy was probably better off than he realized. He had a charming wife, comfortable surroundings, a nice son and an adorable daughter. What more could you ask for in life?

Each of the ladies spent Christmas with their own parents. When Brenda's father saw her he stared at her for a few seconds with a surprised look. "You look different without your eyeglasses, the new hair cut, and you have a very nice complexion." He smiled and gave her a light hug. Her mother looked at her too. "And jolly! You have lost some weight." Then she immediately changed the subject and with delight informed Brenda about the family news. "Your sister has a boyfriend, and he is coming over for Christmas dinner." Then as usual she had to make an irritating comment that made Brenda feel by far the less favored child. Sarcastically she said: "Hopefully I will get to see one of my daughter's get married before I die." She always acted as if Brenda would never get married.

During Christmas dinner most of the family's attention went to her sister's shy and plump accountant boyfriend. The conversation consisted on how good the food tasted and how nice it was to have the family together. Her sister was in love, and the two lovebirds kept on staring at each other and barely saying a word to anyone else. The family seemed to be very pleased with their daughter's boyfriend and their upcoming marriage. Except for meeting her sister's new boyfriend it was an uneventful Christmas, as usual.

Diana's family was worst off than ever financially. Her mother kept on purchasing expensive clothes that her farther could not afford. They were expecting Diana to marry someone dignified and wealthy that would help them with their financial situation. When her mother found out Diana was not dating anybody, she let her know she and her father were very disappointed.

"Diana, with your looks and social background, you could easily marry a prince. Look at your brother Harry; he is dating the niece of a very wealthy count. He is celebrating

Christmas at the count's house as we speak." Her mother's entire conversation went around the same vicious circle: about money and who had lots of it and who didn't. Her father usually had several books he was reading. His concentration on these books was so intense that everyone could tell he did not have a clue about what was going on in his own household. Diana was anxious to get out of there very fast.

George also went to his family home for the holidays. He had four brothers and one sister. He enjoyed his loud family gatherings. The aunts, uncles, and cousins could barely fit in the small farmhouse, but they all had to celebrate Christmas together. One of his cousins was getting married in February and, as a wedding gift, the family had been helping him finish the couple's new farmhouse. They knew George had attended some fancy school in the city, and they asked him to help with the small details.

George was glad to help with the layout, and he would help install the plumbing and electrical when they were ready. The families explained that because they could only work on weekends and the weather had been very cold, the house would not be ready for the wedding. They made plans to complete the house as much as possible, so that when George came back for the wedding he could take a week to work on his part. The couple would be taking a week off on their honeymoon. George could complete his part of the job by the time they got back, and all the others would be there to help him out.

Getting together to help one another is what he remembered most about his family. They didn't have money, but they were rich in kindness and giving. He just wished they were a little more ambitious.

The Gonzalez' family were in a dilemma. Only the first two years of the International Business degree were offered in the U.K. Ralph would have go to Madrid, Spain, or to Saint Louis, Missouri to graduate. The University of Saint Louis had one of the best programs, but he would have to go to the USA to complete his degree. If he went to study in Spain, the family could visit him more frequently. Marie Terre did not have an opinion one-way or the other; she was making a gigantic effort to hide her melancholy from the family. Christmas had always been a joyful experience for her, until now.

Her mother's relationship with the Christmas season was completely different. During the holidays she missed her relatives the most. One year they all went to Puerto Rico for Christmas and New Year's, and they stayed at her aunt's house. It had been a wonderful experience; all of them had a marvelous time. San Juan was full of gaiety, and they partied every single night.

One of the Island's customs during the Christmas holidays was called "Parrandas". They consisted of lots of friends and family coming up to your house sometime during the night, singing and dancing holiday music. It reminded Marie Terre of the carolers. However, the "parranderos" expected to be welcomed into your house and offered food and drinks. They would sing for the family, eat, drink and dance. Then you would get into your own car and follow the parranda to someone else's house to sing, eat, and drink rum and dance there. The Parranda would end when the sun came out the next morning, and by then the group would be gigantic.

Marie Terre wanted to feel that joyful again, and she remembered how bubbly her cousin Claudia sounded when she invited her to the spa in the Dominican Republic. Because of her brother's college education plans, her parents could not afford to help her out with this trip even though her mother had offered to pay for it. But she new Diana had mentioned they would have money left over after remodeling the flat, which they could use for investment or maybe for a well-deserved vacation.

Her cousin Claudia said the spa in the Dominican Republic would cost one thousand dollars per week, all-inclusive. She needed to find out how much the airline ticket would be, and how much money Diana had allocated in the budget. She called Diana on the phone at her parents' house and explained her plans for February. Diana said she would redo the budget and let her know how much money she could count on, and maybe she could also go to New York. Most Europeans loved going to the most amazing city in the world.

Diana was very pleased to see her friend moving on. She had overheard so much gossip about the women that dated William and how devastated they were when he left them. According to gossip magazines, he was so attentive with his lady friends that it gave them the impression of being the special one in his life, the one he would end up marrying. The gossip pages also mentioned he was one of the most desirable bachelors. It was not easy to find a man like him. Most of these poor ladies never knew why he left, or why he never called them again.

The Americans that owned the flat on the fourth floor left the UK and returned to the USA. The ladies gladly moved out of Georges' basement flat and back into the flat on the fourth floor. Diana was the first to return to the flat after Christmas. She had nothing better to do, so she started working on the budget.

George had been very helpful keeping the prices of the repairs to a minimum. He had recommended they purchase quality appliances, but he had saved in areas no one else would have even thought about, such as using the good lumber that was underneath the counters and inside the closets to cover the wood that needed repair in other parts of the flat. He fixed, painted and modernized the old kitchen cabinets; all they had to buy was new hardware.

It gave her great pleasure to see his face when they gave him the electrical saw and table, he was elated. First he did not want to accept it, but he gave in when the ladies explained it would cost them more to get new kitchen cabinets than to get the electrical saw, not to mention that it also saved them precious time.

Brenda walked in to the flat carrying potpies her mother made for the four of them. George was included. There was a knock at the door and Brenda opened it; it was George, with a homemade baked ham. They were inspecting the ham when Marie Terre walked in with pork, sweet yellow plantains, and eggnog. They set the table for four and as they ate they shared their Christmas experiences.

Diana was glad that George was included in Brenda's mother's generosity, but at the same time she felt it was unsuitable to include him. She felt jealous of Brenda talking about him to her mother. As she was thinking about this, she felt silly. She decided to enjoy the food and forget about her fantasies for a while.

Marie Terre was the only one that did not talk much. She only mentioned the dilemma her parents were having about where her brother should complete his college degree, but they realized she did not mention any feelings: not happy, not sad, not good or bad or annoyed. The food was delicious. They devoured the potpies, the ham, and the pork. Marie Terre played with her food. None of them said a word when they noticed she was not eating. As friends, they were worried about her, but they also knew she would eventually get over it.

George felt lonely in his basement flat. He liked having the ladies around and listening to them talk about their activities at work, at the night school, the trivialities about makeup, their good or bad hair days, and every once in a while the comments they made about their families. It was late, and Diana said she was going to rest; he knew it was time to leave. He said his 'good nights' and 'until tomorrow' to them and left the flat. When the door locked behind him, Diana got very excited and told Marie Terre and Brenda that they had about ten thousand pounds each to do whatever they wanted with. Marie Terre could pay for the spa, the airline ticket, and even stay in New York for a few days. This was more expensive, but according to the budget she could afford some days in the big Apple.

Brenda was so excited for Marie Terre that she decided she also wanted to go. Brenda said they could share a room, because Marie Terre had mentioned her cousin would be sharing her room with a friend. Marie Terre agreed, and told them that early the next morning she would make all the necessary arrangements from this side of the Atlantic and let her cousin make the arrangements for the spa for both of them. Diana would have also liked to participate in this spa experience, but figured that by saving some money she could probably help out her parents with their own financial problems. Nevertheless, she was very happy for her two friends. She designated herself as the person in charge of staying in the UK overlooking the remodeling of the flat.

Still in Buenos Aires, Argentina, William studied most of the investment possibilities for the Japanese. It was summer outside; he had received several invitations for summer parties and dinners. In the past he enjoyed these parties, and liked the Argentine woman for their beauty and boldness. But this time he wanted to work as hard as he could to return and see Marie Terre. Too much time had gone by without calling or having communicated with her. He figured if he called now it would be awkward. He did go for a walk on Florida Street. The clothes, shoes, and accessories were exquisite and of excellent workmanship. He wished he knew Marie Terre's size; he would buy her lots of dresses and shoes. He saw a nice looking small purse that again reminded him of her. He walked into the shop and bought it. He figured she would accept this gift.

When he got back to his hotel the amount of messages at the front desk was overwhelming. After buying back the business from the previous investors, he interviewed several potential local investors and decided on a gentleman called Mauricio Ortiz. Along with the other investors they would own fifty two percent of the company in Argentina and he would own forty eight percent.

Getting the paperwork all signed and legal had taken more time than it usually takes in other parts of the world, but he knew it was happening. He was hoping to return to the UK the next day, now that the paperwork was in order. However, he received a long distance urgent call from Camille: with all that was going on with the Japanese he would have to go to Japan before he returned to the UK. He felt hopeless, and hated the feeling. He told himself that as soon as he got back to the UK he would start hiring new top managers that would handle the international affairs for his constant growing business. He needed and wanted others to do the legwork.

To complicate matters even more, the deal in Argentina took another week. The New Year was celebrated with some friends that had a lovely home near the Tigris River.

The new franchise's owners took advantage of William's presence in the country for much needed publicity. The newspapers added the playboy adjective to most of his pictures.

Four days after the New Year he was on his way to Japan. It was an eight-hour flight from Buenos Aires to Miami, Florida. After the two-hour required layover, William took a seven-hour flight to Los Angeles, California. He had a hotel reservation in Los Angeles. He barely had time to take a shower and a much needed nap. From there he boarded an aircraft that crossed the time-line barrier and took him to Tokyo. The negotiations with the Japanese were very profitable, but time consuming. They entertained him to the point of exhaustion. For publicity purposes, they had him dating another international model. He finally arrived to the UK in February.

9 THE CARIBBEAN

Brenda had never traveled on an airplane, and she was nervous. It was going to be a nine-hour direct flight from the UK to the enchanted island of San Juan, Puerto Rico. Diana gave Brenda a natural sleeping pill made of calcium and magnesium. It was a night-flight and the pill would help her sleep. After the airplane was up in the air Marie Terre noticed the back part of the airplane had a middle row of empty seats and the two other chairs next to it were also empty. The stewardess gave them permission to use these seats.

She gave Brenda two more pills with a cup of chamomile tea. She was petite, therefore she took the two empty seats and let Brenda take the middle row of seats in order for her to lift her legs and sleep in comfort. Brenda fell asleep before her dinner was served. She never got to see the movie that was shown on the television, or eat breakfast. The stewardess woke her up just before the aircraft was ready to land because she needed to bring her seat upright.

Brenda sat at the window seat next to Marie Terre. It was about 5:45 in the morning, San Juan time. From the airplane the island looked like a gigantic lit up Christmas tree, full of lights. It was very beautiful, and most of the other passengers were also looking out the windows. After such a long trip you could sense how comforting it was to finally see some land. She imagined how Christopher Columbus must have felt when they finally saw the islands. She felt relaxed and rested, even though her heart was pounding with the excitement of getting to visit this tropical paradise.

The air inside the aircraft was very dry, but when the doors opened and the passengers started to walk outside they got hit with a sudden shock of humidity. Her straight hair started to get curly. She could feel her skin drinking up the humidity. It had been very cold in the UK before they left, and she could feel the warmth penetrate her body. People were speaking in Spanish. In a matter of seconds all of her senses acknowledged she was in a different part of the world. By the time they completed customs and got their luggage, it was almost seven in the morning and the sun appearing through the windows was brighter than anything she had ever seen.

In the airport terminal Marie Terre greeted her aunt and cousin with lots of hugs and kisses, and then she introduced them to Brenda. These people had more warmth and were even friendlier than Marie Terre, and that was saying a lot.

The flight for the Dominican Republic was scheduled for 1:00p.m. They decided to do the check-in for that flight then, leave their luggage, and get something to eat. Brenda was starving. Marie Terre said she ate plenty on the airplane, which was not true. She had not been eating much at all. When the check-in for the other flight was completed, the uncle drove them to a nearby restaurant. They ordered rum and coke with a twist of lemon, "Cuba Libres". Then came big pieces of fried plantain bananas.

"It's really too early to be having lunch or drinks, but we are celebrating with our beloved Marie Terre, who we have not seen in several years."

Then he ordered some Cuban sandwiches that consisted of French bread with ham, pork, melted Swiss cheese, and pickles, among other things. Brenda would have preferred something a little less fattening but once she took a bite of the sandwich the taste was heavenly. Everyone was eating except for Claudia, who could not stop talking about all the activities that were planned at the spa.

Elizabeth, Claudia's friend, arrived at the airport about eleven in the morning. At once she was introduced to Brenda and Marie Terre. At the gate more hugs and kisses and wishful blessings were offered. The thirty-five minute flight to Punta Cana, in the Dominican Republic, was uneventful. A bus was waiting for them at the airport, and they got to the hotel in less than ten minutes. A cocktail and live music were waiting for them at the reception area. The cocktail was a long glass with two little melon balls inside; the drink was a sugar free drink that was quite refreshing.

After the cocktail they were taken to their rooms. The hotel had a building with regular hotel rooms, but they had reserved a small villa with a kitchen, dining, and living room areas, and an interior garden. A small hallway led to the bedrooms. Claudia and her friend had a room with two double beds and a private bathroom. Marie Terre and Brenda each had their own room with one double bed and a private bathroom. Claudia mentioned that these special accommodations were obtained because her friend Elizabeth was related to the spa's owner, and the fact that they made four reservations was also a contributing factor. They were all delighted with the small villa apartment.

Finally, they were able to take a cool shower and get into more comfortable clothes.

At the cocktail, they had been given a list of their daily activities. At 5p.m. they had to get a massage. It consisted of an entire body peeling made out of oatmeal. The massage was exhilarating and reviving. They were told it eliminated dead cells and prepared the skin for a good and even suntan. After the massage, they got a facial with the same purposes. Then they got the most thorough manicure and pedicure imaginable, not one bit of extra skin was left on their hands and feet. Their feet and hands were polished smooth, and then painted in brilliant colors. Marie Terre chose red, and Brenda, bright pink. Brenda bit her nails, so for twenty-five extra dollars they applied a set of acrylic nails.

She could not stop looking at her hands. They looked so elegant, and long fingernails were so glamorous, that it made her feel pretty. It made Marie Terre happy to see how excited and pleased Brenda felt. Brenda said: "This wonderful pampering is like a very big reward for all the work we have been doing the last several months." Marie Terre agreed.

Before dinner they got weighed, and an appointment was made for the next day to get a medical check-up and talk with a nutritionist.

Dinner was at seven thirty, and they were hungry. Separated from the rest of the hotel guests, the spa participants had a long table. The spa owner introduced the guests to one another. Only one other person did not speak Spanish. She was an American lady from Boston called Jennifer. Everyone else spoke Spanish even though they also knew how to speak English. Most of the participants were from the Dominican Republic. Some had studied in Canada, the USA, Italy, and Spain. Their grooming was impeccable. Four medical doctors from Puerto Rico came to the spa to get started on a diet; they actually looked very slim and fit. They told the group they were going on a tour of the vineyards in France, on a helium balloon. Their traveling schedule included a visit and stay at a different vineyards every other day. It was a wine tasting and gastronomic tour. They wanted to taste all the fabulous fattening French meals; therefore the logical thing to do was to go on a diet before leaving for France.

The people at the table mentioned how much pounds or kilos they wanted to lose. Most of them needed to lose ten or fifteen pounds, about eleven kilos. There was one nineteen-year-old boy that needed to lose 100 pounds. This young man's parents had sent him to the spa for as long as it would take him to eliminate the excess weight. He had to stay at the spa until he lost the entire amount. One other young lady also had to lose about a hundred pounds, and she was also going to stay for a longer amount of time. Everyone else was there for two weeks, and they expected to be pampered.

The food tasted fantastic, but in very small quantities. They received two bread sticks, a four-ounce peace of fish and a big plate of salad each. Most of them started complaining that they were hungry. The waiters were instructed to remind them: "Ladies, you are on a diet." Some were so hungry they stole bread sticks from those that had not eaten them, or from the ones who were talking with someone else and not watching their food. These fancy ladies realized that hunger makes people do crazy things, and from then on everyone did not take their eyes off their food. They were not allowed to mingle with the rest of the hotel guests, in order to avoid temptation and order food from other waiters that had not received the proper instructions.

After dinner, they were taken to an outdoor ballroom with loud music. Most of the people went directly to the dance floor and started dancing Merengues and Salsa. The upbeat and exhilarating music inspired them to get up and join the others. No one was allowed to sit down, and someone was always ready to come and get whoever was left out into the dance floor. They were all dancing with one another as a group.

Most of them were expert dancers; Marie Terre was also a good dancer. The others took turns teaching Brenda and Jennifer how to dance. Everyone laughed, danced, some sang, and all were dripping sweat from head to toe. It was so much fun that even Marie Terre forgot about her melancholy. At two in the morning they ended the party and went to their bedrooms. A shower was absolutely necessary, and it felt divine. As soon as they put their heads on the pillows they fell asleep.

A knock on the door woke them up. They were informed to get dressed for a morning walk. It was only six in the morning, and they had slept less than four hours. Marie Terre and Brenda brushed their teeth, put on their sweats, and met the person that was going to take them for a walk. Besides them, the only ones that showed up were Jennifer and two of the ladies from Puerto Rico. The morning walk started at six thirty.

Brenda was still sleepy when she felt the breeze caressing her face and instinctively she took a deep breath. The air was crisp and clean. She looked at the sky and it was a very light blue, almost white. There was not a cloud in the sky. She had never seen sky this color of blue before. The path they were walking on had big red and burgundy flowers called "bougainvillea". They were planted in rows and small benches had been built from rustic wood underneath the roof created by these gorgeous flowers. If you sat on any of the benches you could see the Atlantic Ocean.

The beauty of the row of flowers had her mesmerized. Finally, she turned her head to the left and spotted the ocean. The water seemed transparent, it was a different color blue also, but just as bewitching as the sky. The sand looked like gold dust. Her spirit and mind were moved with so much beauty, and a feeling of warmth and belonging penetrated her entire being. She knew then why the Caribbean islands were called Paradise.

The walk was invigorating and brought joy to her spirit. Breakfast was waiting for them at the section designated for the spa participants. Coffee was served with fat free cream, a small portion of oatmeal that tasted very good, and an even smaller amount of delicious tropical fruits, but it was not sufficient. They were still hungry and wished for more food. She looked around for the others and realized the rest of the participants were still sleeping.

After breakfast they went to the doctor's appointment. Dr. Hernandez specialized in weight loss. He was not very tall and had an attractive, but mischievous face. He greeted Brenda with friendliness and was encouraging.

"You could lose seventy pounds in less than six months, if you follow the nutritionist's instructions, and you will get rid of about six kilos during the next two weeks at this spa." Then he went over to Marie Terre. "And you, my dear, will leave the spa with five less kilos. The nutritionist will also give you the knowledge you need in order to keep the extra weight off forever." As they walked out of the doctors' office Brenda told Marie Terre: "That is the best positive reinforcement I have ever received." Marie Terre agreed. "Yes, his words are encouraging; it makes me want to follow the diet." After the doctor's visit they went to see the nutritionist.

Linda, the nutritionist, had a sweet and understanding voice. She asked them: "What do you eat on a daily basis?" She gave them her recommendations of what foods should not be mixed with others. For example, she recommended: "If you are going to eat a hamburger, do not eat it with bacon and cheese. Eat a turkey sandwich instead of a Cuban sandwich. Eat vegetarian pizza, not pepperoni." Her recommendations were helpful, but were directed more towards a North American diet and not the British. From there they went for a massage.

The price for the two weeks at the spa included three massages per week. Brenda and Marie Terre paid extra to receive a daily massage: it was that good. After receiving the massage it was lunchtime. Most of the other participants were finally awake and started to arrive for lunch. As they sat down several of them were complaining about the person that woke them up at six in the morning. They sounded very upset and hungry. Others complained loudly about the amount of food: it was not enough, and they felt empty. It was obvious many of the ladies that were complaining did not have jobs, and were used to getting their way. Restrictions did not go well with them.

The complaints calmed down and the whole group became very alert when one of the ladies started talking about the many plastic surgeries she had received on her buttocks.

"I went to high school in Canada and the other girls would laugh at my humongous butt. At the age of sixteen I begged my parents to let me have my first plastic surgery. I've had two more surgeries with different plastic surgeons and my butt is still too big for my body."

You could sense the amount of frustration in this attractive woman's voice. Brenda could relate to her comments, since that kind of frustration was very real for her. Marie Terre whispered into Brenda's ear: "Most Caribbean women have big butts. My father made many jokes about the Cuban women's big black beans buttocks." The way that Marie Terre said it sounded so hilarious to Brenda that she started laughing out loud, and everyone stared at her.

"Sorry, I am laughing about something very different. I am in total solidarity with what the young lady is saying."

Another lady got very enthusiastic. "There is a new plastic surgeon in Santo Domingo, the capital of the Dominican Republic. He studied in Brazil with the best plastic surgeons in the world."

Very proudly Claudia said: "I have heard wonderful things about him and as soon as we complete our two weeks at this spa, Elizabeth and I have an appointment with him. I want to have a breast reduction, and Elizabeth wants liposuction to get rid of her saddlebags."

Marie Terre got upset and worried. "Ladies, you are taking surgery very lightly."

Before she could continue, another lady noticed how upset she was and tried to be reassuring. "Going to the plastic surgeon is like going to a beauty parlor." Another lady said: "I had abdominal surgery and even though it was very painful, I do not regret it one bit." Another one added: "I am very happy with my nose job." Somebody else replied: "I am fascinated to see how men turn their heads to look at my lovely breast implants." Most of them laughed at this comment. In a more serious note another lady said: "I got rid of my back pain after my breast reduction."

Each and every one of them had had something done by a plastic surgeon, except Claudia, Elizabeth, Brenda and Marie Terre. Brenda was intrigued and wanted more information from Claudia and Elizabeth. Elizabeth looked at Marie Terre.

"I am aware of the risks involved with any kind of surgery, but I also know that it would take years of exercise and diet to get rid of my saddlebags, and even love handles are eliminated in just minutes with plastic surgery. I go to the beach practically every weekend and have no way of hiding them in a bathing suit." Marie Terre could identify with Elizabeth because, ever since her teens, she had been struggling with her own love handles, those pesky areas of extra fat around her waist. She was very self-conscious of them, and Elizabeth had touched a sensitive button.

At two in the afternoon, the group went for an aerobics class inside the ocean, which was a lot nicer than expected. At three, they had a snack that consisted of carrots and celery. After the snack they could play volleyball or go riding kayaks. From four to five they had another aerobics class. Most of the comments they overheard about the trainer were very good. He had an aerobics class on television and was considered the best trainer in the Dominican Republic.

Jennifer had become attached to Brenda, and walked with her and Marie Terre to the aerobics class. A large terrace with big roman columns overlooking the ocean was assigned to the special aerobics class. Some of the hotel guests were also there. None of the spa participants skipped this activity.

Jennifer was the first one to comment on how masculine and virile the trainer looked, and they also overhead two hotel-guests comment on "How come we never get so see men like that back home?" He started with low impact exercises and kept on building up to high impact. The aerobics class got harder and harder by the minute, but the trainer inspired the group with his dynamic energy. Whenever he saw someone not doing the exercises he would scream "Animo", which meant to cheer up. Brenda wanted to escape before it got to the point where she would collapse in front of the others, but the trainer was coming near her. This gave her the courage to continue and complete the one-hour class.

As soon as the class was over most people collapsed on the floor for about fifteen minutes to recuperate from the strenuous exercises. Marie Terre and Brenda stared at each other realizing just how out-of-shape they were.

That night at dinnertime, Jennifer sat next to Carlos Sanchez, the trainer. She was flirting with him and seemed to be having a nice time. A lot of people were staring at them. Dancing after dinner went on every single day at the spa. This was the best activity, and the highlight of their day.

Even Marie Terre and Brenda did not get up at six the next morning. At lunch, Jennifer informed Brenda that Carlos was getting a divorce. His soon to be ex-wife had a six-year-old daughter from a previous marriage, which he practically raised. He was very depressed about the divorce. He also told her he had studied in the US and wanted to start his own gym. Brenda immediately thought that this was all a big fat lie, or as she would put it, "story time". Over the years she had heard many men tell her they were getting a divorce and the next day they would tell her they were getting back with their wife.

The rumor mill at the spa was faster than a jet airplane. One of the others had told Claudia, Marie Terre, and Brenda the reason Carlos did not go to the night dance was because comments would get back to his wife in Santo Domingo, and it could affect his divorce proceedings. His wife was keeping the house, and he was affected emotionally and financially. Somebody else started talking about how he was a good father and husband, but did not make that much money.

Marie Terre got the impression there was more than one lady interested in Carlos at this spa. She realized he had a great body, and she remembered as a teen reading a book written by Zsa Zsa Gabor called "How to Catch a Man, How to Dump a Man, and How to Keep a Man." It had a whole chapter dedicated to a Dominican man, called "Man Above All Men, Porfirio Rubirosa." This Dominican playboy was famous all around the world. From Brazil to Europe, women adored him, and Carlos seemed to resemble this Rubirosa man in many ways.

At dinner the next night Carlos sat between Brenda and Jennifer. He enjoyed Brenda's British accent, and asked about her life and work. He wanted her to keep on talking so that he could learn how to pronounce certain words the way she did. Trying to imitate the British accent, he repeated words such as "radar" and "tomato", and they both enjoyed this little game. He seemed genuine and caring, but most of all there was a sensuality about him that made her want him.

That night in her bed she could smell him, feel his smooth olive skin, and see the movements of his strong, muscular body. Softly she started to touch herself, thinking about him, and had one of the best orgasms she could ever remember having.

Every night after that Carlos would sit next to Brenda during dinner. He even started going to the night dance and teaching her how to dance merengue and salsa. They exchanged a lot of information about each other. She told him about the immense pain she felt during her school years because of the cold boarding schools, how she dreamed about living in a warm climate, and how she had been bullied for so many years.

She could hardly believe herself. She had told him more than she had her own roommates. But he had also opened up to her, and seemed to mellow when he talked about his step child, and soon-to-be ex wife, his dreams about owning his own gym/spa, and the challenges he was facing. He seemed genuine when he encouraged her to lose weight. He even told her she could have a better figure then any of the ladies at the spa. Very diplomatically and with a caring, soft tone of voice he dropped the suggestion that, with her beautiful green eyes, a jaw implant would make her look like a famous movie star.

The next day, and very determined, Brenda went up to Claudia and asked her to please get her an appointment with the famous plastic surgeon. Then she went to Marie Terre and very boldly told her she was not going to New York with her and explained what her plans were. Marie Terre was not in the mood to argue, since she also felt like getting rid of her forever-protruding love handles.

Without thinking too much about it she went to the front desk of the hotel and asked them to cancel the New York arrangements, as well as the airline tickets, and to leave their return tickets to the UK open. With shyness in her voice she asked Claudia to make an appointment with the doctor for her as well. She had been influenced with the idea of looking better with less effort.

During the last day at the spa their entire bodies were painted in sweet-scented clay. They got another manicure, pedicure, and their hair was done. They felt attractive and ready to face the world. Most of the participants became close to each other. However, everyone was glad to go home or continue his or her journey somewhere else.

The young lady and the teen-age boy were the only two people staying at the spa until they lost the total one hundred pounds. They were devastated with the separation of their new-made friends. The boy had lost twenty-five pounds during these two weeks, but still had another seventy-five to go. The nutritionist was talking with him explaining that a new group of participants were arriving today and he would make new friends, but he said: "I do not want to make new friends. I want this group, these are my only friends and when they leave, I am going to go inside the hotel kitchen and eat all the food I can find."

Marie Terre, Brenda, Claudia, and Elizabeth walked in on this conversation when they came to say goodbye and wish him well. He did not want to say goodbye. He continued pouting like a small child. They were informed that the other lady was locked up in her villa in tears and did not want to see any of them leave.

It was an emotional departure. The participants kissed and hugged each other as if they had been in a war zone together. Most of them had family picking them up. Jennifer and the four Puerto Rican ladies were taken to the airport. A bus took Marie Terre and her group on the five-hour drive to a hotel in Santo Domingo. That night they had wine and pasta with a big fillet dinner.

Claudia told Brenda and Marie Terre: "I practically had to beg Dr. Gutierrez' secretary to give us an appointment. He is a very prominent plastic surgeon and, as a favor to Elizabeth's cousin, the owner of the spa, he gave us an appointment for Saturday. He never works on Saturdays. In fact, his entire family is already at their beach house waiting for him to arrive. Elizabeth finally convinced the secretary to call the doctor and he agreed to see all four of us regardless."

Dr. Gutierrez' office was an Old Spanish style house that had belonged to his grandmother and was now converted into a clinic and doctors office. The decoration was done with old-world elegance and a modern twist of surprise. The waiting room had a large waterfall that fell from the second story all the way down to the reception area. Glass windows separated the interior garden that had a round fountain in the center, surrounded by tropical flowers. The patio walls were covered with Spanish tiles. The doctor was also a painter and sculptor. The artwork on the walls and the sculptures on the end tables were all hand-made by him. He was a magnificent artist.

Marie Terre had lost eleven pounds during her two-week stay at the spa. The doctor let her know he would get rid of her love handles in less than twenty minutes. It was very simple, because she did not have that much.

When Brenda asked him about her chin implant, he told her that first he would get rid of the hook on her nose. Then he would implant a small chin that would make her face look lovelier then any face she could ever imagine. She had lost twenty pounds at the spa, but she still had fifty-five more to go. With compassion, he said she needed to lose some more weight, but that he would perform some liposuction on her tummy. The procedure would take approximately three hours, and he could only operate after a heart specialist gave his permission.

All four of them would see the heart specialist early Monday morning. He had separated Monday morning for Claudia and Elizabeth. He had to operate on all four of them the same day or not at all, because he was booked solid for the next four months.

Early Monday morning, after getting their laboratory work done, the heart specialist provided a clean bill of health for all four ladies. Dr. Gutierrez began with Brenda, since she would take the longest. Then Claudia got her breast reduction, Elizabeth got rid of her saddlebags, and Marie Terre got rid of her love handles.

The rooms at the clinic were decorated with lots of class. Brenda's room had an antique chest and a flower-print love seat that was also a bed. They hired a full time nurse to take care of all four of them. Brenda and Claudia had to stay one extra night at the clinic. Marie Terre and Elizabeth rented a nearby hotel apartment. They also contacted a therapist that was to give them cold wraps around the areas where they had received the liposuction.

The cost of the operation, the hotel, the nurse, and the therapist was less than what Marie Terre would have spent for the ten days in New York. She used her own savings to complete the payment for Brenda's operation. Brenda and Claudia stayed one extra night at the clinic. Both of them had IV's and were in pain. The doctor told them he did not want them to suffer and would give them something for the pain. A nurse from the clinic came to the room and gave Brenda and Claudia a shot that made them sleep like babies all night long.

The next day Elizabeth, Marie Terre, and Brenda waited and received the therapist with anxiety. The cold therapy lightened the burning sensation they had from the liposuction. Claudia's breast reduction did not allow her to lift up her arms and she was instructed to stay as still as possible. Even though she was in pain, there was a permanent grin in her face, and an obvious fascination for Dr. Gutierrez. He was about six feet, two inches tall, with dark eyes and hair, warm, an artist, tender, and very masculine.

Brenda was in a lot of pain. The others were also in pain, but they comforted her most of all because they could only imagine the amount of suffering she was going through. Her face was swollen, and she complained most of all about the pain produced by her chin implant. The doctor had been very reassuring and he was on call for them 24/7. He said in ten days he would take off Claudia and Brenda's stitches, and then they could travel to Puerto Rico. He recommended Brenda stay at least two more nights in San Juan before taking the long trip back to the UK.

For entertainment they watched television, read books and looked at magazines. They made jokes and talked about dresses, shoes, and men. The hotel had a restaurant in the lobby area that delivered delicious Dominican food to their rooms. They had plantain bananas for breakfast, lunch and dinner, cooked in every which way possible.

The most unexpected and delightful phone call came for Brenda. All four young women were thrilled that a man had called. Carlos said: "I am calling to find out how are you all doing, and to tell you that my divorce is final. I would like to have dinner with you to celebrate." She was honest when she told him how sorry she was about the divorce, but that she could not see him now because she looked like a monster. He responded with the most sensual voice Brenda had ever heard.

"I enjoy so much talking with you that I do not mind at all how you look, and you will not be looking that way for much longer anyway. In fact, very soon you will be one of the most beautiful women in the world, and I am not just saying that. I truly believe it. I met you before your transformation, I got to know the beautiful person you are inside, and that is what really counts."

Her heart melted. Nobody had ever called her beautiful, and she felt as if she could love this man forever. The next day Brenda received a lovely tropical flower arrangement that Carlos had sent her. It filled the room with an aroma that made her smile. These flowers became a symbol for a much more satisfying future, one full of self-acceptance.

Carlos called her one or two times a day, and their conversations got more and more intimate.

Brenda became bolder. "I want love in my life, someone that I can comfort and that will comfort me back, someone that will treat me with lots of affection, and fill me with hugs and kisses."

"I want a lady I can feel proud of. I will take her to the most fabulous places. I want someone that is intelligent and smells as expensive French perfumes. I don't want a lady that smells like garlic and onions."

They understood each other, and their affinity increased. He started coming over for dinner. Marie Terre would leave them alone to talk, and she had dinner with Claudia and Elizabeth in their room. On other occasions all five of them talked and made jokes. He also danced with all four of them, and they laughed and sang together. Brenda was learning to speak Spanish very quickly.

Within two days she would have her stitches removed, and leave forever. It made Brenda sad to think about not seeing Carlos again. One night Carlos was sitting next to Brenda on her bed and inspected her nose and chin gently, without hurting her. Very expertly he held her head with both hands and gave her a long passionate kiss, being careful not to hurt her wounds.

He held her hands and brought them to his lips to kiss them, then her shoulders, and continued toward her breast. Her clothes slipped off her body like magic, his clothes made a pile on the floor. When his large penis penetrated her depths he whispered: "This is what I have been dreaming of." His rhythmical movements were ever so slow. He would stop moving whenever he perceived he was about to get an orgasm. He turned her around and continued moving until she reached her climax. Then he had a full explosion of an orgasm himself. She was in ecstasy, and when he held her hand she fell into a hypnotic sleep. She dreamed about being completely transformed, from a caterpillar to a lovely butterfly.

Marie Terre opened the door and found them sleeping together, naked. Without making a sound she went back to the other room and explained her predicament. Claudia was glad for Brenda. Elizabeth explained: "Dominican men are experts in love making. I've been told that as soon as they turn thirteen they are taken to a prostitute who teaches them the art of making love. Friends of mine that have been to bed with Dominican men have told me that it's an experience you never forget, and it can become addictive. As husbands, their culture expects them to have one or two mistresses. Being faithful in marriage is not the custom in this country." Now Marie Terre was worried. But she slept in Claudia's room that night.

At midnight, Carlos made love to Brenda again. She was worried about Marie Terre, and Carlos reassured her that she must be with Claudia and Elizabeth. Carlos noticed Brenda was not in as much pain as he thought. At six in the morning, before taking a shower, Carlos made mad, passionate love to her. He had to go to work but would be back as soon as he got out.

She was happy, and felt fortunate to have experienced sex like she never knew could exist. His lovemaking was brilliant, one of a kind. She did not know if this was love, but she wanted more. At eight in the morning Marie Terre rang Brenda on the phone to find out if Carlos had left. As soon as Brenda said he had, the other three ladies came running into the room to find out what happened.

Brenda was without words, but to the others she looked lovely. They did not know if it was because her face was not as swollen, or because she was glowing. Then Claudia said: "Cubans have a saying: some men's penis can make a woman wither, and others can make her glow. This guy has one that definitely gave you a shimmer." They all laughed at this off-hand, original, and witty quote.

They all needed to take a shower, get dressed, and be at Dr. Gutierrez office by nine in the morning. He was going to pull out Claudia and Brenda's stitches today. That was all that stood between them and a good bill of health to leave for Puerto Rico.

As soon as Claudia saw Dr. Gutierrez, she melted. She had a big, dreamy smile on her face. He was very courteous and gentle with all the ladies, but you could tell he liked

Claudia and she liked him. He examined Elizabeth and
Marie Terre; he said they were doing fine. Very
meticulously he examined Brenda. He seemed to be
pleased with himself, and he let her know that it would
take about six months for the swelling to go down
completely. He took several pictures of her, but he said he
would love to get a picture of her in six months; she was
going to be a beauty. Brenda agreed to let him give her
collagen injections on her lips to make them fuller. After
completing the injections he told her he wanted a picture of
her with makeup on. He sent her to an office where an
expert cosmetician would teach her how to use make up to
enhance her beauty.

He began to pull out Claudia's stitches. She started to
scream, and black tears were rolling down her face. She
had put on lots of mascara, and her tears rolled down her
face in thick, black lines. She looked terrible. She kept on
complaining about how painful it was every time he pulled
out the stitches. He said that in the Dominican Republic
there was a saying: "She who wants a pretty hairdo endures
pulls." They all started to laugh. Then he looked deep into
her eyes. The attraction was there, but he was married,
and she painfully knew that that would be the end of that.

When Brenda came out of the other room she looked
ravishing. The tropical warm weather had made her hair
grow longer and fuller, her tanned skin glowed, the
symmetry of her nose and chin were perfect with the shape
of her face, it made her lovely green eyes so much more
noticeable, as well as her full lips. The entire effect made
her look remarkable. They were all so happy for Brenda
and for their own transformations that they hugged and
kissed Dr. Gutierrez and kept on thanking him for what he
had accomplished. Again he looked into Claudia's eyes,
and kissed and hugged her a little longer than the rest.

Brenda new she was getting cystitis, inflammation of the bladder, from all the lovemaking. Before leaving, she told the Doctor and he prescribed a red pill that would get rid of it. He smiled at her without saying a word. He could tell she had experienced a good Latin lover.

10 SURRENDER IN PARADISE

In the UK, Diana had felt extremely lonely without her friends. She resigned from the night school because it wasn't fun going there alone at night. George had asked her to invest some of his money on something that was not too risqué. She also had to see him every night for the final details on the flat.

One of those nights he told her he needed a week off. He was going to a cousin's wedding, and he was going to help with the electrical and plumbing of a house his family was building for his cousin as a wedding gift.

She could not bear to think she would be left in London without any close friends. The bank had given Marie Terre and Brenda their vacations in February because most employees requested vacations during the summer months. The bank needed some employees to take their vacations in February to balance the year out. She knew they would be delighted if she took her own vacation time in February. She practically had to beg George to take her with him to his cousin's wedding.

George had made some money with the investments she had recommended, and this made him feel obliged to comply with her wishes. He also loved having her around. However, he dreaded having to explain how rustic his family was, and once they saw them together they would definitely think they were an item. It was going to be an odd situation all around.

She more or less knew how his family would react with her visit, but she did not care. She told herself she did not want to be alone, convinced this was the only reason she wanted to go with George to his cousin's wedding.

When William finally arrived to the UK he was in such a state of anguish that he asked his chauffeur to take him to the bank before he went to his own place. As soon as he arrived he ran in and asked the Branch Manager where could he find Marie Terri Gonzalez. She informed him that she was on vacation. He asked about Diana. She said: "Diana works on another floor, for the investment banking department. However, I know her and she is also on holiday." In desperation he ran to the car and instructed his chauffeur to take him to the basement flat. When he arrived he knocked on the door, but there was no one there. He encountered a man George had left in charge of the building. The man, with suspicion, came rushing toward William and asked: "What is going on? Who are you looking for?"

William realized he needed to calm down. As the gentleman he was, with extreme politeness he said he was looking for George and the ladies that had a flat in the same building. The man examined William and he could tell this man was definitely a gentleman, so he pulled out a piece of paper where George had written down the address where he could be reached at. He handed the paper to William and told him he would be there for about another week. He also explained one of the ladies he was referring to have gone along with him. William wrote down the address and thanked the man.

Disappointment transformed his face when he walked back to his car and asked his chauffeur to take him home. Once he arrived to his own place, he looked around and the surroundings felt empty and cold. He took a shower and as he lay in his own bed his emotions took over. He realized he missed Marie Terre with all his heart and soul. Not knowing about her had him filled with pain and despair. All he could think of was he needed to find out how she felt about him. The internal turmoil was so intense he almost believed she had bewitched him. He could only focus on one thing: to see her again. He would do whatever was necessary to make her feel the same way he did. Early the next day William asked his chauffeur to take him to the address left by George.

When the chauffeur arrived at the address, the house was empty. A neighbor saw the big black Mercedes and came running towards them. He told William that everyone was at the chapel for George's cousin's wedding, and gave them directions on how to get there. William walked into the chapel and looked for Marie Terre, but he only saw Diana; she was sitting in one of the front rows. The wedding ceremony had started. He decided to wait for the wedding vows to be over with. In his mind he wished he and Marie Terre were making those loving vows. Following the bride and groom were the maids of honor and the immediate family, and then everyone else walked outside.

Diana was flabbergasted to find William at the chapel door. With mischief in her smile she asked him if he was on his way to the men's room and just happened to notice that he knew someone there. George joined them. He liked William, and he could tell William was deeply bothered. Before giving him information about Marie Terre's whereabouts, Diana questioned him about his disappearing act. What about those pictures all over the news with different models, and above all why had he not called her in almost two months?

William did not like this harassment, but he had to stay calm. She knew where Marie Terre was, and he needed that information. Humbly, he answered all of her questions, and even added a little bit on how he was feeling. Diana saw something in him she had never seen before. He seemed to genuinely care for her friend. George intervened and asked Diana to let him know where Marie Terre was.

"Marie Terre and Brenda are in a small hotel in Santo Domingo. I have the name and phone number of the hotel in my flat in London, and I will give it to you when I get there. I will be back in about a week."

William did not want to wait for another week, but he thanked Diana as he kissed her on the cheek as a demonstration of gratitude for her information, and he gave George a manly hug. After he left, George was worried for him.

"William seems very vulnerable."

William made the necessary arrangements to fly in his private jet to the Dominican Republic. He instructed his assistant to call every hotel in Santo Domingo until she found out were Marie Terre was staying. On the flight from the UK to the island of Hispaniola, William's enthusiasm grew by the minute. The mere thought of seeing Marie Terre again made him delighted in such a way he felt week.

He fell asleep and dreamed that Marie Terre was running towards him, and then nervously she stopped, just before he covered her with his arms and they could not stop kissing each other. The airplane's radio woke him up. It was his assistant, and she provided the information he had requested as well as reservations for a rental car waiting for him at the airport in Santo Domingo.

The rental car agent gave him a map and instructions on how to arrive at the hotel. The agent knew how to speak English and William also knew how to speak some Spanish. The traffic in Santo Domingo was not an easy task, to say the least. As soon as he arrived to the hotel he asked for Marie Terre, but the front desk informed him that the four ladies had left for the airport; they were leaving on the four thirty flight to San Juan, Puerto Rico.

Because of the heavy traffic he knew he would never make it on time to the airport. His own airplane had to be refueled and his pilot had to sleep for eight hours, after the long flight from the UK. He thought he would explode from frustration. He called his assistant in the UK and asked her to call Marie Terre's parents' house and find out her aunts' address in Puerto Rico.

Mrs. Camille Bronson had been working with William since he opened up his first office. She had seen him get out of many situations where he had been persecuted, harassed, and followed by female admirers. But she had never seen him go on a chase like this after any woman. She began to feel admiration for Marie Terre, whoever she was. She had definitely awakened a part of William that many thought was dead.

She had always admired William for his savvy, and that special ability to get what he wanted. She knew that behind the cool, calm, and collected exterior was a soul with so much feeling that he did not want others to see. He needed someone like this. Life needs balance, and it can't all be work and making money. He needed a family and stability.

With all this in mind, she called Marie Terre's parents house. Her brother answered the telephone. She told him that flowers were to be sent to Marie Terre at her aunt's house in Puerto Rico, and she needed their address. Ralph asked if they were from Mr. William Burgess. As soon as she said yes, he gave her all the information she needed, and was glad he had answered the phone. He knew his mother or Papa would never give William this information.

Marie Terre's parents kept all the magazines they had found with pictures of him with different models. It was like flipping a coin; as much as they had liked him when they first met him, that is how much they disliked him now. Each parent prayed that William would stay as far away from Marie Terre as possible. They were very proud people, and as far as they were concern their daughter had to be treated with respect. The pictures spoke louder than words.

At the airport in Santo Domingo, Carlos arrived to see Brenda off. He had not been able to take them to the airport because he had been filming his exercise television program. He was out of breath from running; he had been terrified that he would not get to see Brenda. With tears in his eyes he asked if he would see her again. They both promised to write to each other, call, and visit when possible. When she saw his tears she could not help but start crying herself. She wanted to stay in the Dominican Republic forever. They looked like two wounded lovebirds.

Marie Terre's spirit had been somewhat lifted with the new friends at the spa and the dancing, but she wanted to go to Puerto Rico. She had been so happy there as a teenager. She actually did not know what to expect. All she knew was that something enchanting always happened in the enchanted island.

William's aircraft landed in San Juan at eight thirty the next morning. He rented a car and went to a flower shop, where he ordered the biggest and most exotic flower arrangement they had. He gave them the address and explained he was going to follow the delivery truck, and the flowers needed to be handed to Marie Terre Gonzalez in person. He gave the driver a fifty-dollar tip to follow his instructions as soon as the arrangement was ready.

Marie Terre's family was preparing breakfast when the doorbell rang. The deliveryman explained he had to deliver a flower arrangement for Marie Terre Gonzalez in person. The aunt went to Claudia's room, where all the ladies were staying, and explained that there was a flower arrangement for Marie Terre.

Marie Terre put on a robe, figuring it was a mistake and the flowers were really for Brenda. William was leaning against his car when she looked outside for the deliveryman. In slow motion, she took a few steps forward to get a closer look at this man that looked just like William. She had a questioning expression on her face, staring at him for a few seconds and trying to adjust her eyesight to the morning sunshine. At first she figured it was a look-alike, then she believed it was an apparition or a figment or her imagination, and then she needed proof. With a tone of voice between question and groan, she looked at him in the eyes and called out his name.

"William, is that you?"

Wanting to run into her arms, he took control of himself and walked toward her slowly. At first they just looked at each other and then she realized she was in a bathrobe, and looked like a mess. However, she composed herself, proudly lifted up her head, and looked at him expecting him to say something first.

"Yes, fairest princess. I have been traveling through many far-away lands, and I arrive here today with the most noble of intentions." She did not know what he meant by that. All she knew was that she felt confused and happy at the same time.

Her aunt suddenly interrupted them, asking her to invite her friend in for breakfast. She did not want him inside the house, but he grabbed her hand and they walked inside anyway. She excused herself to go get dressed. When Brenda saw William she was glad for her friend. She went over to Marie Terre and gave her a big hug.

"I am so happy for you! He seems to be genuinely interested in you."

"I am very confused. I can't figure out what is happening. The last time I saw him, we were not dating. We have not gone to bed together. I need to act cool, because he is just a friend. I am the one that makes a big deal out of nothing."

She took a quick shower, put on a pair of jeans, and a summer-pink top. She knew she looked good. It gave her the confidence to act cool, calm, and collected. When she came out of the room, William was eating breakfast with the other members of the family, and everyone was delighted with him. He invited her to the rain forest called "El Yunque". She invited the others to come along, but Brenda needed to rest before they left for the UK, and Claudia and her family had been there many times. She had been there only once, but she definitely wanted to go again, especially with William.

Marie Terre did not talk very much during the one-hour trip to the rain forest. William did most of the talking. He explained every detail of what had happened, all the times he tried calling her, and the difficulties he had encountered. She acted as if she did not care, but deep inside she was taking it all in.

He knew she had not had breakfast, and it was almost lunchtime, so before going up the mountain to the rain forest he stopped in front of Luquillo Beach. The place had lots of small huts with tables where you could eat local creole foods. They ate "bacalaitos," which were delicious codfish fritters. They also ate fresh lobster dipped in garlic butter, and fresh oysters with lemon, among other local treats. She was hungry, and also missed eating this kind of food, so they both ate to their hearts content.

After lunch they went to the rain forest. William first pulled up in front of the beautiful waterfall. The waterfall made her feel like jumping in. It looked clean, cool, and refreshing. The steady stream of rushing water fell between rocks and ferns all the way down into a clear, delicate pool. The sounds of the water drowned their voices, and made it feel like they had stepped into another world.

He held her hand as they walked among the varieties of unique plants and trees that had managed to grow and adapt to the copious amount of rainfall year round. Everything around them was green, lush, and full of exotic beauty. The ferns were enormous, and the symphony of sounds made by the different insects was melodious and enchanting. It felt like being inside a fairy tale.

Marie Terre was pleased with all the explaining he did for not calling her in the past months, and was acting more receptive towards him even though she kept being mysterious and cool. She let him know they should not wander around too far away from the hiking trails, or the picnic facilities. People had gotten lost in this forest. He thought he wouldn't mind getting lost with her.

She wanted to go to the lookout tower, and once they got up there, every direction they looked at was filled with overwhelming beauty. The island had many places they could go to, but he needed to bring peace to Marie Terre, and the rain forest experience had been an excellent choice. He then saw some wild berries, which he picked and fed to her. She started laughing and ran away from him. She could not possibly eat any more.

He dropped the berries and ran after her. When he reached her, he pulled her down and they sat under a tree. She spotted some orchids, and then some bromeliads. She was fascinated with the abundance of vegetation. She also knew this was the ideal place to forgive William for not calling her in a couple of months.

She tried to stay cool, but as they talked they kept on touching each other and getting closer and closer. The conversation took an intimate tone, and their brows were within inches from each other. All of the sudden their lips were tenderly touching and slowly, very slowly, they started a soft, tender kiss. Their chemistry took over and their passion was so intense, they were clinging to each other. The kissing turned into lust and an intense desire overtook William, until he could not take it any longer and without thinking, started undressing her. She could feel how hard his male organ was. He gently kissed and then savoringly sucked her breast with want.

Her hot Caribbean blood was ardent with love and desire; her body was responding with such vehement passion that she was flooding over with immense wanting and loving for this man. She could not think of the importance or consequence of things. As he penetrated her she went crazy with passion, and could not hold back a scream, as she felt closer to her orgasm. When she came, he could feel her writhing and enveloping him, with so much satisfaction and pleasure that it brought the unexpected arrival of his own climax. After their convulsions, they held on to each other very tight, and kissed one another with love. They knew they had attained perfection.

All of a sudden they realized they were in a very public garden. Other people could pass by at any moment. They had been lucky no one had seen them, or heard them. They both got dressed and walked to the car without saying a word, but he held her hand so tight that it started to get numb. He finally asked her if she could spend the night with him. She let him know it would not be proper, or practical since they were leaving for the UK the next day.

He drove back to his hotel; he was staying at the Caribe Hilton. His hotel room had a fantastic view of the ocean and part of the city. She walked to the balcony to admire the beauty of it all. He walked behind her and put his arms around her waist, and also admired the sight. This was the perfect setting for their encounter. The waiting, the anguish, were now in the past. He would never let her go again. He began kissing her and then they made love, this time in a proper bed. Before they knew it, it was almost time for dinner. William called the hotel concierge and instructed him to have the Boutique in the lobby bring size four or six dinner dresses to his room. Marie Terre did not want to accept dresses from him, but he insisted they needed to go out for dinner and she had to have the proper attire. She selected a simple summer blue dress that made her look like an angel.

They went out for dinner at the Swiss Chalet, and ate a fillet mignon for two. The place was very romantic, and William almost ate with one hand: he kept grabbing hers. After dinner they went dancing to the Hotel San Juan. It had been a perfect day, filled with romance and tender loving kisses. They declared their love for one another and promised never to be separated again.

The next day the ladies canceled their flight to the UK and William picked Brenda and Marie Terre up at her aunt's house to return to the UK in his private jet. The inside of the jet was splendid. It had ten leather seats and a bed in the back of the aircraft. Bill, the pilot, was very friendly and delighted to have extra passengers aboard. This trip had been so precipitated that they had not hired a flight attendant. But he knew that William would explain all the details concerning the flight once they could walk around the cabin.

Marie Terre felt somewhat intimidated by all this. It made her think she was out of place around William. This was definitely not what she was accustomed to.

Brenda was in physical and emotional pain. When Carlos had been near her she felt no pain, but now all of her body started to ache. William and Marie Terre pampered her all throughout the flight and had her take over the only bed available.

During the flight William tried to convince Marie Terre to move in with him, once they got back to the UK. She explained that in her culture that would not be proper.

They needed to date and learn about each other before any commitments were made.

William knew that most women would have jumped at the idea of moving in with him, especially after they had traveled in his private jet. He did not know why, but the stance she had taken about not moving to his place overjoyed him. He knew he was in love with her, and he liked the old-fashioned stops she presented in their relationship with her Victorian concepts. It was like playing a delightful game for the first time in his life.

With mischief and boyish playfulness, he mentioned he had tried to resist the temptation of getting her another gift, but he just could not control himself.

"In order to avoid upsetting you again, I am tempted to give the gift I got for you in Argentina to my assistant, Camille."

He practically made Marie Terre beg him to give her the gift. She had to give him several kisses before he gave her the small handbag he had purchased in Buenos Aires. Once she saw the lovely hand-stitched night bag, she kissed and hugged him and let him know how much she loved it.

William was not expecting such an outflow of gratefulness for such a small thing. He had to know why her reaction with this gift had been so different than with the small pendant. She tried to figure it out and be honest.

"This gift makes me very happy because it lets me know you were thinking about me during your busy work travels. The other gift was perfect for another kind of moment, but it did not seem appropriate to accept diamonds from a man

I did not know that well, and we were not even dating." What she said was not very convincing, but he gave her credit for at least trying to give a plausible explanation.

11 BACK HOME

George did not have a radio in his old car. For entertainment during their trip to his hometown, Diana and George began singing several of the Beatles' catchy songs such as "Yellow submarine". Diana knew the words but could not follow any kind of tune. George's family sang in most of their meetings and he had a good musical ear. Diana's lack of musical tone was funny to him.

"You are lucky to have a College education, because if you had to sing to make a living you would not make sufficient money to even feed the chickens."

Diana knew this was true and liked the fact that he was sufficiently bold to make the silly remark, but nevertheless she punched him in the arm for criticizing her. He started laughing.

"You call that a punch? You only give cotton punches."

She punched him much harder then. "What about that one?"

"OK, that was a little better." He started to caress his arm. Then out of curiosity he asked: "Have you ever been criticized before in your life?"

With pain in her voice Diana answered.

"Believe it or not my mother still criticizes me. She tells me how I need to talk, walk, sit, do, and say."

"I can't believe it's that bad."

"It's only when I see or talk with her. But I get my revenge by asking her: 'When was it that the Good Lord gave you the power to judge and condemn at the same time?' She does not like this question very much, but I think I have used it so often that it seems to go in one ear and come out the other. What really gets me is that when I lived in her house, I tried so hard to please her! But she was always unhappy. It was as if she only wanted to see the bad side of things. She never saw the good things my father and I did for her. I stopped trying when one day she told me that nothing that I did was of any value."

In solidarity with what she was saying George held her hand, but as soon as he realized what he had done he let go. She liked him holding her hand.

"What about you, were you often criticized?"

"I think everyone has been unfairly criticized at some time or another. In my family, we had to work from morning until night. My father repeated several times a day: 'Work is what puts food on the table, so everyone must work, work, work.' We were valued for our hard work, because it put more food on the table. But the sad part about it was he also liked whiskey. Money was for food and his whiskey. My mother never got to have nice things, and I resented that. The day I get married I want to share whatever I have with my wife and children. All the good things in life."

Diana's hart melted over each word he said. Listening to him made her realize he had the moral values she longed for.

George drove Diana to the Inn were she was going to stay.

"I am going to explain your presence in town to my family, because if I don't, they are going to think there is something going on between us and they will tease and make fun of us to the point of exhaustion. I will call on you for dinner. I do not want for you to eat all by yourself."

She assured him it was not necessary; it was late and she wanted to rest. She would see him the next day. He stared into her eyes.

"It breaks my heart to leave you alone in this unknown place."

Her heart was pounding much too loudly for comfort. "Go to your family. I was the one that insisted on coming over here. I would have been more lonesome in London than I am here." Then without thinking, she added: "...because I know you are close."

And for the first time since the night-school blunder, she kissed his cheek. He squeezed her hand before he left. She was staring at him when he looked back to see if she had already left, and for that instant their souls met and all they did was smile at each other from afar.

As soon as George greeted his family he gave them what he thought would be a good explanation for Diana's presence.

"I am remodeling a flat for three ladies that live in the same building where I work as superintend. I told them I had to interrupt the remodel to work on my cousins' new home. One of the ladies insisted on seeing for herself the kind of work that I do and she drove here with me to see how I work on my cousins' home."

One of his brothers said: "But you already remodeled a flat in that building. This lady that drove over with you could have seen that flat when the Americans are in the USA, because you have the keys."

The silence was so intense you could hear a pin drop. All eyes were on George, expecting to hear what he was going to answer to that. So George looked at his family and said: "I did. I showed them the flat that was already remodeled, but this particular lady said she wanted to see every detail of my work. She wants to know exactly how I install the electrical and the pluming: she is very meticulous."

The jokes started immediately. "Yeah, I bet she is very meticulous!" "Which parts of your work does she want to see in detail again?" "Are you sure she did not drive all the way over here to have her own plumbing and electrical repaired?"

Everyone started laughing, and George took the opportunity to try and change the subject. But it was not that easy. The jokes turned into a full-blown interrogation: "Are we going to meet her?" "Did you invite her to the wedding?" "How old is she, is she married?" He shut them up with a loud remark. "The lady is a client of mine and it's none of your business to ask all those questions, so that is that, and I do not what to listen to any more questions about this client."

Everybody was quiet for a moment, until one of the cousins added: "You gave us too many explanations about your mystery lady, and that is why we are all suspicious. There's something you do not want us to know." As George walked away from his family he didn't look back when he angrily said, "Just forget it".

The bridegroom ran after George. "Because you are the best man, we waited for you to arrive for the wedding rehearsal. It's going to be tonight. The maid of honor is looking forward to meeting you and being your partner at the wedding."

George was too tired and worried about Diana to listen to his cousin. He answered, "yes, yes", only to get him off his back. During the rehearsal he felt like a robot. He followed directions and only thought about what could Diana be doing all by herself. As soon as the rehearsal was over, he told his family he was exhausted and needed to go to sleep. He did not even notice how enthusiastic the maid of honor had been when she met him, and throughout their brief encounter.

His family's rustic silliness convinced him he could not take Diana to the wedding. George arrived at the Inn about ten in the morning to have some tea with her. She was already sitting near the fireplace with a cup of tea and did not see him walking in. He took advantage of the moment to stare at her. He could not help but compare her to his humble and loud family. She was so calmed and poised, her lean body made her seem like a majestic portrait with the sparkle of light from the fire reflecting on her golden hair. She was so beautiful he imagined her coming from another dimension; he could not believe so much beauty could share the same space he was in. Then she turned her head and smiled at him.

"Good morning. I hope you had a good rest. I am sorry that you may not go to the wedding, but my family is already making assumptions that there is something going on between us, so it's best that you stay in the Inn and I will see you after the wedding."

Diana had never "not been" invited to an event. This was so new to her that more than ever she wanted to go to the wedding.

"I am not going to stay in this Inn all by myself. I brought a nice dress for this wedding, and if you don't want to make your girlfriend jealous of me I can explain to her why I am here."

George started to laugh, but it was a nervous laugh.

"That's ridiculous, I have no girlfriend, but if I take you to the wedding my family is going to think that you are my girlfriend. They are going to make your life impossible, asking questions on how we met and when are we to marry."

Like a spoiled child she said: "I don't care what they think, or ask, or how rustic they are, I am going to the wedding with you, so let me know at what time I need to be ready."

George felt lost, but content at the same time. He was fascinated with her imposing manners.

"I will pick you up at 2p.m."

She answered calmly and composed, but inside she was gloating. "Very well, please sit down and have some tea with me."

Like an obedient child he sat down and felt in ecstasy.

Diana's attire was a conservative black and cream knitted dress with a round neckline; it accentuated every curve of her figure. In the black area of the dress she placed a small Cameo, She paired the dress with a long, cream cape that made her look like the cream of society.

When Diana saw George for the first time in his black dress suit she thought to herself: "My God, he is a real Adonis!" As they looked at each other they began to giggle, with the nervous laughter some people get when they want to say something that they know the other person knows. They knew that, as a couple, they were a smashing hit.

George was the first one to say something. He did not want to seem ordinary and say something Diana most have heard many times before, so he said: "It's the first time I have seen you all dressed up for a party, and it becomes you."

She could not remember ever having felt this happy, like a teenager on her first date, giggling and nervous. "And you seem to have been born to wear a suit."

This was the most amazing complement he had received in his entire life, only because it came from Diana.

When they arrived at the chapel, George instructed Diana to sit on the second row of the benches. He went to the front and stood next to the groom. The groom stared at Diana from the altar while he talked to George.

"I wanted to give you the good news that my future wife's sister fancies you, and is expecting to be your date during the wedding. What are your plans with the mysterious lady client? Are you going to give anyone here the opportunity of trying to conquer her, or is she all yours?"

Georges' body trembled to even think about anyone considering Diana as a possibility, but he was at a loss for words. He was still thinking about what to tell the groom, when the organ started playing and the maid of honor walked in followed by the bride and her father.

Diana noticed that during the ceremony the maid of honor kept on smiling and making eye contact with George. She also realized that his necktie matched the color of the dress she was wearing. A nauseating sensation in her stomach made her realize she was jealous of this young girl. She started examining every detail about the girl's hair, dress, how she carried herself, and how sickening the girl's flirting with George made her feel.

When she looked over to George, she noticed he was intensely staring at the back door. She turned her head to see what he was looking at and to her amazement it was William. She immediately guessed he wanted to see Marie Terre. On the other hand, George could not believe his own eyes. His first thought was that something terrible had happened, and then he panicked thinking that William could be interested in Diana.

As soon as the ceremony was over, George walked with the maid of honor clinging to his arm towards the door where William was standing. He managed to disentangle himself from the maid of honor's grasp and joined William and Diana. He was relieved to know that William was interested in finding Marie Terre.

George was hoping that William would stay at the wedding or at least take Diana to the city with him, but William was too anxious to leave and find Marie Terre, and Diana did not want to leave the wedding party. In fact, she seemed more upset with William than usual and was taking it out on him.

The maid of honor tightly grabbed George's arm and said: "You must be part of the group or you will ruin the pictures." He knew Diana overheard, and could only hope she understood the situation with the photographer as he was whisked away by the girl.

The chapel had a connecting reception room for celebrations. At the wedding reception the bride and groom sat in the center of a long table. Her parents were at one side of the table and his parents were at the other side. George was to sit next to the maid of honor for all the wedding photographs.

The maid of honor was totally infatuated with George. She was trying her very best to make him notice her. She found out what his favorite food was, who were his best friends, and what he liked to do for entertainment. She had been asking about him for days before his arrival, and after the rehearsal she told her sister she wanted to marry this wonderful man with all that city education.

As best man, George's toast was simple but with the expected emotional undertones that brought tears of joy to many of the guests. The maid of honor was so nervous, she drank the entire content of her wine cup in a gulp. Someone filled her cup and again she drank it, and this went on all through the toast. By the time everyone started dancing she was not walking straight and looked inebriated.

She insisted on dancing with George and even tried to kiss him on the lips several times. She continued to drink alcohol, and when George took a stand and told her "stop grabbing me, control yourself, and stop acting like a fool", she started crying and wailing like a mad woman. In a distressed voice she repeated over and over again "I love you, and we are going to get married, please don't leave me alone, I need you, you are my soul mate!"

Like everyone else at the reception Diana stared at the spectacle. But in her mind she figured this was why George did not want to bring her to the wedding party. As soon as others came to console the maid of honor George walked over to Diana and in an upset tone of voice asked: "Would you like to leave now?"

"Oh yes!"

During the car drive to the Inn they did not say a word, but as soon as they arrived she slammed the car door.

"You can explain to your girlfriend that there is nothing happening between us."

"I told you I do not have a girlfriend. I just met the girl last night."

Sarcasm dripped from Diana's lips. "Sure. And she is already madly in love with you, and you are her soul mate."

Having said that she walked into the Inn and left George astonished. He told himself: "She has no right to be upset with me. The girl is not my girlfriend and Diana was not my date." Then he started laughing out loud. "She is jealous! I think she likes me."

Then it hit him. He was the superintendent of her building. They were worlds apart. "I must remember that she is a lady. When we get back to London she will be with her own kind."

The next day George went to the Inn to tell Diana he would be working the electrical and plumbing with his brothers and cousins.

"I want to go. I promise not to interrupt your work, and if you need anything from the hardware store I can go and pick it up. I can also go for refreshments and serve as a messenger. I want to explain to your girlfriend that there is nothing going on between us."

George started to believe she deserved to spend time with his people. "Perfect. You will see for yourself how my family dynamics work."

George was wearing his work outfit and she had on American blue jeans. George walked Diana inside the empty house and as soon as the others saw her they started whistling and making silly comments. George had to yell to make himself be heard.

"Stop that. The lady is here to see our work."

It was admirable to see how they all respected him and continued working in silence. Diana was terribly bored watching the men work until she overheard one of them explaining to George how he needed to drive to the hardware store for more wires. Immediately she said: "I will go and get them, and if you want sandwiches I will also get you some."

The men felt relieved to know the lady would do that for them, so they all put in their orders for the sandwiches and wrote a note for what she needed to pick up at the hardware store. One of the teenage boys that could not drive volunteered to make the trip with her and show her the way. As she drove George's car she felt relieved to be looking out into open space. She needed the fresh air and to do something useful, instead of just watching the guys work.

The young boy was tense and did not talk at all until she started questioning him.

"What is your name? How old are you? What is your favorite subject in school? Do you have a girlfriend?" He started to loosen up as he answered each and every one of her questions. He became friendly as he told her about his girlfriend. She took advantage of the conversation.

"Has George been seeing the girl that cried last night for a long time?"

"Oh no! He just met her the night before. I heard she had been asking about George long before she met him, and when she did it was love at first sight. The girl seems to be used to getting what she wants, and she wants him, but he is not interested. Her family says he lives in a fantasy world, that his ambitions are to ridicule people like us, and that is why he did not even notice the poor girl."

Diana did not say a word, but she was very pleased with this information.

With that particular feeling of happiness she walked up to each and every one of the men and gave them the sandwiched they had ordered. After eating, the men started singing. They had good voices, but forgot some the words of the songs. Diana would tell them the words and they continued singing. This scenario repeated itself until the electrical and plumbing was completed. They kind of bonded with Diana, even though George tried to stay as far away from her as possible.

That night George's mother prepared an exquisite meal for them. The group had accepted Diana and made her feel welcome. She felt comfortable helping set the table and washing the dishes after dinner. After a long day of work and singing there was little cause for arguments. They took advantage of their leisure to learn more and ask George questions about his work. Dinnertime gave everyone the opportunity to be at ease.

Diana observed the family interactions and realized George was correct to say his family was rustic. But she thought: "If he were to meet my family and see how they act, he would be so grateful for his. My people look as if they swallowed a stick. If he was ever to see them, he would realize that the ease and care in this family is much more suitable for me."

Before she could get used to country living, it was time to get back to London and meet her friends. Brenda and Marie Terre were scheduled to return within the next three weeks. She knew what she had to do. She gathered her wits about her, and started to plan her future. She had three weeks to make it happen. And it would all start that same night.

And the three weeks flew by, and they were better than expected.

Diana was happy to have her friends back in the UK with her. She was amazed to see Brenda's beautiful transformation. Marie Terre was also glowing, all bright eyes, and with a lovely suntan. Getting rid of her extra five kilos made her look taller. She walked in holding hands with William. Even he had a special something going on. The three friends hugged and kissed and talked at the same time. It seemed like the mutual admiration society. Diana had no suntan, but there was something different about her. She was also glowing. The friends had a lot of catching up to do.

Before William left for his own place he gave Marie Terre a big kiss on the lips and asked for her phone number. They both started laughing: it had become a private joke between them. Diana let them know their flat was still not completed and the Americans were arriving to the UK the next day, therefore they would be staying in George's basement flat again. Marie Terre gave William George's phone number, as well as her office phone number.

Diana sat her friends down. "Before the two of you fill me in with every detail about your world travels and Marie Terre's romance, I want to tell you about the current events in my own life."

She told her roommates everything that happened from the time she decided to accompany George to his country family wedding, to the day she sat in his family's kitchen after the construction work.

She went into detail explaining: "I was fascinated just observing the interaction among the family members. I loved what I saw, but most of all I carefully studied all of George's movements. Deep inside I had always felt a physical attraction towards him because of his extreme good looks, but when he was in his own surroundings he was so confident, active, and sure of himself I just fell for him. He was a total gentleman at all times. I realized that if I wanted to have something with him, I would eventually have to make the first move."

Diana looked at her friends to see their reaction, but all she got was two pairs of eyes looking at her with expectation. They really wanted what was best for her, and needed the details. With some hesitation she continued. It was extremely important for her that her two best friends get a true understanding of the situation. She wanted them to accept her new reality concerning her relationship with George.

"I calculated all my moves. Like Diana the conqueror, I invited him for dinner at the Inn where I was staying, knowing that my bedroom was right upstairs. At first I felt embarrassed because I was planning on seducing him, but I knew there was no other way. He would never make the first move. During dinner I could not keep my eyes off his strong, calloused, large-knuckled hands. My imagination had his hands sliding up and down my back, caressing my hips, thighs, and, well, you can imagine the rest."

"Do we have to imagine it?"

"Come on! This is no time to stop the story!"

"My desire for him was so intense that I had to make myself come back into present time and concentrate on how I was going to seduce him and take him up to my room. I ordered a bottle of wine for the two of us. At first George was suspicious of my unusual behavior, but after two glasses of wine his body, mind, and soul also seemed to be crying out for me. One thing led to another, and we confessed our mutual attraction.

George said he felt it had been cruel how he had suppressed his own feelings toward me, and he could not believe that I was now coming on to him. He also knew the world was cruel. The difference in our social backgrounds was so big he was convinced that a relationship like this would not work, and it would only get our hearts broken. That night George let me know that my friendship meant the world to him, and he would never do anything to compromise it. I was the one that put one hand over his and told him I wanted to live in his world full of caring, love, and happiness.

He pulled his hand away from mine and got a little upset. He told me: 'I have the feeling you are not getting it.' Then he became loud, and frustrated. 'Life is not that easy! I left my family because I felt suffocated by them, imposing their own values on other people's lives!

Having family members, such as aunts and uncles, cousins, friends, and neighbors getting into everyone's private life and into each other's business is the most demeaning thing in the world. They have their own opinions and do not respect the opinions of the individual. It's all a group situation and one can't outrun the group. I love and care for them, but I want a life of my own. I want to make something of myself. I want more. I want to see the world and enjoy the good things in life. I want some of the things William has.'

When I saw how angry he was I became even more attracted to him, because it demonstrated he is a man of character. I am sorry to say this, but I have resented my father for not standing up to my mother's constant demands. I was also fascinated by his adventurous side, which I had no idea he had.

I told him we could build our own world together. With disbelief he stared at me and said: 'I am totally lost. This situation does not seem real to me. I don't believe in fairy tales and this is definitely a fairy tale. How could the most unreachable, adorable lady give her heart to me?' He later on told me that at first he was petrified. He had held back his desire for me for such a long time that all he could do was stare at my face, but then he stopped reasoning and let his love for me take over.

I myself am not quite sure how it happened, but all of a sudden his strong hands were gripping my body as our lips rushed against each other. The kissing was so dizzying that I thought I would faint. I desperately wanted to get upstairs. How we made it to the room only heaven can tell, because I for sure cannot remember how we reached the bedroom.

Once we finally made it there our longing bodies were prepared, and my knees were about to give when he picked me up in his arms and gently laid me down on the bed, caressing and contemplating me as if to immortalize this moment in eternity. He undressed me as I was undoing the buttons on his shirt and his belt buckle. He caressed and kissed my body, and then skillfully he pressed down on my sensual, wet desire. Our ecstasy felt like a state of rapturous amazement. I fell asleep in his arms. But when I woke up the next morning he was not there. I found a note on the nightstand that said: 'Thank you for the most amazing night of my life. Love always, George.' I wanted to be with him forever."

Marie Terre and Brenda were both fanning their faces and letting out little sounds of encouragement. They were certainly happy for the two of them, but wanted to know more.

"George showed up at the Inn when I was having breakfast and told me he wanted to stay with me forever, but if he were to spend the night away from his family they would all inquire and try to investigate what had happened. He wanted to keep me for himself and not give them more information than was necessary. The next day we left for London and have been living together ever since.

George somehow doubted that he could reach his long life dream of making a better life for himself and his future family: our future children and me. We did some brainstorming and came up with an idea. We are using the profits from the investments I made for George in the Stock Market, and my own savings from the money I earned at the night school. We are going to remodel the many flats in London that need repairs. We made an educated guess and decided to take our chances in real estate.

Holding hands, we walked the streets of London searching around until we found and bought an old dilapidated building that George is fixing up. Each flat will be sold individually. Actually, we have already sold two of the twelve flats, and it's still a work in progress."

She looked at Marie Terre and Brenda. "So, what do you think?"

Brenda smiled. "And we thought we had the big news!"

Marie Terre said: "We better not travel without you again. Next time we will come back to meet our nephews!"

The three friends fused in a long embrace, looking forward to sharing the new chapters of their lives.

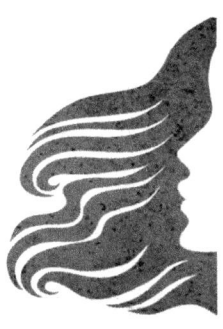

12 NEW BEGINNINGS

Marie Terre could not believe all that had occurred in Diana and Georges' life during the twenty-eight days she and Brenda had been away. Her mother always said travel was a life changing experience, and this trip had certainly changed all five of their lives in a very positive way.

Brenda's supervisor and co-workers at the bank were astonished to see her transformation. They kept on staring at her with amazement, and they told her how lovely she looked. For the first time in her life she had been called beautiful, lovely, elegant, and so on. But she did not care. She felt miserable; she missed Carlos, the blue sky, the transparent Caribbean water, the white sand, the laughter, the dancing, and even the food. Her supervisor said that she was so pretty that she should apply for a position as an accounts officer. Without giving it much thought she went to the Human Resources department and requested the position. They took the application and informed her they would revise her personnel folder and get back to her in a week or two.

Diana and George made an extra effort and completed the flat two weeks after Marie Terre and Brenda got back to the UK. All it needed now was new furniture. Diana was not interested in decorating the flat because she had too much work. Every night she would go with George to the building they had purchased. She would inspect it, provide her input, make a list of what needed to be done or what materials needed to be obtained, and she would also help when possible.

William wanted to see Marie Terre every single day. He had lots of social activities and she needed to get the proper wardrobe for each occasion. She was fortunate that Williams' assistant, Mrs. Camilla, liked her and had the local boutique stores bring a selection of outfits for her to look over. After work Marie Terre would go to Williams' office to try on and select what she liked. Once she picked out what she wanted to wear for the occasions, she would take a shower in William's office and off they went.

Brenda felt so lonely that she decided to take Spanish classes at night school. She wanted to write to Carlos in Spanish, plus she did not want to forget the little Spanish she had already learned. A couple of weeks had gone by and she received a call from Human Resources. At the meeting she was informed her folder had been carefully revised, and because of her amazing credentials they offered her the position of Branch Assistant Manager. She knew she deserved this position and wanted to celebrate, but she felt alone. Diana was living with George, and Marie Terre had given in and was staying at Williams' place.

The three friends had been meeting for lunch whenever possible at the cafeteria. Her friends were very happy for her promotion, and they wished her all the success in the world. They invited her for dinner on Saturday. All five of them would go. Knowing that she would be without Carlos made her stomach ache. It was a pain she had never felt before.

William had a house in the city near his office. It was in a lovely street lined with trees. The front of the house had a tall wrought-iron gate, cemented with brick pillars and an intercom with a surveillance camera on the wall next to the latch. The house front wooden doors were wide and opulent. The front hall had a Greek statue under the large staircase. The decoration was sumptuous, with fine antique furniture. The framework on the expensive paintings was extravagant, with intricate hand-carved details. The accessories and the fireplace mantel all came from centuries ago, and then there were the luxurious window treatments.

It was all too profuse for Marie Terre's taste. It looked more like a luxury hotel than a home. Marie Terre loved whipped cream, and she had dreamed of decorating a flat with white furniture, lots of real plants, and simple drape panels on the windows. It would be a place where everyone felt comfortable; where you could spill wine on the floor and just clean it off without the inconvenience of damaging a plush carpet or breaking something precious, and above all, where children could play and not be afraid of breaking something. She wanted a home like the home her parents had given her.

Mr. & Mrs. Green, Williams' butler and housekeeper, did a wonderful job keeping the house crystal clean. They had seen many gorgeous women come and go from this house, and in only a matter of weeks they all disappeared into oblivion. When they met Marie Terre, they were proper but without warmth of affection. In fact they were as cold as ice.

This petite immigrant did not compare to the dramatically beautiful ladies that had fallen madly in love with Mr. Williams, but she did have a quality they had not seen in the others: she seemed very self-assured without being conceited. She talked with authority. They never heard her talk with double meaning, and she did seem to provide Mr. William with a suitable environment. He was more upbeat and enthusiastic about things when he was with her.

William suggested they celebrate Brenda's promotion in his house. It had been a long time since he had guests over, and he also enjoyed George and Diana's company. Diana and George immediately said yes to the invitation. They enjoyed going out for dinner, but at this moment in their life they could not afford it. They were in financial hot waters, but did not want anyone to know it.

In her new position at the bank, Brenda got to interact with more customers than she had before, and a couple of single men had asked her out. She went to lunch with Robert. He was a tall, not bad looking accountant from one of the best firms in the country, but she found him boring compared to Carlos. However, she did not want to go to dinner at Williams' house without a date, so she invited him. Robert was elated. He had read about William's success over the years and had an innate desire to meet this accomplished man.

Upon arrival to Williams' house they sat in the living room and started their evening with some Port wine from Spain. Some of the side dishes brought in by Mr. Green included pâté with crackers, sausages, and fresh shrimp. After an hour or so of small conversation, they all went to the charming dining room with its warm fireplace and, of course, old-world opulence. The first plate of fish with white wine was a perfect starter, and the main course was a delicious fillet mignon cooked with red wine and mushrooms, accompanied by roasted vegetables and mashed potatoes. The dessert was Mrs. Green's specialty:

a delicious chocolate soufflé covered in a strawberry and brandy reduction. Everyone seemed happy and ate to their hearts content, except for Brenda.

The celebration was for Brenda, but she looked dull and gloomy. She went through the motions of eating when in fact all she did was nibble. She would pick up a small bite at a time and eat squeamishly. The others had noticed this but did not say anything. They did not want to embarrass Robert.

With great delight, George was providing the details of how he and Diana had purchased the building and the work it entailed. William was listening with admiration. He liked George and was glad for him. He suggested that as soon as this project was complete, they should take the profits and invest as much as they could. Then they could repeat the process in Spain. The properties there were still affordable, and once Spain entered the European Common Market, the property prices were going to skyrocket. George gave Diana an inquiring look. By now she could read him like a book. She would let him know she loved the idea of moving to Spain for a year or two.

Robert was marveled with the conversation, and asked William for his recommendation. He also wanted to invest in real estate. William suggested he invest in one of the flats that George and Diana were selling.

After dinner they had a Crème de Menthe and coffee. As the conversation flowed, William and Marie Terre held hands and every so often, gave each other a small kiss and smiled at each other. In the kitchen Mr. & Mrs. Green commented that Mr. William seems to be smitten.

"I have never seen him like this before."

"He actually looks very happy."

Brenda listened to the conversation without saying much. She remembered her childhood dream of living in sunny Spain. Now with all her heart and soul she wanted to live in the Dominican Republic, a third world country, with lots of electrical and water problems. Most houses there had an electrical plant and a cistern, to deal with the lack of reliable utilities. Yet she had been so happy there!

Just thinking about Carlos, the blue sky, and the warm weather made her light-hearted and it showed. She knew she had to do something about the way she was feeling. She had conquered other obstacles in her life already. She had been fat, and now she was not. She had been ugly, and now she was attractive. Now she needed to do something about her love life.

Knowing that it was in her disposition and power to do something about the way she was feeling, that she was in control of her life and destiny, made her elated with pride. She knew she had to aim high in order to obtain what she wanted. She still did not know what she was going to do, but one of her main goals tonight was to get into a good mood and enjoy her friends company and the exquisite surroundings. At his point her attitude changed and she actively participated in the group, and even found the jokes enjoyable.

William picked up the habit of making jokes out of little things from Marie Terre's father. After dinner he made a few. George, who was an expert at making jokes, started with his own round of jokes. They were all laughing so hard their belly ached. Brenda also got in the mood and everyone was happy to see her in a high spirit.

William had gotten into the custom of calling Marie Terre at work in the mornings and again in the afternoon. But one afternoon he called her several times and she was not at the bank. He started to re-live the anguish he felt during the two months he had been traveling and had not spoken with her. At first not knowing where she was worried him, and then it gave him heartache.

An emergency had occurred at the bank. One of the tellers was crying her heart out because she had given a client an extra 900 pounds. She knew she would lose her job over this mistake. She had called the client over the telephone and the client said, "Mistakes are paid with money" and hung up. As assistant Branch Manager, Brenda wanted to protect the teller. She decided to visit this client and talk with him in person. She asked Marie Terre to go with her to the client's house.

The client opened the door of his house, but did not let them in. He admitted that the teller had given him an additional 900 pounds, but he was not going to return the money because just as he had told her over the telephone "mistakes are paid with money." Brenda and Marie Terre tried to make him sympathize with the teller, since she would lose her job over this mistake. There was nothing they could say to have him give in. He just shrugged and with a lot of sarcasm refused to comply, and then shut the door on their faces. At this point they finally gave up, but Brenda was so furious that she told the client through the closed door the next day she would close his account with the bank. They did not need clients like him. He opened the door again and this time he slammed it on their faces.

William had his chauffeur drive him to the bank. One of Marie Terre's co-workers informed him she was with

Brenda running some errands. To calm his nerves, he decided to walk around the block until she was back. As he was walking the sidewalks he started remembering how he became a social climber back in his teens, when his parents were going through harsh times. He looked back on the attractive, very well to do ladies he had dated, and how their money would have put him in top society had he married any one of them. It made him feel good about himself knowing he had done it on his own, without compromising his integrity to a loveless marriage.

Love could only mean Marie Terre. He loved her very much, and wanted her to know that he would do anything for her. He looked into the window of a friend's jewelry store, and as if in a hypnotic trance he walked in and asked to see engagement rings. He fell for an emerald cut, five-carat solitaire. He purchased the ring, with the condition that if the lady it was intended for did not like it, she could return it. He put it in his pocket and walked back to the bank.

William walked in front of the Bank's glass door and looked inside. When he saw Marie Terre had finally arrived at the bank, and was on her way out the door, he became giddy. But as she approached, he could see she was very angry, so he controlled himself and gave her some space. Without even asking him what he was doing in front of the bank, she walked at his side following him toward his car. Along the way she gave him all the details of the horrible incident with the client. She could not stand people without honor, respect, and responsibility toward others.

He had never seen her so upset. He listened to every word she said, and her ethical values make him feel very proud of her. When he pictured what happened his admiration for her grew even more. It made him want to give her the ring right then and there. During a moment of silence, William invited her for dinner or cocktails. She explained it would be best if they took a long walk so she could cool down, and then they could go to his place. However, it started to rain and they drove to Williams' place right away.

The fireplace in the parlor was lit. She walked straight to it and for a long time stared at the crackling fire. It helped calm her down some. The fire was soothing and it warmed her body and mind, allowing her blood to flow back to a normal state.

In the wine cellar, William selected one of his best champagne bottles. Upstairs he picked up two crystal flutes and walked into the parlor. Marie Terre was still in her own private place, and he respected that. He stared at her for a minute or two. He was enchanted by her pure and simple ways. Quietly, he approached her.

"Do you want company?"

"I want to know what you think about the whole situation, and of this deceitful client."

He walked closer to her and put his arms around her shoulders.

"I understand how you feel, and I want you to know that your feelings about the situation are very appropriate. I would have reacted the same way. In fact, maybe I would have struck the man with my own bare hands. I would have given him a blow on the head and another one on the neck." He lifted up his fist in the gesture of a strong, valiant man.

When Marie Terre saw his scrunched-up face, she realized he was trying to get her in a better mood. She decided she had been upset for too long, and it was time to play.

"I love strong, valiant men. I would have liked to punch the guy out too." William's comment made her feel better. She felt accepted, respected, and cherished. She smiled sweetly at him, and put her arms around his neck to give him a soft but loving kiss.

The telephone rang. Brenda wanted to tell Marie Terre her great news. She had just finished a meeting with the top management of the bank, and managed to save the teller from being fired. This was possible because the teller knew how she made the mistake and who had the money. She explained what happened when she and Marie Terre went to visit the client, and the reason Brenda told him they were closing his account.

The management weighted her experience and the teller's, and decided the amount of money lost did not justify the loss of a good employee, who would for sure be extra careful from then on. They actually congratulated Brenda for her proactive measures to try and recuperate the money.

Marie Terre congratulated Brenda on her success and thanked her for calling and letting her know all was well, with the teller and herself. The well being of her friend made her feel much better, and ready to celebrate. As soon as she hung up the phone she ran to William and happily gave him the good news.

As William poured the champagne Marie Terre started joking with him, letting him know how strong, robust, vigorous and powerful her brave and courageous man was, and how as long as she was near him she would never fear anything. Then she also lifted her fist letting him know that she would also defend him with all the power in the world. He told her jokingly her blows would feel like caresses. They laughed, hugged, and kissed.

Then William became very serious. He picked her up from the floor and sat her down on the love seat, and sat down next to her. For a moment she became very frightened that something was terribly wrong.

"I want you to know how much I love you, and I can't continue living without you. I need to know if you also love me, because if you don't love me I will do anything and everything in my power to win your love. I will allure you with kindness to win your heart, and when I have it, I will love you even more."

She loved him more then she could ever imagine you could possible love someone. It felt as if she had loved him forever. As he was proclaiming his love to her she realized that it was so obvious to herself that she loved him, she figured she had demonstrated her affection with actions, but had never said it in words. She held his face with both hands, kissed him.

"I adore you."

He kissed her with his heart and his soul bared. Then with gallantry he bent on one knee, and pulled a small box out of his pocket.

"Then, if you love me so, would you make me the happiest man in the world and marry me?"

She wanted to say yes, but she hesitated. It was too soon. She wanted to get to know him more. Then there was all the doubt drummed into her by Diana, her mother, the many photographs of him with outrageously gorgeous models, and the two months he had disappeared. Fear turned into panic, she was motionless staring at the box but did not dare open it.

He could read her like a book; he took the box from her hand.

"What are you afraid of?"

As customary, whenever she got nervous she talked too much. Tears were spilling from her eyes as the words from her mouth.

"I am afraid of your traveling. I do not want to be alone. I am also worried that I do not look like a model, and models seemed to be your type."

He explained that she had every right to feel fearful of the travel, but this last experience had provided him with the insight to develop a division within his office that would have an International Staff servicing his franchises in other countries. In fact, he had been hoping her brother would graduate soon so that he could be in charge of the Latin America, Caribbean and Mexico division.

As far as the models are concern, they used each other as a quid pro quo for publicity reasons. He was the oldest of the brothers and he wanted his children to play with their cousins. And the naked truth was he loved her and could not live without her.

In her mind she said; yes, they both wanted children, yes, she also wanted to stay with him, and yes she wanted to marry him. Then she smiled and pulled her hand out so that he would give her the box. He pulled the box away from her and said no, he wanted her to first say yes to the marriage proposal.

When she said yes, he got up and walked a couple of steps away from her, and told her he could not hear her. She said yes again, and he walked further away. She said yes again. She then ran over to him and grabbed his arm, kissed him and at the top of her lungs said, "Yes, yes, yes."

Before handing her the box he let her know that she could change the ring if she did not like it, cost was not an object. When she opened the box with the five-carat emerald-cut diamond solitaire, she knew it was a quirk of fate.

She felt like a real life princess, her fairy tale now a reality. This ring was more magnificent than any ring she could have ever imagined or dreamed of. William slipped the ring on her left hand's ring finger. He stared at her, as her eyes were mesmerized by the engagement ring.

1

3 THE ENGAGEMENT PARTY

George had resigned from his position as Building Superintendent. He was working about fifteen hours a day fixing the building they had purchased. William had sent him several clients and most of the flats were sold. This was fantastic, because it gave them the working capital needed for the materials, supplies, and payroll for the several employees he had to hire. William had mentioned George needed to see another building that was for sale and maybe do the same thing again.

Diana could get him a small business loan with the bank, but first he needed to get incorporated and hire even more personnel. For their first building they had hired a structural engineer they liked and trusted for the inspection of the buildings structure. If that was in good shape, George knew he could plan the rest. For the interior design he still went to the night school to get young minds that liked designing contemporary facilities inside the walls of old structures. Diana and George would select the designs they liked the most.

George moved into Diana's room in the ladies flat. She had kept the private smaller room with the large walk-in closet. Brenda and Marie Terre were sharing the large room, but Marie Terre had practically moved in with William, and she was involved in several projects that gave her little time to show up. The flat was still not decorated. It only had beds for them to sleep on. It seemed like no one had the time or the interest in buying furniture and accessories for the recently remodeled flat.

Brenda had been following the instructions given to her by the spa's nutritionist and the pounds were easily melting away. During the weekends she went shopping for clothing that would fit her new figure and position as Assistant Branch Manager. This was the fun part of her new life: selecting a wardrobe that fit properly and shop for the accessories that went with it. Her co-workers started to call her glamorous, and she liked that. During weeknights, when she did not have her Spanish lessons, she stayed at the office until late. She hated going home to an empty room. Top management was very impressed with her hard work, but most of all they liked how knowledgeable, prudent, and conscientious she was.

Marie Terre made it very clear to William that before they told anyone about the engagement he had to ask her father for her hand in marriage, and for his blessing. It was customary, and she would not deprive her father of that joy. With a big grin on his face he complied with her requirements.

It had been very difficult to keep the ring in its box until they met with her parents. She had called her mother giving her all the details. She needed to prepare her father for what was expected. Lillian was nervous and frightened about this engagement. They hardly new this man, and the articles in the magazines described him as a womanizer. Again, Marie Terre had to reassure her mother: what she read in the news were publicity tactics, and William had proved his love for her and wanted to marry her.

"We are getting married six months after the engagement announcement."

Lillian was scared for her daughter. In order to control her fears she decided to focus on the wedding reception. She had dreamed of making all the arrangements for her daughter's wedding, but with William as the groom she knew they would probably get a fancy wedding planner.

That Saturday, William and Marie Terre arrived at the Gonzalez house at noon. William had brought a case of the bubbly for the celebration, but as they walked into the house everyone was so sober that he left the case in a corner. The family knew what it was all about so they sat down in the living room in front of the fireplace. In silence each family member stared at William, expecting him to start the conversation. He read the body language and went directly to the point.

William lifted his shoulders as he looked at Mr. Gonzalez in the eye and explained his honorable intentions of wanting to marry his daughter, and humbly requested his permission to do so. Mr. Gonzalez first wanted some kind of explanation about the rumors concerning the models he had dated. With patience William answered all of his questions. Mr. Gonzalez emphatically stated that he would consent to this wedding and give them his blessing only if he agreed to always treat his princess with all the love and respect possible. His princess had a home and a family that would always look after her well being, if ever he could not. William agreed to everything Mr. Gonzalez said.

"I promise to honor, love and protect the princess with all my might."

Her father looked at Marie Terre.

"Do you love this man?"

"Yes, with all my soul."

Ralph was elated and screamed, "Congratulations!" Lillian's eyes were all tearful, but in her mind she was praying for the couple's happiness. Amongst the hugs and kisses, the champagne corks started to pop. Lillian had cooked a succulent Cuban meal for the occasion and the dinner table had been set before they arrived. William finally opened the little box and put the ring on Marie Terre's finger. Everyone's eyes popped open. They were amazed by the size of the stone.

During the meal William talked with the family about their plans. Marie Terre had agreed to leave the bank and work on the development of an international division for his business, which would provide support to the franchises they had around the world. Some of the franchises included travel agencies that also provided hotel and car reservations. They were hoping that Ralph would agree to join them once he graduated from university.

The family felt privileged to be sharing their table, the conversation, and above all their daughter with this brilliant entrepreneur. They started to realize how Marie Terre's good fortune was going to change the fate of the entire family, and they prayed to God that it would be for the happiness of them all.

Marie Terre could not wait to tell her friends about her engagement. After lunch she called Brenda and Diana to let them know William had asked her father for her hand in marriage. She promised to fill them in with all the details on Monday. Now she had to help her mother pick up the table and wash the dishes.

Brenda received five letters from Carlos all at once. She organized them by date and started to read. Each and every one got more and more romantic. She read all of them several times. The last letter read as follows:

"My dear Brenda, my love:

I wish I were a poet and had the ability of expressing with verses all the love that flows from my heart. The days and weeks go by and my love does not dissipate, it just grows stronger. Years may go by before I see you again, but time can't make me feel indifferent toward this terrible absence. I love you when you are near me, and when you are far away I long for you even more. Only with you I assuage the afflictions of my soul.

Please, please let me know when you will be coming back to the Dominican Republic. I am trying to save some money so I can purchase the airline ticket and travel to whatever part of the world I may find you in. I am also filming additional workouts for the television program. I want to have a month off from work and use the days off to share them with you.

I saw your internal beauty before anyone else did. Now that you have become, and look just like a Hollywood movie star please don't forget who really loves you and wants to be with you always. I long to kiss and hold you in my arms and whisper how much I love you.

Write to me and let me know how you are doing. I am heartsick without you.

Send my regards to Marie Terre.

With everlasting love, yours always,

Carlos"

Brenda could not believe this was actually happening to her. It sounded too good to be true. But his letters had filled her with hope of someday living with love. She remembered his expert lovemaking, and that warmed her up. She also longed for him, for his touch, and the joy that she remembered sharing with him in that paradise. She answered his love letters with letters that were not so floral, but that also expressed her caring and feelings toward him. She did long for him, but could not express it the way he did. In her letters she let him know Marie Terre was engaged, and the wedding date had not been set but it would be in approximately six months and she would love to go with him to the wedding.

William asked Camille to find a competent person that would organizer his engagement party and wedding reception. After asking around and calling only the best, she selected Ann and introduced her to Marie Terre.

Marie Terre let her know that her mind was not into organizing a party or a reception. She wanted Ann to work the details with her mother Lillian. Her justifications were that she had presented her resignation at the bank with a two-week notice, and she was much occupied leaving everything in order for the new employee. She also had her heart set on the project William had assigned her, the international department of the company. This made her feel closer to him and his world. In reality, she was avoiding the turn of events in her life.

Again, Brenda went to the Human Resources department and requested a transfer to a small branch the bank had in the Dominican Republic. A personal representative sat down with Brenda and explained the position required ample knowledge of Spanish. Brenda told her she had been studying Spanish and was getting better.

"A transfer could entail a lower salary. However, it would be great for your career if you request to be part of the International Staff. Most employees envy these positions, but only a precious few get the opportunity. The benefits for International Staff include a higher salary, living expenses, plus a first-class round trip airline ticket back home once a year."

She could not promise Brenda anything but she would look into it and try to help her out. In the meantime she needed to continue to learn Spanish. Brenda was so excited walking out of that office! The possibilities of living with Carlos and also making a stupendous career move were blessings that she would pray for.

Ann and Lillian were in constant discord: they were in disagreement about the place, the size, and the colors. Whatever Ann said Lillian would say the opposite. Ann complained to Camille, and as usual she said she would handle it.

Camille invited Marie Terre for tea, and politely explained that her wedding day should be the most important day of her life. She could delegate, but she needed to be more involved in the process.

"But I don't want to be planning a party! I need to focus on the new International division, because I don't want William traveling so much."

Camille understood then. "I assure you I will help you on both ends; the new division, and the wedding. However, your involvement in the reception arrangements is essential. I think you will agree, William deserves to have the time of his life the day he finally marries you."

Marie Terre finally realized it was their wedding, and right then and there decided she was going to do everything in her power to make it fabulous.

William let Marie Terre know she could pick her dress or entire wardrobe from whatever designer she fancied the most. It could be Guy Laroch, Arnold Scasi, Channel in Paris, Carolina Herrera, or Christian Dior. There were no limits.

The engagement party was an intimate affair that only included; William's brothers, Paul and Henry and their wife's, Elizabeth and Laura, Marie Terre's family and her best friends, Camille and her husband, and a few of Williams friends.

William's sisters in law were snobs. Everything they wore had to have a designer tag. They had already met Marie Terre and looked down on her department-store wardrobe and her petite figure. They had always figured that William would marry a model, or at least one of their fabulous friends. When they first met Marie Terre, Laura told her if she could have one wish in her life, it should be to be taller. Marie Terre answered she did not wish on trivial things like that, and if she had only one wish in her life she would wish for her family's good health and happiness.

Behind Marie Terre's back the sisters in law commented that most people in the Caribbean islands practice witchcraft, especially in Haiti, and since Marie Terre had been to the Dominican Republic, which borders with Haiti, they were sure she had placed some kind of spell on William. Marie Terre was on her way to the powder room, when Elizabeth and Laura saw and followed her. Once they were inside, with sarcasm in their voice, they commented that William seemed to be under her spell. It seemed she had done some kind of witchcraft on him.

Marie Terre knew about the comments that are made about witchcraft and the people from the Caribbean islands, so she decided to amuse herself and play a joke on them. Perspicuously she asked them if they wanted to know how to make a love potion, and they agreed. She had heard about these love potions and had an idea about the recipe.

"To make a good love potion you first boil one dozen white roses in a pot with water, then you add some witch hazel to it, and a tablespoon of honey. You light up four white vanilla candles and place them on each corner of the room where you are to pour the enchanted water, once it is cooled down. The enchanted water needs to be poured over your head three times. The water most roll down from your forehead towards your back. While you pour the enchanted water, you most repeat the name of the man you love, and if you don't have a particular man you want to enchant, then just say to find the man I want to marry. The results are obtained in less than one month."

The in-laws were gasping. On her way out of the powder room Marie Terre repeated: "In less than one month. It's magical. You will get the man you love, but afterwards you have to keep silent, or it could reverse on you."

Marie Terre knew William adored his nieces and she wanted to get along with his brothers wife's, but is was the little things like what she just did that made her feel she was in control the situation. She liked and wanted harmony with his family members. Her own family was very close. But every time she saw her sisters in law they would make a face demonstrating their aloofness, and treated her insipidly and coldly.

Once she made them a homemade carrot cake and when she gave it to them, they said "thank you," but made that face that let her know they did not like her or her gift. That same day a friend brought them a red rose and they went overboard thanking their friend and demonstrating lots of affection. They avoided speaking with her, but whenever they did it was in a flat tone of voice and with total unconcern.

Marie Terre could not understand their graceless manners. She wanted warmth and family union, but they were very cold toward her. What she had just told them about the love potion was not true. It was a total invention, but they already thought badly about her and what she just did would confirm their own idiotic perceptions. Like it or not, she was going to marry William, and if they wanted to see him in good spirits they would start treating her better.

After a while, she got upset with herself for not having more self-control. She knew she had to keep on trying to build a relationship with them: they were going to be family. Her parents had taught her that family means helping each other in every way possible, and that communication among family members was essential. She had to make an effort to communicate with these in-laws, even if they only paid attention to themselves.

Marie Terre finally had a heart-to-heart talk with her wedding planner. Ann explained she was her personal assistant for the wedding coordination: her job was to make her wedding memorable for her and her guests. But first she needed to understand Marie Terre's ideas in order to build on them. She promised Marie Terre once she found out what her needs were, and how she envisioned her own wedding, she would take careful care of the details. Marie Terre finally grasped the idea, but most of all she found in Ann an ally that was conveniently there to help her, even if it was only for a limited time. And she needed to use this opportunity to her advantage.

Brenda called Marie Terre and read Carlos' last letter to her. They both started giggling and started to sing, "Fairy tales can come true, it can happen to you, if you're young at heart." Once they both stopped laughing, Marie Terre told Brenda that William was sending his private plane to San Juan a week before the wedding to pick her family up. Carlos could fly to Puerto Rico and take the jet with her family to the UK and be at the wedding. Brenda felt happy and grateful at the same time. She decided to call him and have him start taking all the necessary steps at work and with his finances. He needed to make the proper arrangements as soon as possible.

It took Brenda a good fifteen minutes to get an international line and make a telephone call to the Dominican Republic to talk with Carlos. He was thrilled to hear her voice. Then he became emotional and told her how much he missed her and loved her, promising to see her as soon as possible. Brenda found it all a little melodramatic, but she found herself enjoying the novelty of this exuberant emotions.

From having no love in her life to suddenly live this excesses with a man as hot as Carlos made her want to soak into this extravagant drama. She was not clear if this was love, lust, carnal pleasure, or the passion she never knew was in her. With him she felt sprightly and enlivened, even though she knew very little about him and his culture.

Diana and George were living an exquisite romance, a true friendship, and were entrepreneurs in their own business. Their sex life was great, and life smelled like roses, except for her parent's refusal to admit him as their daughter's possible husband. They refused to have him visit them, challenged her judgment, declined any notion of their daughter's romantic involvement, and he was perceived and talked about as a business partner.

George and William had become good friends and talked about practically everything, from money and business to what would please their ladies the most. George was constantly on the lookout to improve his business and the way he projected himself towards others. He was a very intelligent man, but a country boy. He felt he did not have the same birth worth as William; therefore he had to work hard on cultivating himself. He needed to become polished, elegantly dressed, and well mannered.

He started practicing pronouncing his words with the same enunciation and articulation William did. He even got William's tailor to make him a small wardrobe. When the four of them went out for dinner he was treated with respect, and that made him feel comfortable with his lady and her friends.

William had a big surprise for Marie Terre, but he had become a little worried about her reaction whenever he gave her a gift. He first wanted to test her and see if she would go for it. He was sure of one thing: that one of her favorite hobbies was visiting museums. For the weekend, he invited her and her friends to the City of Bath, in North East Somerset, England.

There were many fascinating museums in Bath, and it was also famous for its hot springs, spa water, its Roman history, and its Georgian architecture. You could also find activities such as fishing, shooting, and canoeing. He told George and Diana the city of Bath could serve as an inspiration for their business. He filled them in on the surprise, but made them promise to keep it a secret from Marie Terre.

When the weekend arrived, they were all excited about the trip. Once they arrived in Bath they found some splendid parks to view the city from. It was a feast for lovers of fine architecture. Before deciding on which museum to visit first, a Mr. Thomas casually walked over to William and greeted him. William introduced him to the others. Mr. Thomas gave the others his business card. He was in the real estate business. Mr. Thomas invited them to see a lovely fourteen-century Tudor house that sits on twenty acres of land and is for sale. Marie Terre loved seeing old houses, so they all agreed to follow Mr. Thomas to the house.

On the way to the estate Brenda pointed out a local stable for horse riding, and they all agreed they would go for a ride once they saw the property. Mr. Thomas stopped his car in front of an old, very ornate iron gate. As the car approached the house, Marie Terre mentioned the garden needed to be manicured, but she loved the rolling fields of magnificent trees, the vineyard, and the old tennis court.

William hinted on the possibilities of a croquet lawn, and a flower garden with fountains and ponds. Once they were inside, William kept on asking Marie Terre how she felt about the space and how would she arrange it. The more she walked around the house the better she felt about it.

She mentioned the ballroom could be used as a family room for eating, listening to music, and reading, and when they had a big ball then the furniture could be moved and everyone could dance. They all laughed because they knew how much she loved dancing.

The house was in terrible condition, but George became William's ally. With great enthusiasm he talked about how he would incorporate the convenience of modern living while still keeping the lovely attributes of the house and its historic content. He was sure he could create a comfortable family home that was practical and convenient for the lifestyle William had accomplished.

William looked into Marie Terre's eyes and mentioned how lovely this place could be for children to grow up in. They could have an area for them to play games, relax, watch television, or for studying. That was when she realized that something was happening. She looked at the man she loved and then she looked at the house and she let him know that yes, this house could be made suitable for them. Then, totally out of character, William yelled, "Let's buy it!"

He was so happy she went along with everything he said. It was going to take lots of good coordination and skillful undertaking to keep up with the details of the wedding preparations, then the development of a workable international office, and now the restoration of this palace. She thought about her father, and how proud he was going to feel to know his princess was going to live in a real palace.

George got the contract for the restorations of the property. His instructions were to use only high-end quality materials and get everything approved by William and Marie Terre first.

George and Diana could definitely use the money, but they knew this was going to be a monumental job that had to be done to the utmost perfection. This would be an important job because of their friendship with William and Marie Terre, and because this would put their work on the limelight for future restorations.

They could become very famous if they fixed up this old house back to its original splendor, and also convert it into a cozy home for a contemporary family. They welcomed the challenge with open arms.

They were all too excited about the plans for the house to even think about going horse riding. They went to a nearby pub and only talked about how they wanted the house to look like. William said that the materials for the house had to set a unique standard, such as the use of natural stone for the Roman bathrooms. Marie Terre said they could go to Spain and get ideas.

She wanted her bedroom decorated with Spanish details, and the guest rooms could be more French. But, the library definitely had to look British. George and Diana made it very clear that they were going to look over the plumbing for the bathrooms and the kitchen, and the electrical installations for the entire house. The decoration was up to Marie Terre and William.

Marie Terre had an expression on her face that spelled overwhelmed. She could not even talk, but William came to the rescue. As had become the usual, William read her expressions like an open book. In a soft-spoken voice and with tenderness, he kissed her and assured her she would have plenty of help.

The decoration of a house was something to be done slowly. It was an ongoing process, not a one-time situation. He had a way with her that made her feel everything they decided to do together was going to be easy and perfect, even if it required hard work. She felt delighted and blurted out the words that had been dancing in her head for a while.

"What do you think of us getting married in Puerto Rico?"

"I love the idea! Let's get married where we made love for the first time. The enchanted island is the ideal place for the celebration of our enchanted wedding."

George and Diana had never been to the Caribbean and they thought it would be fantastic. Brenda was elated, just thinking about going back to the warm sun and to Carlos' arms made her tremble with joy. She knew that all Carlos had to do was cross the Caribbean Sea. Little did she know he had to get an American Visa from the USA embassy in the Dominican Republic, and that was not an easy task. Many had died crossing the ocean in fishing boats. Those who survived found themselves arriving to USA soil illegally and without the proper documentation.

On Monday morning Brenda went to the Human Resources department to find out about her possibilities of become International Staff in the Dominican Republic. She was informed that first she needed to go for an interview with the Personnel Director, and if he approved her then she would need an interview with the CEO of the branch in the Dominican Republic. Her airline ticket would be paid for. If she was accepted it would take about a month before she could actually leave.

14 THE WEDDINGS

Ann flew to Puerto Rico to make the wedding arrangements. She was pleasantly surprised to find how helpful the hotel manager and the assistants were. They provided details of how they conducted and catered to top of the line weddings. They helped her design a special menu for the celebration, with lots of champagne and strawberries, as Marie Terre and William specified.

She spent a week at the San Juan Hotel and Casino before making a commitment. She tasted the exquisite cuisine, looked at the ballroom several times, and enjoyed the luxurious accommodations and the finest white-sand beaches with their breathtaking natural beauty. Her evaluation of this beach front resort made her feel confident to plan the most glamorous and spectacular wedding. This hotel had been called the most exciting hotel in the Caribbean, and yes, she could feel its pulse, day and night. It had a lasting beat that injected the soul with the desire to enjoy life to the fullest.

She took a taxi to Old San Juan and got dropped off in front of the Cathedral. She needed to inspect it for the wedding ceremony. Before entering she sat on a shady spot in the Nun's Square, facing the graceful, Gothic inspired structure built in 1540. It had lovely stained glass windows, and was the heart of the beautiful city of San Juan. The city was founded in 1521.

She started walking around this picturesque place and could not help but admire how well kept the cobblestone streets were, as well as the hanging balconies. As she walked forward, she saw a lovely chapel that had a small park next to it. She made a note to include this park as part of the wedding photo shooting. As she continued walking she could see the ocean from the hilltop as well as the fort, with its massive walls that surrounded the city.

She kept on until she arrived at the Castillo de San Felipe del Morro. In 1933 the United Nations declared it a World Heritage site. Morro means "promontory." It was built by Spanish troops to defend the island against enemy ships and to protect the ships that came from Spain, and used the city as a middle ground. It was another great spot for pictures.

After all that walking she got hungry and decided to stop for lunch. She looked into different restaurants that were on the way and found that many of them had delightful interior patios. She had lunch at a restaurant that overlooked a lovely plaza and another church.

After lunch she got lost and had to ask for directions on how to walk back to the Cathedral. The people were friendly and helpful. She knew the wedding guests would find this a charming place to visit. She arrived to the Cathedral and reserved the wedding date.

Carlos had a hard time trying to get a visa from the USA embassy in the Dominican Republic. After trying for several days, he took the Wedding invitation to the embassy and explained that this was the reason he needed a visa. The employees at the embassy looked the invitation over and recognized William Burgess name. Carlos was granted a visa, and treated with extreme courtesy. He did not know what happened, but was relieved to have his visa and know with certainty he was going to see Brenda again.

For many years he had an on-and-off mistress called Carmen. She was tall and dark, with a very small waist and big hips. Carmen worked as a masseuse and absolutely adored him. He had never even considered marrying her, because he knew she would always be there for him. On the other hand, Brenda represented status. She had a European culture, a college degree, a good job, and he could make her look extremely attractive. Most of all he knew he had the charm to make her fall madly in love with him. In his world she was a very good catch.

At the bank in the UK Brenda was provided with an airline ticket to the Dominican Republic. She was allowed three days off work for her job interview in Santo Domingo, the capital of the Dominican Republic. She did not say a word to Carlos. She wanted to give him a big surprise, and she did not want to call him until after her job interview. She was so anxious that the flight seemed to take forever. She wanted this position very badly. It would give her the opportunity to live near Carlos and get to know him better. It would also give her the opportunity to learn a new culture and practice her Spanish, plus it was a great career move. She could not sleep at all on the airplane.

A bank officer picked her up at the airport and took her to the hotel to freshen up. Her interview with the CEO was at four in the afternoon. The CEO was originally from Colombia. He had been in the Dominican Republic for a year, and was already looking for some other country to move to. He was a relatively young man with a strong personality. The first question he asked was why she wanted to move from the UK to a third world country.

Brenda was very honest answering the question: all her life she had wanted to live in a warm climate. When she went to the spa in Punta Cana she fell in love with the people and its culture, and wanted to learn more about this country. She knew it was a smart career move for her, and it would be advantageous for the company to use her skills, knowledge of Spanish, and experience from the UK.

He agreed on everything she said except her knowledge of Spanish. She needed more practice. However, that was not a problem because all bank employees had to know English before they were hired. Most of the International Staff he had contracted arrived from Latin America, Mexico, or the USA. Hiring somebody from Europe would enrich everyone's work environment. He told her she could practice her Spanish when she moved here, but first she had to talk with the personnel director and start working on her papers, job permits, and her residence.

The personnel director was a forty-year-old native from the Dominican Republic. She was very cordial and understanding of International Staff affairs. At the end of the interview they got along as if they had been long time friends. The personnel director was also requesting a new position in the USA. Her daughters would soon be going to college, and it would be very educational for them to study in a different part of the world. Globalization was the "in" thing now, and the more cultures and languages you knew the better off you were to qualify for offshore positions all over the world.

She started filling out Brenda's job papers, and all the other paperwork needed. She explained the company would pay a maximum of two thousand dollars for living expenses, but not to her. It would be paid directly to the landlord. Brenda walked out of the interview with her heart pounding, and looking forward to this new chapter of her life.

The same bank officer took Brenda back to her hotel. Very attentive, he gave her his business card and volunteered to take her sightseeing or out to dinner if she was interested. Brenda expressed her gratitude for his hospitality but declined the invitation. As soon as she was back at her hotel room she called Carlos and told him she was in Santo Domingo. After the initial surprise, without hesitation, he told her it would take him twenty minutes to get to her hotel. He was ecstatic, and his voice demonstrated his excitement about seeing her sooner than he had expected.

Brenda was resting on the bed when she heard a knock on the hotel door. When she opened it, there was Carlos with a big smile on his lips. For a few seconds he just studied her, observing her reaction. She was self-conscious, and a sensation of uneasiness came her way without knowing how to react. He noticed this and suddenly he grabbed her by the waist and started kissing her with immense passion. He pulled her hair back and kissed her neck, her eyes, her lips, over and over again, and then he slammed the door with his leg. He kept on kissing her until they reached the bed. All these months of longing for him made her fall under his spell in total ecstasy; her release came with immense pleasure.

After they finished making love, they started all over again. This time it was less sumptuous, but he explored her body with such precision, he knew exactly where and how to make her feel maximum arousal. His performance was so exquisite that it made her feel an amazing amount of pleasure, to the point where she reached explosive, multiple orgasms.

Around nine that night they went out for dinner. Brenda gave Carlos all the details about her transfer. She explained that most of the International Staff work abroad for two years, or until they find a replacement. If she wanted to stay in the country, then she would get paid according to the position and salary rates in that particular country.

Carlos said he would love to be her landlord. He could purchase a place near where she was going to work and she would get to select it. Brenda wanted to help Carlos out, but she was very scrupulous and told him she would fist talk with Human Resources to find out what rules and regulations they had for the rental of her living arrangements.

The three days they spent together were amazing. They took long walks at the Playa Chica beach. Carlos took her to splendid restaurants. They went dancing every night and to her amazement, the love making kept on getting better and better. Brenda had never danced, laughed, or enjoyed life as much as she had in these few days. At the airport Carlos seemed very sad to see her leave. However, he knew she would be back soon, and they would be able to get to know each other better. He was also looking forward to go to the wedding in Puerto Rico.

Carlos was a very presumptuous man that liked to look good at all times. The first thing he did as soon as she left was to visit a friend of his that had been a tailor in New York City, and now had his own business catering to the very rich in the Dominican Republic. For a decent price his friend would help him out with the proper wardrobe for the wedding.

Marie Terre's future sisters in law had been very catty about William getting married in a little island in the

Caribbean. Their own weddings had been splendid, almost as good as any royal wedding had been. They criticized and made fun of Marie Terre and poor William.

Even Diana's mother thought it was ridiculous to celebrate such an important occasion so far away. However, most of the guests had already been to both of William's brothers' weddings, and this one was going to be totally different from the others.

Openly, many friends expressed how thrilled they were to have been invited to the Caribbean, and how exotic and very romantic it was to celebrate a wedding in the enchanted island. It was the talk of the town. Everybody thought it was a fitting start to their enchanted life as a couple.

Little by little, the guests started arriving at the hotel. Most of them had never been to this island and when they saw its natural beauty, they gasped at the colors, the sky, the water, the people, and even how the air smelled and felt different. They were pleasantly surprised with the hotel amenities and the odd but delicious food.

Marie Terre had selected a very simple strapless wedding dress that made her look like a ravishing, elegant, living princess doll. The train fell with a cascade of Italian embroidery, and it was about a meter long. Claudia, Brenda, and Diana were maids of honor. All of William's nieces were part of the wedding ceremony.

Lillian was the most anxious of them all. As Marie Terre got dressed, she started to cry and couldn't stop. Claudia found them a wonderful hairdresser that also did their makeup, but he had to keep on retouching Lillian's, because her eyes were already red.

To her own surprise, Marie Terre was cool, calm, and collected. She even helped her friends out with their own dresses. Before she left the room, her mother kissed her and gave her a lovely embroidered handkerchief and a rosary, which she held under the amazing flower arrangement made of tropical orchids.

Her father knocked on the door. Lillian opened it and they gave each other a tender loving kiss, then he took his daughter by the arm and helped her all the way until they got inside the limousine. During the ride towards the Cathedral he did not say much. He was afraid if he started talking he would also cry. He noticed how calm she was and was not about to change that.

Ann hired a body of violin musicians that played at wedding ceremonies. When Marie Terre walked into the Cathedral the unexpected harmonic sounds of the violins caused an emotional and impressionable effect on her. She looked at her father, the man she had been strongly attached to for all of her life, the person that had always been there for her and had cuddled her up whenever she was afraid, and had protected her from all the evils of the world, loving her unconditionally. Now he was going to give her away to a total stranger, one who would change her innocent and simple world the way she knew it.

She looked at William standing in front of the orchid-laden altar, this good-natured adorable man that had grown essential in her life. From today on, she would be intimately united with him, and he would become her everything. As she was walking down the aisle, the violin music got more intense, the guests were all staring at her, the fully decorated Cathedral looked adorable, and an unforeseen emotion overtook her.

She could not help herself when tears started rolling down her cheeks. She started to shake, and her nose got red. She did not know if she was overjoyed with happiness, terrified of having to live up to the prince's standards, or if it was just stage fright from all the guests staring at her from the benches.

She wiped her tears with the handkerchief her mother had given her, and realized she had been born to be William's princess. She knew she had the talent to follow her destiny as a new member of his family.

William always had the upper hand on most situations. However, when he noticed the tears on Marie Terre's eyes, he got a lump in his own throat. He wanted to run over to her and hold her in his arms to console her, but he had to wait until her father gave him his beloved daughter.

When it was time for him to pronounce his vows he was speechless on account of his emotions. Then she gave him her magnetic smile, and he knew everything was going to be splendid. After the vows were said and the priest had pronounced them man and wife, he piously kissed Marie Terre on the forehead. This was his way of telling the world that she was the most genuine, pure, and entirely deserving woman he could have possibly married

As the 200 guests entered the ballroom, the live band was playing such catchy Latin music that many of them started dancing before they reached their tables. Others talked about how much they admired the amazing tropical flower arrangements on the tables, as well as the very different and exquisite wedding decorations. The guests could select from a special dinner menu of different kinds of seafood, all cuts of beef, lamb, and chicken. The food was prepared with exotic spices that made it taste so unique, most of the people could not believe they were eating seafood and meat.

The table arrangements included both of Williams' brothers, their wife's and children to the right of the table; and Marie Terre's mother, father, and brother as well as Diana, George, Brenda, and Carlos to the left side. Claudia and the rest of her family were sitting at a nearby table. Many of the guests were intrigued about Marie Terre's family, but their intrigue faded away as soon as they saw Carlos. Most of the ladies were much more fascinated with him.

His clothes fit him like a glove, and they had to admire his spectacular body. Some of them mentioned he was exactly what you would call a "Latin Lover." The older people said he reminded them of Rodolfo Valentino. But they were really flabbergasted when friends and family started dancing to the rhythm of the local band and they saw how he could move.

While sitting at the table he seemed to have a pleasant disposition, even though he was somewhat pretentious. However, when he started dancing he seemed to care nothing of what people could say. He was delightful to watch.

Dancing merengue got most of the guests in a good mood. Some of the ladies wanted to dance with Carlos, and he taught them a few basic steps that would get them by in any dance floor without much difficulty. At the fall of night, and after several champagne glasses, some of the ladies started flirting with Carlos.

Brenda had seen the attention he got from the ladies at the spa, but she had treated it as something incidental to his fame as a TV personality. She had been very casual about it then, but these were her people, and she was consumed with jealousy. Now more than ever she wanted to be with him until the end of time.

Diana's parents, as well as her brother, were at the wedding. Her mother told her father: "I am so glad the wedding is not being held in the UK. By no means would I want our daughter to be seen in public with George." Their repulsion for him was so great that they contradicted, objected, and repelled Diana and George every time they made an approach, preventing any kind of closeness from either of them.

Diana was so upset with her parents she asked George to get married in this tropical paradise the next coming weekend.

Because of her family's demeanor towards him, and also their marked difference in social status, he had not dared to ask her to marry him. Now he felt elated to know she wanted to. It was an immense relief to have her say it so bluntly. However, after evaluating the current state of affairs, and because he was too astute to be deceived, he let her know he definitely wanted to marry her but he needed to know if her intentions were to take revenge on her parents because of the way they had been treating them.

Diana looked at George with love and admiration in her eyes: she put her arms around his neck and let him know she could not think of a life away from him. She wanted to be with him in the good and bad. She knew they would get married eventually, and this island was the idyllic place to exchange their vows of everlasting love. All that worried her was his family, and if it would hurt their feelings not being invited to the wedding.

George knew at this point that it was not a good idea to have his family and Diana's together in the same place.

"I think it would be a good idea to get married as far away from them as possible, and if you want to, we can have a second wedding in my own hometown with all of my relatives present."

She kissed him several times, saying how much she loved him and how happy they were going to be, and how when they got old with arthritis they would come to this island on their wedding anniversary.

Diana was so excited she couldn't wait, and ran over to Ann.

"Could you please find out how much it would cost to have a simple wedding ceremony and reception for about twenty five persons or less by next weekend?"

Ann was very pleased with herself for not having a heart attack right then and there. She explained that more than the cost she should be worried about the fact that the hotel needed months in advance to prepare for a wedding ceremony. However, she saw the look of disappointment in Diana's eyes.

"I will see what I can do about the availability of the facilities, and how fast we can put the wedding arrangements together."

William, Marie Terre, her family, and many of the guests laughed, danced, and were delighted to learn several new steps of salsa music. The joy that surrounded them was the perfect finishing touch for their enchanting Puerto Rican wedding. For their honeymoon, William had leased a yacht with its captain that would sail the next day to nearby islands in the Caribbean.

Before they could leave the wedding reception, Diana told Marie Terre and William about her wedding plans for next weekend. They were thrilled and happy for Diana and George, and let them know with many congratulations and good wishes.

"I promise we'll be back for the wedding ceremony, and as our wedding gift we invite the two of you to cruise the other Caribbean islands with us. The pleasure craft I leased has plenty of room for all of us."

Diana looked at George and they both agreed excitedly, and proceeded to thank William profusely.

"This invitation makes it clear: it's a good omen to get married next weekend in this adorable paradise."

The next day Diana informed her parents about her wedding. Her father tried to reason with her.

"You are making such a harsh move because of the way we have been treating George."

Her mother refused to admit Diana could possibly be in love with George. Diana felt as if she was in a court of law and not in front of her closest family. Her mother got very angry.

"You think you're in love, but this is just a taste for the unknown. You never got acquainted with rustic peasants before, and this is all just an infatuation with a country clown."

She continued to challenge Diana's judgment, and tried to force her to back off her decision.

"There is no way I am ever going to let you drive me back into your ridiculous, make-believe life. Your desire to impress the so-called 'high society' makes the entire family feel miserable. I deplore your way of life, and I am going in a totally opposite direction. My life is going to be filled with love, communication, understanding, and hard work, because these are the things that are important to me.

I don't give a damn about what others think of me, about the latest fashion, or who belongs to the jet set and who does not. You live your life according to the gossip tabloids, not to your own spirit. I despise everything you stand for. You are a fake, and you cannot force me back into your fake existence."

She looked at both her parents. These people had given her the gift of life, and had raised her to be who she was now. She could not conceal her disgust and anger at their current attitude.

"You may go to the wedding if you want to, or you may decline. Either way I am getting married next weekend."

Diana slammed the door as she walked out of her parent's hotel room.

The situation was worthy of tears, but she did not want anyone to see her crying. She ran into a public bathroom and cried her heart out. When she felt in control again, she washed her face with cool water. Her eyes were red, and her nose was a mess, but she felt relieved.

As she walked out of the ladies room, she found her father standing outside the door. He wanted to talk with her. They both walked outside of the hotel and when they reached the white soft sand, took off their shoes. During the first fifteen minutes they walked in silence, the warm sun and cool breeze relaxing them.

"I am sorry for the way your mother talked about George. But I do need to confirm you are sure of this decision, and that you are not marring him just to upset your mother."

"When I am with George, I feel complete. We compliment each other in many ways, and we share ideas that become real projects. In addition to the construction business, little by little we have built a life together. More than anything in the world I want to share my life with him not only as his associate and friend, but also as his lifelong companion.

There is a joy and simplicity in George's family that, sadly but true, I have never felt within my own family. I want to build a life that incorporates joy and laughter into my daily life and household. I would not even dream of bringing up my children in a household like the cold, anguished one I grew up in, sorry.

When I see George's unpretentious relatives, and the children happily playing around, I want to have that. I want my children to share their love and innocence freely."

Diana's sincere words moved her father deeply.

"I loved your mother so much, I tried to give her everything she wished for as well as the lifestyle she dreamed of. I was so involved in pleasing her that I overlooked how it affected my own children. I am so sorry for not having been there for you, but I promise I will do whatever it takes to make it up to you. And if marrying George is what makes you happy, you have my blessing. It has always been my dream to walk you down the aisle on your wedding day. I humbly request the privilege of doing so."

Diana hugged her father and couldn't help the tears. He had always been so sweet, but weak whenever her mother wanted something. She felt for the first time in her life he was on her side, and it felt good.

He saw in her eyes the need for a talk that was long overdue.

"My beloved Diana, again, please forgive me for shutting you out of my life and not realizing how miserable you felt within our family. I did not take responsibility for my role as a father. I was so wrapped up in my own petty problems; I did not realize you needed me to be there for you. I saw you as a beautiful, determined child with the willpower to live as she wished. Your brother was so attached to your mother; I took for granted you were also close to her.

I felt like an outsider in my own house. The only way I was able to live all these years with your mother's nagging was to shut her off, and without realizing it I had also disconnected from you in the process. My entire life was a detachment routine.

I enjoyed my work as a college professor, but the salary was never sufficient to satisfy the lifestyle your mother ambitioned. When we first got married I worked overtime and gave extra night courses so that she could buy the outfits she needed for the different events that were constantly in her agenda. But the more I earned, the more she wanted. It was a never-ending story.

When I was home all she talked about was how I should get a job with some big corporation that would pay a decent salary. But I saw how many of our friends were drinking too much, or traveling too much with these so call "nice jobs". Four of my college friends actually confessed feeling totally miserable with their careers. I felt privileged to be in a job I enjoyed doing so much.

I started to disconnect. I figured if your mother was so desperate for money to buy things and keep up with the social class she dreamed of, then she could work and make the money she needed. She never did.

I don' know how many times I need to say it, but please forgive me for not being there for you. I am here now, and this will all change. I am going to be talking with your mother as soon as I get back to the room, and I promise she will be part of this wedding."

Diana's father finally confronted his wife.

"Diana has her own life to live, and she is going to live it according to what she perceives is right. She has to be respected as an adult. She was not born to act as her mother's puppet, but as her own persona, in her own right, and it is our responsibility as loving parents to be there for her. We are going to the wedding."

For the first time in his life he finally put his foot down. His wife was furious, but she felt proud of her husband for defending their daughter. To a certain extent she was relieved she would not have to worry about organizing a big wedding. She also felt that the Caribbean agreed with her. She felt less tense and less worried about what people could say.

Brenda was elated. Her two best friends got married with the men they loved on the same trip! She wished them the best, but couldn't help but feel a little left out. Her relationship with Carlos seemed to be blossoming, but it was definitely too soon to be thinking about long-term plans. She just wished to be as happy as her friends eventually. For now, she had to adjust to her new life.

Claudia helped Diana find a stunning dress, made by a local designer, for her wedding day. She looked amazingly beautiful; she could have easily been the envy of any top model. Ann had to improvise a location for the wedding ceremony and reception, and she rented a lovely white tent with gold trimmings to be placed on the soft, sandy beach.

Her father walked her down a red carpet placed on the sand between two rows of chairs. The vows were exchanged beneath the canopy of an ancient tree, with the sky and the sea as a breathtakingly beautiful and dramatic background. As night approached, stars filled the sky, and the dark sea with its rhythmic waves made a roaring romantic sound that would remain in their memories for a lifetime.

Ann had used many decorations left over from Marie Terre's wedding, and it made the small reception tent look dazzling. William was the best man and Marie Terre the maid of honor. George looked so charming, even Diana's brother had to notice.

"Well, mom, one thing you have to admit is that you are going to have the most beautiful grandchildren in the UK."

Diana's father added: "Just look at them. You can see they both glow with love for each other."

Her mother did not say a word, but after the ceremony she walked up to the newlyweds.

"I wish you the very best."

Diana and George were very happy to have finally received her mother's blessing. Diana would never know how her father managed such a dramatic change in her mother. It was one of the most pleasant wedding gifts she could ever dream of.

The buffet was intimate and cozy. When the music started, everyone got up and went straight to the improvised wooden dance floor with the excuse to practice the new dance steps they had learned at Marie Terre's wedding. Even Diana's mother and father were dancing and laughing.

Diana and George were pleased to see this, but most of all they were happy to know that from now on they were family. Marie Terre and William danced holding each other very tight. Brenda danced with Carlos all night long, and was very pleased not to have anyone cutting in to take him away from her.

15 THE BIG MOVE

As soon as they arrived back to the UK, Marie Terre moved into William's place. Diana and George were still working on some of the flats they were remodeling, and it was easier for them to move to a flat in that same building. Brenda handled her job transfer, executing the process very quickly. In two more weeks she would be with Carlos, and she was looking forward to starting that fantastic adventure.

The weekend before leaving, and with lots of enthusiasm, she went to visit her parents to tell them of her move to the Caribbean and her promotion. She put on a black pantsuit with a white turtleneck sweater. She still needed to lose about twenty-five more pounds, but she was looking good.

As soon as she arrived to her parent's house, her mother told her all about her sister's wedding plans and how they were expecting her to be there for the ceremony and reception. Her father actually looked at her, and told her the outfit looked good.

Receiving a complement form her father was so unexpected, it actually brought tears to her eyes. She thanked him profusely. Immediately she wished she hadn't.

"Young lady, I said the outfit looks good. You should accept the fact that you have never been an attractive woman. Intelligent yes, but not attractive."

He did not even look at her when he said this. He didn't notice all the changes she had gone through and how much better she looked. In the past she felt sad being ignored like this. Every time it happened she went into a drinking binge. Now it only made her want to leave.

Thinking about her move to the Caribbean made her feel good about her fate. The only bad thing about it was not having her friends nearby. The separation was going to be very difficult, but they had both started their married lives, and she had to move on.

Before saying her good-bye's she told her mother she would try and make it to her sisters' wedding. Her mother just repeated: "I just want you to respect your sister by participating in her wedding."

The flat that started their friendship had never been decorated. None of the three friends could bear to sell the flat that had turned into a life changing experience for all of them. They signed a contract with Sara, a real estate agent, to have it rented. The money was to be deposited in a bank account they opened under all three names.

Brenda's farewell dinner was held at Marie Terre and William's place. It was a celebration for a better future, but it was also a sorrowful moment for their friendship. Between hugs and sobs they promised ongoing communication with each other for as long as they lived, from wherever they happened to be. The pact was sealed with honesty and genuine caring for each other.

In the Dominican Republic, Carlos found a big, colonial, Spanish style house not far away from where Brenda was going to work. The house was perfect for his business. It was on a busy main street, with a big back yard that could be converted into parking spaces. The second floor had four big bedrooms and a terrace off the master bedroom. It could easily be converted into a one family residence.

He could use the street level entrance for his training room, a spa with a sauna, massage booths, showers, and even a small space for a beauty parlor. It would be a perfect fitness center.

He convinced the owner to sell him the house without getting a bank mortgage; he could not afford the high interest rates. He would pay the man an equivalent of two thousand dollars a month and the property would be paid for in little less than two years. The owner did not like the idea of getting monthly payments, but it would provide him with a fixed income for almost two years. However, the deciding factor was that the house had been on the market for some time and it had not sold.

Most people were buying apartments in new high-rise condominiums that had water tanks and a big electrical plant, and where the tenants shared maintenance. If a person wanted to have regular running water and electricity in their house, it was essential to have this kind of equipment installed on the property.

Big houses were getting harder to sell because of the high maintenance costs. The house owners' accountant suggested it was a good deal, and Carlos' offer was accepted.

Carlos was aware of all the fine-tuning and slyness it would take to carry out his plans, but it was the chance of a lifetime and he was going for it. In little less than two years he would have the house paid for, and he would convert his spa into a big business. This could all happen if he made Brenda the happiest woman on the planet. He could use the money from his salary at the TV station to entertain and keep Brenda happy. Whatever money he made from his aerobics classes he would use to upgrade the facilities.

Because Brenda was a single person, the Human Recourses department recommended renting an apartment instead of a house. Most buildings had 24-hour security, and they had special employees that handled electrical and water outages problems. However, it was her choice to live anywhere she wanted to. Carlos had already advised her to tell them the maintenance of the house would be taken care of by the landlord, and to say she fell in love with the colonial style house.

Brenda was relieved that she did not have to say any of that. They were more interested in getting her residency paperwork done and her car loan settled. She was offered the option to hire a chauffeur to drive her around until she felt confident driving on the other side of the street, and in the big traffic jams that were common within city limits. They gave her a list of car dealers she could see. Once she had selected the new car, they would work out the car loan details.

During Brenda's first two weeks in the Dominican Republic, she stayed in a hotel, and Carlos stayed with her.

He would wake her up in the morning with lots of kisses, saying tender nothings and then they made passionate love. More of the same got repeated before going to bed at night. He took care of all her needs; he helped her select the new car, and worked as her dedicated chauffeur.

On her first weekend they went to purchase furniture. She had so many things on her mind; she didn't want to make more decisions. She wanted to relax. Plus the house was so big she did not even know where to begin, and yes, she missed her friends. At work she needed to learn new operating procedures according to local law. She also had to make decisions on how to improve and make the bank operations at the branch more efficient. It was a great relief when Carlos offered to take care of the house decoration.

On her first Saturday back in the Dominican Republic, Carlos took her to a lovely beach front restaurant on the road to the airport. On both sides of the restaurant they had big white canopy beds, with small tables were you could eat, drink, relax, and observe the immense calm ocean, as well as the small sailboats that where passing by.

It was exactly what Brenda needed; the entire atmosphere and Carlos' lovemaking made everything she was doing worthwhile. In tall, frozen glasses they drank a very cold beer she had acquired a taste for called "Presidente." Its texture and taste was very appropriate for the warm weather, the place, and the occasion. Completely at ease, they laid down on the canopy bed and had several dishes of tropically prepared seafood that tasted delicious. It was a day made in heaven.

Part of Carlos' savings went into hiring an architect to design the house remodel. He added another carport at the side of the house that matched the Spanish architecture. It was separated from the main house entrance with double wooden doors that opened into an interior patio with a fountain, perfect for entertaining. Surrounding the fountain was a matching attractive stone staircase to the entrance of the new apartment on the second floor.

One of the bedrooms was torn down and converted into a kitchen, a half guest's bath, and a dining room that opened up to the large hallway, converting it into the living room. He also designed all the spa facilities for the first floor.

On paper it looked fantastic. All of his savings went into building the second story apartment, and construction started at once. He had laborers working day and night to have it completed in less than a month, which was the time Brenda had to move out of the hotel she was living in. However, it actually took about four months to have it totally decorated and move-in ready.

Brenda had given Carlos the money to purchase the furniture they needed. He explained that because of the tropical climate the best choice was to have furniture built from local mahogany trees, since the wood would last longer and it was also lovely. He got a well-known carpenter to custom-build the furniture, starting with their bedroom set. The man was an artist, and built slick, contemporary designs taken out of any magazine. It cost less than buying any kind of imported furniture.

During construction of the second story apartment Brenda and Carlos lived on the first floor of the house. They converted what was originally the dining room into a temporary bedroom with a bed, two night stands with small lamps, and a television set Carlos had from what had been his old apartment. He made sure Brenda saw and approved all the designs before making a selection. This made her feel part of the project, even though he was the person doing most of the legwork.

She had to admit the designs were impressive; she found them tasteful and gladly approved them. He also hired a cook and a housekeeper to do the cleaning. When Brenda arrived at night from work their part of the house was impeccably clean. The housekeeper also hand-washed and ironed her clothes on a daily basis.

Carlos still offered his aerobics classes in an old wooden house he rented. He offered one class from seven to seven forty five in the morning, and then he would go do his television program. He offered two other classes, from four to four forty five, and from six to six forty five in the afternoons.

Carmen, the masseuse, also worked at the wooden house. He saw several clients in the privacy of their homes during the day. As soon as he completed his last aerobics class he would take a shower and get all dressed up in order to be ready for whenever Brenda called.

He would pick her up at work every day. Sometimes they went out for dinner and other days the cook would have dinner ready for them at home. It all depended on what Brenda wanted and how she felt. In the mornings, after making love to her, he started taking her to the wooden house for the morning aerobics class. After her aerobics class she would take a shower, and Mary, the beautician, fixed her hair and gave her a ten-minute make up. At work she always looked radiant.

Brenda always had the ability to look at problems and find solutions. One of the goals she had been given when she was hired to work in the Dominican Republic was to increase the bank's portfolio. In other words, they needed more clients. The excuse other Managers had given for that particular branch's lack of growth was the country was very poor.

Brenda looked around and yes, she saw lots of poverty, but she also saw lots of European and American expensive cars on the road. The country was booming with new construction: condominiums and hotels were coming up everywhere. The houses being built were big and expensive, so money was flowing, and the people purchasing these cars and homes had sophisticated tastes and needs.

She had to find out with whom these people were doing business, and if all their needs were being met. She needed a new profile of possible clients and their perception of the bank; were the products her bank was offering the proper products to fulfill these clients' needs?

She asked her secretary to request an estimate from a local marketing company for a study of what the local clients banking needs were, and how clients and non-clients perceived them as a bank. As soon as she obtained the cost estimate she submitted it to the New York head office. The study was declined. The reasoning was her branch was too small to justify such an exorbitant expense.

Even though it was not part of her daily duties, she decided to do the study herself. She called different marketing departments in the UK, USA, and Puerto Rico. Most of them sent her samples of different marketing studies made locally, and some made internationally. It took her a couple of months to study them carefully and make up a simple local questionnaire for clients and non-clients. The personnel director translated the questionnaire into Spanish.

She instructed her officers to very respectfully ask the clients if they would mind filling out a small questionnaire. When the branch was somewhat idle, the officers would take turns going in front of the building to ask persons going by if they were clients or not, and if they would mind filling out a small questionnaire.

When she had the results, she requested the main office's help to change the bank's image according to what the questionnaires' revealed. She provided some of her ideas on how to attract more clients. Most of all, she wanted clients to be aware of, and have a clear perception of how the bank could provide the products that would fulfill all of their banking needs.

Headquarters was so impressed with her results that they promoted her to Vice President of Marketing in the Dominican Republic. She was in charge of developing new products that would increase the portfolio, but most of all she had to figure out how to increase the net profit. If she proved her ideas and changes made a difference and actually increased the net profit of the bank, she could someday aspire to become Corporate Executive Officer.

For her new assignment Brenda was scheduled to take several Marketing courses, some being offered in New York, Florida, and the UK. She was thrilled with this new endeavor, but she was also worried about the net profit. She had learned in business school that you don't make a company spend money unless you are confident they will get it back with lots of profit.

She had not made many friends at work; most people treated her at a distance and called her "jefa", which means boss. However, Carlos took her to the best restaurants, nightclubs, and shows. Without her realizing it, she was mingling with the jet setters of society in "La Capital." They started receiving dinner invitations as a couple.

Most of the conversations were about politics, of which Brenda new very little. She missed her long heart-to-heart conversations with Marie Terre and Diana. She talked with Carlos and he was a great listener, but he did not share his own thoughts. For him, life was all about working to make money, looking good, and a constant party.

He had the cook make her a special low-fat diet, and she was doing aerobics classes three days a week, lifting weights the other three days, and they slept in only on Sundays. Saturdays she got a massage, facial, manicure, and pedicure. He even found her a seamstress to make her wardrobe. He told her to get expensive shoes and designer purses when she went for training courses outside of the country. The fact was she was in the best physical condition of her life, her body was slim and trim, and her wardrobe had to be taken in practically every other month.

Carlos made love to her every single day. She never knew that such a good thing could get to be a little too much. One of the things she started enjoying was how men stared at her, and complimented her whenever she walked by. The expressions of flattery from others had become so endearing that she was working out harder than ever, and executing her make up with care. Before walking out of the house she would correct her dress, fix her make up, and be sure everything was nicely combined.

She would call her friends and tell them the many activities she was involved in. There was one thing she kept repeating in every call: "I am living a life better than that of any royal lady."

16 THE FRANCHISES

At William's business, Marie Terre was thrust into the limelight. Camille had been very helpful explaining how the franchises worked. They had several reservation offices all over the world providing traveler's assistance with hotel accommodations, car rental, limousine service, tour packages, and airline travel reservations, among other miscellaneous travel-related services. The franchises paid a fee for business sent to them.

The most difficult part of the business was keeping the owners of the franchises informed on discount rates for VIP's, companies, and organizations, because some of these companies had discounts that applied in their own country but not anywhere else, and other companies had discounts that applied internationally. William himself had negotiated the VIP discounts with many large corporations.

Another important aspect of the business was keeping the employees well trained on the different codes used by the travel industry. The owners depended on them. In the past, William went to the different countries and helped prospective owners find the ideal location, get a bank loan, and then trained the owner on all the aspects of the business. The owner would then train his new employees.

Many of his franchises started small, as mom and pop businesses. The problems started to show when an owner sold his franchise. In some cases the new owners were wealthy businessmen with other large franchises that benefited from this kind of operations. Therefore they relied on the employee's knowledge of the business to continue operating. However, headhunters started recruiting for the competition. Employees that knew this kind of operating procedures were well in demand.

Some franchises were sold to foreign corporations. The owners had the responsibility to comply with local law, if not the franchise was taken away from them. Sometimes litigations in court took months. But, the franchises needed to continue operating until they found someone else to purchase it. In other words, they needed someone to keep them well trained and updated.

All three brothers had been working with William's franchises, but now that the franchise division was well established, they felt all it needed was follow up. They had wizened from the franchise business. Developing and selling malls was by far more profitable than the franchises, and the prospect buyers were mostly powerful people that needed to be taken care of as soon as possible.

After noticing some of the problems the franchises were facing, Marie Terre decided first of all she had to hire regional managers to periodically visit the different franchise operations, and help them out in case they needed it. William had franchises spread all over the European countries, USA, Mexico, Latin America, and the Caribbean. She would start with at least four managers, local to the markets.

Her fist step was to get the franchises' profit and loss reports from the accountant and determine how much these managers would cost the company in salary and travel expenses. Once she had a good idea of the numbers involved, she contacted the best headhunters in the USA, Mexico, Argentina, and Puerto Rico. She specified she was looking for people to work on their own, without direct supervision. At the end of the year, in addition to their salary, they would receive a ten percent bonus on all increased business.

It was cost effective for her to travel and interview the candidates in these four countries. She finally hired those who demonstrated a genuine desire to make the business grow and therefore perceived the ten percent bonus as the most appealing aspect of the job. All the people she interviewed were men. She made a point to let the headhunters know that in the future, she also wanted to hire some women, even though she was very grateful and satisfied with the candidates that had been selected.

For the first trip William organized his schedule to be with Marie Terre. He wanted to show her around the lovely streets of Buenos Aires, and share with her the best beef and wines. After work they met at Florida Street and did some shopping of well-crafted leather goods. He also took her to see the opera "Rigoletto" at the famous Colon Theatre. At the end of the opera, Marie Terre had tears rolling down her face when Gilda fell back dead.

During the weekend they went to the flea market and saw tango singing and dancing on the streets. The music was so intense it made them want to sing and dance with the others. Part of the street show consisted in asking someone from the audience to dance a tango with one of the performers.

The attractive petite brunet invited to dance the first tango did an excellent job. She danced like a professional. After the dance, she was interviewed and asked where was she from. When she said from Arecibo, Puerto Rico, William and Marie Terre looked at each other and started laughing. William mentioned that for being such a small island the people sure got around all over the world.

That night, before going to bed, Marie Terre opened a bottle of Argentine wine and put on a long beige and white silk negligee. After having a little too much to drink she grabbed William by the hand and started dancing tango with him until they both fell to the floor laughing. These were the little things that made life with her so much fun.

He began kissing her with tenderness, and then immense desire. He could not get enough of her. She was a part of his soul, and his entire being responded to her kisses, her smell, her touch. Everything about her made him feel as if he were in heaven.

After the exhaustion from making love wore off they finally climbed into bed and fell asleep in each other's arms. The next day they made love again. It was Sunday and they were leaving for Mexico City on Monday. He told Marie Terre he would love to stay in bed all day long but he had to take her for a boat ride on the Tigris River. During the romantic boat ride, they again professed their immense love for each other.

In Mexico City they went to the theater to see the Broadway Show "Cats." The choreography was splendid, the lights were amazing, and the explosion of movement, sound, and energy slowly penetrated the audience to such an extent that as they were walking out, they could hear people saying their friends and family needed to see this presentation. City nightlife was full of live music and entertainment, but they were going to get up early the next day to visit museums so they went back to their hotel.

Marie Terre felt at home when visiting the impressive museums found in Mexico City. At one of them she could not stop staring at Montezuma's handmade headpiece, made of hundreds of peacock feathers. She was trying to figure out the amount of labor invested in the making of the head peace. But what impressed her most was the fact Montezuma had a different headpiece made for him daily. She told William she wanted to know more about this amazing culture.

As was becoming a custom he had anticipated this. He had already scheduled a visit to the pyramids for the next day. With love and tenderness she kissed him on the lips and he held her tight to his heart. Then they walked into the museum shop and she purchased several souvenirs to take back to her beloved friends.

The next day they climbed the amazing pyramids of "Teotihuacan", which means a place where gods are born. The tour guide said it was almost as large as the Great Pyramids of Giza in Egypt. Marie Terre was fascinated with the pictures of butterflies and birds decorating the carved columns and patio in the Temple of Butterflies. A local precious stone called obsidian decorated some of the bird's eyes. Marie Terre purchased more pre-Colombian artifacts than she could carry. William just smiled and asked if she was going to start a museum of her own.

That night they ate, drank and enjoyed the catchy music of the splendidly dressed Mariachis at Plaza Garibaldi. Throughout the trip they talked about their lives before they met, their likes and dislikes, and above all about their feelings toward each other, and how they wanted their lives to be like when they grew old together.

It was a working honeymoon. She was learning a lot about the corporate world and he was learning a lot about feelings, communication and commitment.

Back in the UK, William felt he was the most fortunate man alive with Marie Terre's love and affection. He gave her carte blanche with the international franchises' office. Marie Terre's responsibilities meant more to her then just a job; it made her feel as if she was part of some common design as Williams' wife.

At work, she projected her good nature and positive outlook towards others. This made her a joy to work with. However, she was constantly looking for ways to make her team more productive. Whenever she confronted difficulties at work her modus operandi was to think in a very positive way. She would tell herself she had the tenacity to do it, she was demanding of herself and others, and was confident that all was going to turn out fine as long as she maintained her high spirit.

Before placing different management techniques in practice, she would bounce them off on her friends to get their reaction. She kept her best friends informed of practically everything going on in her life, specially her work projects, by calling Diana every weekend and Brenda at least once a month. Their feedback about her projects and the way she managed her job affairs were the best coaching she could ever receive.

To top it all off and make her fairy tale live even more complete, she found out she was pregnant. Having a baby with the man she adored, she knew their lives and love would go into eternity.

That night at dinnertime Marie Terre played with her food and declined a glass of wine William offered. He noticed she was nervous, and asked her a couple of times if something was wrong. She just smiled and said "no". She was anxious to give him the good news but knew he would not eat if she told him before dinner.

She waited until he had completed his meal to inform him she had received a phone call from her doctor. William eyes opened wide in terror, thinking something could be wrong. His mind was faster than her words. All he could think of was if she was ill, he would search the deepest corners of the earth to find the best doctors and make her well again. The thought of losing her was so horrible that it made him panic.

With a trembling voice he asked her what the doctor had said. A big comforting smile appeared on her lips.

"We're having a baby."

So much was said in those few words! His entire existence changed in a second. He got so emotional that tears swelled in his eyes. He picked her up in his arms and carried her to their bedroom, where he kissed her flat belly and started talking to the soon-to-be baby.

He wanted her to stop working, but she was very blunt explaining how she wanted to work until at least a month before the baby was born. She let him know how happy her job responsibilities made her.

In all honesty, it also made him happy to have her nearby all day long. They decided to keep the pregnancy a secret until she started to show, except for her two best friends.

INGRID BORGES

17 THE IN-LAWS

Every time Marie Terre met with her sisters in law she felt they liked her less.

She tried to get on their good side and be liked by them, but they seemed to have a secret agenda when it came to Marie Terre. The sisters in law felt William raised Marie Terre from the dunghill and was not to be trusted. They were constantly finding faults; the way she dressed, acted, talked, or whatever it was she did. They criticized her without even trying to get to know her.

William's brothers, Paul and Henry, told their wives for the general interest and unity of the family they needed to socialize more with Marie Terre, and should invite her for lunch one day. They were annoyed with the idea, but felt they needed to comply with their husband's request. One day they finally invited her for lunch at a well-known restaurant. As soon as they were seated they ordered a bottle of wine. Marie Terre was not drinking at all, but she did not want to act rude so she had one glass of wine that sat untouched.

Elizabeth had no such inhibitions, had too much to drink, and started flirting with one of the young waiters. This behavior annoyed Marie Terre. She suggested they leave, but before they got to the door, Elizabeth went over to the young man and kissed him on the lips. Other people at the bar recognized her and soon started spreading rumors about a drunk Mrs. Burgess trying to seduce a young waiter. The rumors spread to the gossip columns, but did not specify which of the three wives had been involved in the flirting.

Henry read a comment made by a gossip column and called Paul to let him know they had to talk with their wives about it. Paul was Elizabeth's husband. He had noticed she had been drinking too much lately, so he suspected his wife and confronted her. With spite in her voice she said it was not she but Marie Terre, the immigrant spic, who had the drunken scene at the restaurant.

Elizabeth was desperate to hide her misconduct from her husband. She showed him a nasty article written in another gossip column. The article had a picture of the three Mrs. Burgess sitting at a table in a restaurant, and at the bottom of the picture it read: 'It seems like a wanna-be lady does not know how to hold her liquor, or maybe it's her hot blood that keeps her in heat for the nearest young stud.'

"Who else is a hot blooded lady wanna-be?"

Paul believed his wife and immediately called Henry to inform him they needed to talk with William about his wife.

That afternoon William's brothers stormed into his office and showed him the article. Furiously they blurted how they expected William to control his wife.

William was fuming.

"How dare you even think Marie Terre is capable of doing such a thing?"

Both of his brothers screamed right back at him insisting it was she.

"You are a pair of loons! Marie Terre is not even drinking any more! She is pregnant!"

"I'm no loon! But you, my brother, are certainly a complete and total fool! Can't you see the kind of woman you married? She is so beneath us! She certainly doesn't have our upbringing."

"William, Paul is right! And you will not put our family's reputation in jeopardy because of this wanton!"

Both Paul and Henry turned around and walked out the door, giving a good slamming for good measure.

Because of Marie Terre's pregnancy, William did not want her to get upset over this incident. He was well aware how gossip columnists exaggerated most of the things they wrote about, so he usually paid no attention to what they wrote. However, his brothers' attitude about the situation was very upsetting. He decided to get to the truth of the matter on his own.

He took a picture of both his sisters-in-laws and his wife to the restaurant where the incident had occurred, and asked to talk to the headwaiter. William was blunt and to the point. He showed him the pictures right away.

"Do you recognize these ladies?"

The headwaiter was so nervous his voice would not come out; he nodded with his head.

"Which of the three ladies had too much to drink?"

The waiter pointed to Elizabeth. The next question was whom did she try to kiss. The headwaiter pointed to the young handsome waiter staring at them from a couple of feet away. William walked over to the young man.

"Who tried to kiss you?"

"I did nothing to encourage the situation. I was just an innocent bystander."

"Just tell me which one?"

The waiter pointed to Elizabeth. Once he had all the evidence he needed, William turned around and left the restaurant. The waiters took a big breath of relief.

Elizabeth was ready to go shopping when William's car arrived in front of her house. William's presence daunted her, and his questioning was so insufferable that she confessed, sobbing miserably.

"No one doubted Marie Terre! That is why when my beloved husband asked me, I said it had been her. I never thought this would get to you. And I only did it to save my family's peace and integrity!"

"I feel sorry for you and my brother, not because of your mistake, but because of your deception. You have no backbone to confront your own mistakes and correct them. You are not even crying because you are sorry for having deceived the family and for accusing my wife of something she did not do. You are crying because you feel sorry for yourself, because you have been discovered in your lie."

William knew he had to tell Marie Terre about Elizabeth's betrayal, but he needed to find the correct moment to do so. In order to protect her from the gossip columns he invited her for a small cruise of the Greek Islands. Marie Terre did not know what to think about this sudden, one-week vacation in the Greek Islands, but she had always dreamed about going to Athens and visiting the Parthenon. Without asking many questions she packed their luggage.

There was a very special restaurant William wanted Marie Terre to visit. It was high in the mountains and had a spectacular view of the ocean, the city, and to top it all, the food was delicious. As soon as they arrived to Athens, William told Marie Terre they had no time to unpack; they needed to take a taxi to the restaurant he wanted her to see. This trip had been so unplanned he had totally forgotten to make reservations.

The taxi driver stopped in front of some steps that led up the mountain. As he pointed to the top, William told Marie

Terre they had to walk the rest of the way up to the restaurant. Once they had climbed the staircase up the mountain, they encountered a married couple with two children and seventeen blind people.

William and Marie Terre walked around them, and found the restaurant was closed. They admired the splendid night view and the cool breeze. They kissed each other with love and tenderness as they had promised to do every time they found a place they enjoyed and wanted to revisit.

Marie Terre overheard the approaching couple speaking in Spanish. They were trying to figure out how they were going to get back to the city. Without thinking about it, Marie Terre asked in Spanish if they needed help. They explained a guard had just informed them that day was a holiday in the Greek Islands, the restaurant was closed, and they had no telephone to call a taxi to pick them up. They had to walk down the mountain to get back to the city, and helping the seventeen blind people down the mountain was not going to be an easy task.

William had been so absorbed in his own dilemmas he had not even figured out how they would get back to the hotel. But without hesitation he told the lady they would help. The blind people were able to hold the staircase rail without much effort. It was when they arrived to the street level that they would need help.

The steep, slippery road had no sidewalks, and some people started slipping and falling to the ground. Marie Terre had high heels on, and she also slipped, but William lifted her up before her body ever touched the ground. William looked around and realized they had to walk all around the mountain, following the road, before reaching the city to get a taxi. It was not a good idea for everyone to hold hands because if someone slipped, they could all fall down.

The husband and wife team were experts handling the blind, each one of them helping four blind people each. The two children held a blind person on each hand. Marie Terre and William observed how they were handling the situation and proceeded to help by following the same procedures. William instructed Marie Terre to walk behind him, so in case she slipped she would fall on him. She and her two blind people were the last ones in the procession line.

They had been walking for about fifteen minutes when they encountered a man walking a dog out on the street. He stared at the group walking around the mountain and when he realized what was happening, he waved at Marie Terre to stop. At first she was apprehensive, but he was walking a small dog that seemed harmless, and she loved dogs. She did not stop, but stared at him to see what he wanted. Then she told William.

"Please stop! There is a man waving at me to stop, but it's all Greek to me, literally. I don't understand what he is saying."

Even at a moment like this she took the time to make a joke. When William looked at the man he waved for him to come closer. William asked the others to stop for a moment. He wanted to find out what the man was trying to say. No one in the group knew a word of Greek, so they needed to communicate with hand signals.

William kept on following the man's hand signals until he pointed to a staircase hidden in the bushes. When he saw the staircase he yelled to the others to come and follow. He looked at the Greek man and with a big smile and lots of warmth in his gaze, he thanked him without saying a work.

The staircase was a direct line toward the city; it was going to be much faster than walking around the mountain. The blind people were experts walking down the steps, which made everyone more relaxed. The group started making jokes and laughing. The husband and wife team walked up to Marie Terre and William to thank them for their help.

"We had been debating on how we were going to make it down the mountain, then the two of you arrived and you were the answer to our prayers."

Marie Terre was curious to find out why they were traveling with seventeen blind people. The wife explained that her husband had been blind, but he got a cornea transplant and was able to see again.

During his years in the institute for the blind, most of the blind people were content with their lives; the one thing they missed in their productive, useful life was traveling. As a couple, they felt very blessed to have found each other and to have two healthy, adorable children.

"God has given us so much, we made a promise to take blind people that wanted to travel on a vacation. In Spain my husband gets a month of vacation time per year, so we made a promise to dedicate one week of every year to the blind. And we all look forward to this one-week, because the joy and happiness they experience is extremely rewarding. These trips make our lives complete."

Marie Terre's heart swelled. Meeting these people that engage in quixotic humanitarian enterprises made her know how good mankind could be. The news media only talked about horrible things humans do against each other, but they almost never publish the kind of work performed by people like these. These people made a difference in other's lives.

She believed in social causes, giving back, and making good things happen for others. She would have to think of something she could do for the improvement of society.

Once they arrived to the city, the Spanish group thanked William and Marie Terre for their help, and proceeded to wave at different taxis. William and Marie Terre were starving. They decided to walk around and find a restaurant, but it was after midnight and most of the restaurants were closed.

They noticed a hole-in-the-wall place, where a man with a big beard was cutting roasted meat from a spit and serving it with onions, tomato, and lettuce inside pita bread. Then he wrapped it up and handed it to a young man in front of them.

William walked into the place and, after the man with the big beard had given the young man his change, lifted two fingers and pointed to what the young man had just paid for. Marie Terre could not believe William was going to eat that. She let William know that the man's hands were not clean, and he had also handled money before handling the meat and the other ingredients. William was so hungry that all he said was "Try not to look so closely."

Once he had the food in his hands he looked around for a place to sit; all the tables were taken by men in big long beards, sandals, and long robes, and they were all staring at William and Marie Terre as if they had just landed from

Mars. William saw a staircase and decided they could sit on the steps. Before they reached the staircase, two of the big bearded men got up from their table and pointed to their now-empty chairs. William smiled and bowed his head in a gesture of thank you; the men bowed their heads back, and then they moved over to another table with two other big beaded men.

Marie Terre was so hungry she decided to taste the food, and when she did it was divine, every ingredient mixed to perfection. Once they had finished eating, they waved goodbye to all as if they had been friends forever. The big bearded men stared at them, and then they all waved back with a big smile. The experience was a pleasant surprise, and something they would tell their grandchildren.

The next day they visited the Parthenon. For Marie Terre, it was a dream come true. She was all smiles and laughter. William took many pictures of her sitting, standing, and walking around the impressive Minerva temple.

That evening they took the cruise ship to the different Greek Islands. The food was as good as they expected it to be and then some. Marie Terre and William ate more than they usually did. The food was so tasty and different that they overdid it, which made Marie Terre suffer with unexpected nausea. The movements of the ship, the overeating, and her pregnancy gave her motion sickness, but she refused to stay in the cabin. She had to see the wonderful Greek Islands.

Each island had its own personality. Marie Terre found them to be very colorful, with lots of friendly people at the ports, and many vendors with their donkeys loaded with lovely souvenirs. She compared them to the Caribbean islands she had visited during their honeymoon. The colors were different; the Caribbean had that intense green vegetation from all the rain and sun it receives year round.

She knew it was not a legitimate comparison. They were all different and perfect, with their divine right and just claim to be classified as paradise. William and Marie Terre hugged and kissed during their long walks along the narrow, picture-perfect Greek island's streets. Their hearts were filled with joy in sharing their pure and never ending love.

Marie Terre liked a pair of earrings made in silver and lapis lazuli she found in one of the jewelry stores. William wanted to get her something in gold, but what she liked about these earrings was the Greek design that would always remind her of this sudden, adventurous trip to the Greek islands. William pleased his wife and paid the one hundred dollars for the earrings.

He knew that sooner or later he had to tell her about Elizabeth's mischief about the events that happened at the restaurant, and the gossip columns. He was having such a wonderful time, he did not want to bring that cloud of deceit into their lives, and he kept on postponing it.

It had been a fantastic week. They would have loved to have the time to go to the restaurant at the top of the hill, but after the cruise ship arrived back in Athens they only had a few hours to get to the airport and catch their flight back to the UK.

During the flight, and as gentle as possible, William provided Marie Terre with the details of the incident at the restaurant. This only confirmed what she thought about Elizabeth and Laura, and how they felt about her. However, she let William know that in order to maintain the family union she would forgive Elizabeth, but only if she apologized. Deep down in her heart she knew Elizabeth would never apologize, unless she was forced to.

As soon as Marie Terre arrived to the UK, she called her beloved friends to tell them about her wonderful trip to the Greek Islands. She really didn't want to talk badly about her sister in law. All her life she had been told family is sacred.

She firmly believed the family clan protects and helps each other out, like haven, a refuge. It was natural to have disagreements and discord, but they were kept within the family circle. Even if you disliked a family member, you never made negative comments about him or her to any outsider, because this was your own child's aunt, uncle or cousin. She was very diplomatic when she asked Diana if she had heard of comments in the gossip columns.

Diana wanted to talk to Marie Terre about the gossip that was circulating around, but had not done so before out of respect. She did not know if Marie Terre was aware of the gossip, and if she did know, maybe she did not want to talk about it. However, as soon as the opportunity presented itself she was willing and able to speak up about how she perceived the degrading situation. She was furious.

"Both of your sisters in law are cheats and frauds. You need to be aware of the kind of people you are dealing with."

During her teen years she had met several people like Marie Terre's in laws. She disliked generalizing, but people like Elizabeth had certain characteristics visible to any one who took the time to observe them. She was the kind of people that do not care to cultivate their inner self, or to help others.

"They will not help a faithful servant in need of a salary advance. On the other hand, they donate lots of money to charity to get the best table at a party, or to get public recognition for their contributions. They are very vain: more worried about their physical appearance then the health of a family member.

Their biggest ambition in life is to buy the best jewelry, the best car, house, more servants, and more important invitations... It's ok if they have the money to do so, but they act as if material things define who they are s a person. They actually have no interest in their personal improvement.

To make matters worse they have a tendency to look down on people that can't afford the material objects they have. Once they are in this path they become so blinded by the glitter of the jetsetter's life that they forget to share. Because having the best car, house and material things is more important to them than giving a niece or nephew a gift that would make them happy."

 When Diana perceived that this negative conversation was not helping her friend, she changed her tone.

"We are lucky to have cultivated our friendship between the three of us, because whatever happens in our lives, we have each other. We can also count on one another to bail us out if we ever get into any kind of trouble, or even if we make the mistake of entering the vicious cycle of greed."

Marie Terre felt very saddened by the entire situation. She wanted all negative energy out of her own life: it was bad karma. She wanted to bring back the positive, the joy, and the warmth of sharing good things with others. That night, before going to sleep, she remembered all the things Diana had said.

She promised herself she would live her life with some kind of purpose, performing small but positive deeds that in some way could enrich the life of mankind. She decided she would make a difference to others, in a positive way, doing good deeds.

Marie Terre put her thoughts to action. She created a tuition fund for employees with college-bound students who needed help paying tuition. She also implemented a program that encouraged creative work; if ideas offered by employees were implemented, they got a bonus from the profits made by the new operating procedures.

Offering these real benefits and a support system at work made her employees bring out their loyalty and creativity, and work seemed more exciting in the office. She made sure to keep her friends up to date. Both Diana and Brenda were very supportive, and admired her kindness.

Finally Marie Terre asked her friends what they thought about her implementing a day care nursery at the office, so that working mothers could bring their babies to work and breast-feed them. That is how she prepared them for her own pregnancy news.

They knew Marie Terre would be the perfect mother. She was always nice to children, and her openness and natural tenderness made her an ideal caregiver. Motherhood seemed like the utmost accomplishment of a lifetime, and as friends they were thrilled for her. But as ambitious professionals, they also suspected motherhood could be very demanding.

Diana and George hired several designers for the reconstruction of the Burgess family's home. They requested the architects get their inspiration from modern comforts, love nests, and places for joyful occasions. The master bedroom was the most romantic chamber. The ballroom sported raised cathedral ceilings of about 20 feet in height, where they could host all kinds of parties and gatherings.

Remembering how Marie Terre would get up and make her friends do aerobics, they created an exercise room overseeing a patio where they could plant vines and fragrant plants. The terraces were paved with local stones that created an oasis of serenity. The grounds provided a safe place where children could enjoy nature and play in the open air.

Several local historians and news reporters visited the site to ensure the renovations were kept in tune with the house's original architecture, and that it conserved its cultural value. The articles written about the house were very generous, filled with praise.

"Congratulations for a job exceptionally well done. The renovations are in compliance with the law of the land. It's very gratifying to see how they are preserving the historic value of the house without being boastful or ostentatious. Within the old building's limitations they have skillfully created all the comfort of contemporary living."

"At last, a young generation of entrepreneurs has arrived to stir up the so-needed updating of our old buildings. With ample understanding of our heritage, and in keeping with the times, they have integrated new living arrangements into our city."

The commendations brought more visitors, and soon the predictions were that George and Diana's company would have an abundance of success.

The building in which Diana and George were living in was also undergoing renovation. It was built with every possible attention to comfort and convenience. Most of the flats had already been sold to many of Williams' acquaintances. After the fabulous publicity offered by the news articles, all of the remaining flats were sold in a matter of days.

Diana knew they had to take advantage of all the free publicity they were receiving. On the other hand, George felt they had too much work as it was. Because of the articles in the newspapers, they were getting offers from several old buildings owners that wanted to remodel them, or sell them.

They started to find out these old buildings had become more of a liability than a profit for many owners. Tenants that could afford to pay would not rent a flat in a rundown building.

George had a big "SOLD OUT" sign placed in front of his building. However, every day about four or five prospect buyers would walk up to the building requesting to buy a flat. In fact, some of the previous owners had already sold their flats with a profit, and asked George and Diana to keep them in mind for the next building they renovated.

William suggested they use the profits from the flats to buy more buildings, fix them up, and sell the flats out just as they did with this one. George respected everything William said and treasured his suggestions, but the pace of events was so accelerated that he felt somewhat overwhelmed, and told William he would think about it.

Diana was ready to start her move up the entrepreneurial ladder. She hired a marketing consultant to help them out. The consultant suggested they open a street level store. There, they would have sketches with the remodeled flats designs and before-and-after pictures. A real estate agent would gladly keep the shop for them, gathering information from prospective clients.

Every time a new building was purchased, she would do all the marketing strategy. Ever since Diana could remember, her mother had been talking about the good neighborhoods and the not-so-good neighborhoods. She even knew the list of the inhabitants of certain places; people were willing to pay for vicinity where certain residents lived.

She explained to George that this was their moment: it was now or never, they had to buy and work on other buildings, and hire more employees.

He knew this was the goal of his ambitions. Therefore, he followed her command. They only purchased buildings they could preserve historically, that passed their careful inspections, and in the locations suggested by Diana. Their success and personal fame started developing stature and grandeur, not only in the UK, but also in the world. They received two offers to remodel buildings in New York City.

Brenda took every opportunity to visit the UK. She would take courses there, and during their vacation, she and Carlos would coordinate with her friends to visit and all three couples would vacation together.

Every time they arrived, she looked even more stupendous. Her figure was lean and firm, with a constant, even suntan that made her dazzling green eyes sparkle. She always arrived with the latest hairstyles and makeup, and her outfits fit perfectly.

Many of her bank clients had told her the way she spoke in Spanish was peculiar, and sounded as if she were reciting a poem. She received lots of complements from men. Finally she was receiving the compliments she had yearned for all of her life.

At work, she obtained another promotion. Her co-workers respected her professionalism and called on her when they needed expert advice. Her love life could not be better. There was a glow about her that let others know how fortunate and happy she was.

When they returned to the Dominican Republic, Carlos tended to puff-up with pride whenever he talked to his friends about the places they had visited in Europe. During his conversations with friends he had to be the center of attention; if someone had been to that particular country he would raise his voice and not let others share their own experiences.

Brenda did not see any of that. She was living her fairy tale.

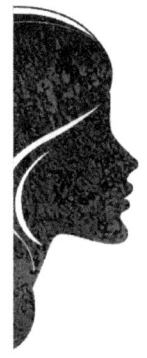

18 BABIES

At six in the morning Marie Terre started having contractions. As soon as she woke William up, he jumped out of bed, took hold of his Rolex, and following the doctors instructions started timing the minutes between contractions. When the contractions were twenty minutes apart he called the gynecologist. The doctor said he would meet them at his office; he wanted to examine her before they went to hospital.

After thoroughly examining her, he informed William she should be in labor during the evening hours. He should take her to hospital when the contractions were ten to fifteen minutes apart.

William took her back to the house and sat in front of her. He kept looking from her to the wall clock and back. If it wasn't such a serious moment, he thought it rivaled the silliest scenes from the best comedies. Diana arrived at their house minutes after receiving the call from Marie Terre. George was at work but would meet them at the hospital that afternoon. Marie Terre made several jokes about how funny they looked counting the minutes between contractions.

At four in the afternoon they arrived at the hospital. Marie Terre was rushed into the delivery room. At 6p.m. her pains were in full blast but the baby would not come out. The doctor instructed the nurses to take her to the x-ray room. He needed to see the position of the baby. At about midnight the doctor talked with William; the baby had turned around and was coming feet first. During nine months, that baby had been in the childbirth position, so the doctor decided to wait and see if he would turn back into the childbirth position. He thought Marie Terre was too young to have a scar, and he did not want to expose her and the baby to the unexpected complications of an operation.

The Gonzalez's family had already arrived, and was in the waiting room with Diana, George and William. After more than twenty hours of labor, William begged the doctor to perform a cesarean section on her. At five in the morning an adorable baby boy, named John, came into this world. The gynecologist came to the waiting room and informed William and the others that baby and mother were in perfect health and that Marie Terre had been very brave. For several hours she had been in intense labor pains, but never did she scream.

Diana hardly ever cried, but she could not hold back her tears of joy when she arrived at the nursery room and saw John on the other side of the window. William insisted on staying by Marie Terre's bedside until she woke up from the anesthesia. He wanted to be the first person to tell her they had a 3kg, healthy baby boy.

She seemed tired but overjoyed with the information. Once she was transferred to her private room the baby was placed in her arms. She looked at him with such devotion, and then she looked at William.

"He is so beautiful, he is perfect."

As soon as Diana walked into Marie Terre's hospital room she kissed and hugged her. Marie Terre told her how grateful she was to have her and George present at such an important event in her life, and how much she wished Brenda was also present. All three friends had been there for each other in their most important moments.

Without giving it much thought she told Diana that Brenda would be the baby's godmother. That way she would have to travel to the UK. With tenderness in her voice she looked at Diana and told her she would be the godmother of her second.

The three friends had seldom felt jealous of each other, and this would not be the exception. In fact Diana also felt the need to have Brenda included is this miraculous event. With tears of joy she smiled at Marie Terre, giving her another big hug. "I am counting on that."

Marie Terre called Brenda from the hospital room and asked her to be the baby's godmother. Brenda was speechless for a moment. It was the biggest honor anyone had granted her, and she promised to execute her duties as a godmother to the fullest.

A nurse walked in and started ordering visitors out of the room. Mother and baby needed their rest and the room looked like a parade stand. Because of the cesarean section, Marie Terre and Baby had to stay in the hospital for a whole week.

More than a wedding planner, Ann had become an event planner for William's immediate family and friends. Camille called Ann to organize the christening. When all the details were ready, Brenda took some days off from work for the christening and to visit with Marie Terre, William and baby John. When she held John in her arms, a warm rush of emotions swept through her. All she could think of was, she also wanted one.

Carlos arrived two days before the christening, and as soon as Brenda saw him she blurted it all out.

"I want to have a baby. Let's get married."

After a few minutes of silence he finally said something.

"Yes."

"I want to have a small wedding in my parent's hometown, with my friends and relatives."

"And then we can have a lavish wedding at the oldest cathedral in America, and a reception at the Country Club in the Capital. But I just want to make you happy. I'll go along with whatever plans you make."

Deep inside he knew it was time to formalize their relationship. He felt that had it not been for Brenda, he would have never gotten his dream of having a spa. He felt he owed her, and a man must pay his debts. She had been so involved in her own work and promotions that she had not even given it a thought, but many months had gone by without either of them uttering the word love, not even now. It had not crossed their minds.

Ann came to the rescue and in two weeks organized a simple but tasteful wedding reception at Brenda's family home. She took a truckload with tents, tables, chairs, flowers, a caterer with lots of food, and a lovely wedding cake. Brenda spoke with her parents over the telephone and gave them all the details for the wedding arrangements.

When she arrived at her parent's house, they didn't recognize her. They were speechless. For the first time in her life, her father called her beautiful. This was the best wedding gift she would ever receive. Her sister had a lovely baby girl that was a bundle of energy. Her mother wanted to know how many plastic surgeons had intervened in her new appearance. Brenda changed the subject and directed them to the chapel where Ann was expecting them for the wedding rehearsal.

Carlos missed having his own family participate in the wedding reception, but to a certain point he was relieved they were not there. During the reception Carlos kept to himself. It was Brenda's friends and family and her day to show off her new and improved self, and he felt happy for her.

In private some of her relatives asked what she had done to look so well. She told them she lost fifty kilos and her husband made her exercise every day. During her formative years in this small village, her relatives and neighbors had treated her as the ugly duckling. Some looked at her with pity and others had nicknamed her the four-eyed cow. Today they could not stop staring at her because of her good looks, and the exotic, attractive man she had married.

It was a glorious day for her and she was enjoying it to the maximum. What pleased her most was sharing with her everlasting friends and knowing how happy they were for her. The day after their wedding, they returned to the Dominican Republic. They had to return to work. The year after they would go on a honeymoon.

Diana and George were so thrilled with baby John they decided to also have a baby. Nine months to the day, they were rushing Diana to the hospital. Unlike Marie Terre, Diana was two weeks early from the date the doctor gave her. As soon as she was taken into the delivery room she had twins, a boy and a girl, which they named Manuel and Madelyn. The first couple of months their hands were full taking care of the twins. Like Marie Terre, they built a nursery in their office and hired a nanny, with mother overlooking the babies' care.

In November of that same year Brenda had a lovely baby girl with her green eyes, and her father's olive skin. Carlos was delighted with his beautiful baby girl. He hired a live-in nanny to take care of Teresa.

In order to select the godparents of the newborn children, and avoid preferential treatment, they put pieces of paper with their names in a bowl. The results were as follows: Marie Terre was to be Madelyn's godmother, Brenda got Manuel, and Diana would baptize Teresa.

December was a splendid month to visit the Dominican Republic. There was a cool breeze, perfect for people that live up north and want to get away from the cold winter months. Friends and family were delighted to fly in William's jet to the Dominican Republic, and all three children were baptized in the oldest cathedral of America.

Ann had arrived one month ahead of them and made all the arrangements for the christenings. To her surprise, she got new ideas from the people at the hotel. The lovely flower arrangements prepared to decorate the cathedral looked very exotic, but deep down they were traditional. The cathedral's columns were draped in lovely green leaves with big roses inserted every other branch.

The materials used were all natural, except for the white gauze that looked like window dressings for the old statues of saints. As the soft breeze moved the gauze slightly from one side to the other, barely touching the palm tree branches and the orchids, Ann felt as if she had been transported to another time and place. It was definitely a tropical paradise; so different it seemed to be many centuries ago.

The cathedral was packed with Carlos' friends and relatives. As soon as the priest had baptized all three children they had a very big party at the Hotel Santo Domingo. A world-renowned Dominican designer had recently remodeled the hotel. The simplicity of the design, and the way it integrated the natural beauty surrounding the hotel, provided an experience that would linger on in everybody's memories.

Lillian could not keep herself from staring at the calm blue sea and sky. Her emotions took over and she started crying. The experience she was living reminded her of her beloved Cuba. As her husband was consoling her, she asked him if they could get a small place in one of the Caribbean islands.

"I would love to live near my sister in Puerto Rico." He promised to look into it.

19 FIVE YEARS LATER

The twins were four years old. Diana and George's business started making money in New York City. They had been living in Manhattan for the last two years, and had acquired an impressive amount of real estate; their company was turning over millions. They both felt honored to help their parents financially and provide them with the things they needed, even if it meant they had to live so far away.

At least once a month Diana, Marie Terre, and Brenda had a conference call. In many occasions it lasted over an hour. All three ladies longed for that one-hour visit on the telephone; they would keep each other updated on all the events occurring within their families and in their own careers.

During the years they had made many acquaintances, but they only shared their most intimate disappointments, longings, and future dreams with each other. They could act like clowns, explaining to each other how totally foolish or utmost ridiculous they had behaved over something unimportant. Sometimes they acted like silly teenagers, and their silliness had coherence only to them. They consulted major decisions with one another because theirs was an alliance.

William and his brothers had a dispute over the daycare center Marie Terre had installed in the office. His brothers wanted it out of the office, saying it was "unprofessional". They also argued about her belief in helping others and making connections affecting their own profits.

Marie Terre's happiness was more important to William than money or anything his brothers could tell him. He decided it was best for them to separate. The attorneys prepared the business separation agreements. The two brothers kept the purchasing malls business, and William kept the franchises as well as the mergers and acquisitions; this last one required his expertise.

After finalizing the business separation, the family became distant and never got to share special events with each other. Both brothers blamed Marie Terre for the brake-up. William told Marie Terre it was time for his brothers to go their own way. He never told her the real reason for the separation, since he knew that to avoid a family dispute she would leave the company, and he loved having her and the children by his side. In fact, he had stopped doing mergers and acquisitions because they required lots of traveling, research, and were extremely time consuming.

After graduating from college, Ralph, Marie Terre's brother, started working with the franchises. He moved to Puerto Rico because it was middle ground between Latin America, the other Caribbean islands, and the USA, where most of the franchises were located. Her mother and father also moved to the island because of the warm climate and to be near her sister and their son.

Brenda's two-year assignment as international staff was over. She had been offered good positions as international staff in other countries, and she could transfer back to the UK and get a permanent position there, but she kept postponing it. Because of her excellent job performance, her salary was not changed. But after three years they gave her a permanent position without the international staff benefits, such as the once a year trip to the UK and the rental bonus.

Carlos had converted the first floor of the big house into his dream Spa. The facilities were very well decorated and had a sauna, aerobics hall, massage room, a hairdresser, and a makeup artist. With the rent he received from Brenda, he had paid off the house. The business was doing splendidly and he also received substantial commissions from referrals he made to local plastic surgeons. He has recently purchased another house, where he lived with Brenda and their daughter, Teresa.

Marie Terre and William's happiest moments were when they shared time with their children: John, who was five years old, and Philip, their second child who was four years old. During the summer months, her parents and brother stayed with them at the "Palace", as her father called their Tudor house. It was joyful times filled with caring memories.

As soon as the grandparents left, Diana, George, Brenda, and Carlos would also visit with them. On other occasions they would all go to New York City. They all took their children to Radio City to see a Disney movie and the famous Rockets.

Once during the Christmas and New Year holidays they all went to a resort in the Dominican Republic. Lillian was fascinated with the resort: the food was fantastic, the friends and family were together, and no one had to worry about cooking, or having sufficient towels for the guests, or preparing the New Year's party. Everyone felt free to do as they pleased.

Lillian and Mike would have breakfast at six in the morning and go to the beach with John and Philip. Ralph would sleep all morning and get up for lunch, then go to the swimming pool. Marie Terre and William played tennis with their friends and with the children in the afternoons.

At night they made reservations at one of the restaurants had dinner all together. They reserved the best restaurant at the resort for the New Year's dinner. The party hats were in black and gold, and they were given whistles and different paraphernalia to make loud noises when the New Year arrived. Even the children were awake; they received the New Year with kisses, lots of love, good wishes, and dancing.

They were leaving to La Capital at noon and their flight out of the country would be in two more days. That morning Ralph got up very early and told William and Marie Terre that he had to speak with them.

He explained the franchises were no longer profitable and it was going to get worse. Most executives had their secretary reserve their airline tickets, hotel, car rentals and whatever, using the internet.

Many major corporations realized how much money they could save, and the word was out they were not going to be using the franchises anymore. Only some small countries that didn't have internet access were still using their services.

He had spoken with a large pharmaceutical company that made an internal audit and found that by saving one penny per day with car rentals alone, they would save thousands of dollars a year.

William and Marie Terre were very well aware of how access to the internet had affected business; they had not communicated it to Ralph so that he would not worry about his position.

Ralph felt much relieved. He told them a large British Pharmaceutical that recently opened a plant on the island had offered him an excellent job opportunity. William and Marie Terre were also relieved to know he had another job offer; they suggested he accept the job he had been offered as soon as possible.

Most of the franchises that were still profitable also offered travel visa services. William knew he had to sell or dissolve the corporation, because eventually operating costs would be larger than the profits. He also knew that young dynamic professionals, that charged less than he did, had started making a name for themselves doing mergers and acquisitions.

The sad part was how fed up he felt with that line of business. In fact, just a few weeks before he received threatening notes from a person that had lost his job in a previous hostile takeover. He had to figure out some other business strategy in order to keep his current lifestyle and protect his family.

William had rented a small bus and driver for the trip from the resort to La Capital. Teresa, Brenda's three-year-old daughter, insisted on going in the bus with all the others. Brenda also wanted to go with her friends on the bus. Carlos agreed to drive back alone in his own car and left a few hours earlier.

The bus drive took four hours. They decided to drop Brenda and Teresa off at their house first, before going to the hotel where they would spend the night. When they arrived to the house, it was flooded with police cars and some news media. Carmen the masseuse was also there with her three children, crying hysterically.

The passengers all got out of the bus to find out what had happened. Brenda immediately asked the police why they were at her house and where was her husband. The police informed her that her husband had been kidnapped and the kidnappers wanted a fifty thousand-dollar ransom, or else they would kill him.

Brenda's body started shaking in shock. Diana and Marie Terre held on to her before she could fall. No one understood what was going on.

William asked Brenda for the house keys, and also asked the police officer in charge to come into the house and explain what was going on. Even Carmen walked into the house with her children. The police officer had a tendency to talk more than he should.

"The country is suffering from an epidemic of kidnappings. Any person that seems to have some money is being kidnapped for ransom. For this reason the very elite have their own bodyguards. The same thing is happening in Mexico City."

William was exasperated. "How did the kidnappers make contact?"

The police officer showed him the ransom note. "They contacted Mr. Carlos Sanchez's woman, thinking she was his wife. Carmen came to this house to talk with the real wife and no one was here. Then she asked a neighbor for permission to use their telephone and call the police. As soon as my partner and I arrived she gave us the note and explained what had happened."

Carmen was covering her face as she continued to cry hysterically. William stared at her with bewilderment. The police officer noticed it, and decided to be helpful. "Carmen is the mother of Carlos' three children, and they live on the second floor of his Spa."

Oblivious to the reactions around him, the police officer continued. "We talked to the neighbors and it seems that for about two months the kidnappers had been watching Carlos' business. They had seen him come and go to Carmen and their children, which were living in the second story apartment he had originally built for Brenda, his wife.

Today, when he arrived to the big house, he parked his car on the sidewalk because apparently he was leaving right away. The kidnappers took advantage of the position of the car and grabbed Carlos from the back, covering his head with a pillowcase, tying his hands behind his back, and putting him in the back part of a minivan. It all happened so fast, the neighbors never got to see the kidnappers."

"All the kidnappings that have occurred in the country in the last six months have created a great indignation in the public opinion. The police commissioner himself has just made a public announcement on television, saying he would personally handle this case. He called for backup from every police station in the Capital. He will see to it that the disgraceful people who committed this hideous crime will get punished with all the power of the law.

Carlos' television program has made him a beloved, well-known public figure in most households in this country. I was informed that after the Commissioner's announcement, the police department has been bombarded with telephone calls offering to donate money for the ransom, and demanding the police do something about this despicable action against law abiding citizens. The television channel where Carlos worked has his picture on the screen, requesting his safe return."

William could see all the reporters surrounded Brenda's house. The police officer continued: "Every radio station in the country stopped its programming and begged the kidnappers not to harm Carlos and to let him return safe to his family." Even people on the streets were screaming: "You must let Carlos go!"

Brenda was in such a state of shock that she could not even cry. Both her friends had their arms around her.

"My life as I know it has collapsed in a matter of seconds. I can't believe Carlos had three children with Carmen. He has violated the sacredness of our marriage."

She put her hands on her chest, like it was difficult to breath. She looked pale, and shocked.

"This pain is so unbearable I feel I can't breath. This infidelity is totally unexpected. He made love to me every single day! Where did he get the energy to have another woman and three children?

I had been under the assumption our love was eternal. I always believed our family was blessed and our marriage would last until death do us part. This is incomprehensible; never in my wildest dream would I even believe Carlos could betray what we had together. Where are his moral and his ethics? He is such a stupid, insensible, dull, crack-brained, gross human stud."

Deep inside she felt ashamed for not caring about his safety.

She could not stand the commotion any longer and like a zombie, walked to the privacy of her bedroom. Diana asked George to take care of the twins and followed her to the room, then Marie Terre asked her parents to take care of the boys and of Teresa, and she also went to Brenda's side. In total silence they both put their arms around Brenda, holding her with all the love and understanding only true friends can share; she finally started crying with screaming sobs until exhaustion finally took over, leaving her motionless.

The next three days were a total nightmare. Ralph was the only person who did not cancel his airline flight; he would try to help from Puerto Rico. More than ever, Brenda needed as much help as she could get.

The cook and nanny arrived the next day, they were both hysterical, and had to be consoled by the neighbors. Carmen was in such bad conditions that she had to be taken to the hospital, and her parents took the children.

None of her friends commented on Carlos' behavior. Diana and Marie Terre's children all slept on the floor of Teresa's room. Marie Terre's mother and father took the guest room. George and William took turns sleeping on the sofa in the study, and Diana and Marie Terre stayed with Brenda in her room.

Carlos' mother came over to the house; she was a sweet, humble woman that adored her son. She came to console Brenda and start a rosary of prayers for his safe return. Brenda was furious.

"There will be no praying in this house because as soon as he appears I am getting a divorce."

"I cannot believe you would leave my son for having a mistress. All men have mistresses, and you are the wife! You can't possibly want to break up your family for a person like Carmen. In England the kings have their mistresses and the queen does not pack her bags and give up her position as a queen because of that."

As Brenda was listening to this sweet lady's talk, she could not help but feel like a total stranger to her surroundings and to this culture. She tried to be as polite as possible when she asked her mother in-law: "Please, offer the rosary of prayer in your own house." The old lady sadly left what had been her son's home.

From the back of the van Carlos had overheard the kidnappers talking about how they needed to plan picking up the ransom money. He started to scream. "Kill me right now, because no one, not my wife or any of my family have that kind of money." They hit him over the head to make him shut up.

The kidnappers were overwhelmed with the commotion and the amount of news coverage Carlos' abduction had created. The radio, television, and the first page of every newspaper in the country talked about indignation and getting him back safe and sound. They started to panic. Negotiations seemed impractical or impossible to obtain.

After analyzing the situation very carefully, they realized they had no way of getting the ransom. Knowing the idiosyncrasy of their culture, and after finding out from the news media how well liked Carlos was, they actually believed someone would kill them when and if they found out they were the abductors. If they killed Carlos, every person in the country would be looking for them and someone would eventually get rid of them.

For their own protection they decided not to request a ransom and to leave Carlos alive. One thing they had to their favor was that Carlos could never identify them, because he had not seen their faces.

They had to find a remote spot where they would not be seen and leave him there. They drove all the way to the border with Haiti and on a solitary road, making sure no one could see them, they waited until the sun was almost down, and then dumped Carlos inside a ditch and accelerated the car as fast as possible, without turning the car's headlights on.

Carlos lay inside the ditch like a flounder, his hands and feet still tied to his back. His entire body was in pain, but that was the least of his worries. He was expecting to hear the discharge or at least the fire lock of a gunshot, and he stayed very still for a few minutes. Almost not breathing, he pretended he was dead.

When he realized that his captures had left, he screamed for help, but no one heard him. For hours he tried to untie his hands. In desperation he pulled at his wrists, but they were bleeding and had gotten very swollen; he was disabled. It was extremely difficult, but he remembered what he would tell his aerobic class participants: "animo", which meant courage.

His own words gave him the fortitude and tenacity to try and stand up, but when he did he bumped his head against a branch and knocked himself down. It had been a painful blow, but he felt lucky because half of the pillowcase covering his head was falling off to one side, and with one eye he could see the moon and stars.

He tried to focus but all he could see was blackness. He felt like an unfortunate wretch. He tried to concentrate on hearing something, but all he could hear was the sounds of the wind and the silence of the night in the country.

To improve blood circulation to his legs he pressed one leg upon another and the rope started to feel loose. He continued twisting his legs until in one contortion he freed one leg out of the ropes. He took a very deep breath and realized he had to get out of the ground and find someone that would see him.

He got up on his own two feet and, with help from the branch, he finished pulling the pillowcase off his head. The main difficulty was getting out of the ditch without his hands. He knew it was no time for doubts; he had to overcome the difficulties, but first he prayed to God. He thanked God for being alive. He promised God that if he got out of this ordeal safe and sound he would be a better man, and he would make amends for the sins he had committed. Overcome by exhaustion, he fell asleep.

By daybreak, Carlos woke up to children's voices playing hide and seek. He screamed for help several times until a five-year old boy saw him inside the ditch and called the other children. At first the other children kept on hiding. They thought it was the boy's trick to get them to lose the game, but his insistence made them realize it was something serious. The other children got out of their hiding places, timidly peeped inside the ditch, and they saw Carlos.

Carlos begged them to help him out of the ditch and to call their parents for help. One of the children ran to his house and told his mother that there was a weird-looking man inside the ditch, with blood on his hands and that they were tied to his back. She ran to the ditch to find out what was going on.

When she arrived two of the children who tried to help the man had also fallen inside the ditch. Another child had also gotten his mother and when she arrived she recognized Carlos from the television. They told Carlos they would go get help.

In about fifteen minutes the two mothers arrived in a police patrol car. One of the officers went inside the ditch and freed Carlos' bloody hands with a knife. Carlos felt relieved, it mitigated his pain, and he stretched his fingers moving them and bringing circulation back to his fingertips. About ten other people had heard about the incident and were standing by observing the rescue.

The officer inside the ditch first lifted one child and handed him to another police officer waiting outside the ditch. Then he lifted the second child and finally they helped Carlos get out of the hole. The sightseers clapped their hand once he was standing on the side of the road. One of the mothers had brought a bottle of peroxide to cure his injured hands, and as she poured the cool liquid over his bloody wrists, he felt an immense gratitude to be alive and well.

The police officers felt very proud to be the ones to find Carlos alive. They called the police Commissioner, providing him with all the details. The Commissioner instructed them to escort Carlos' ambulance to a good hospital in the Capital.

He held a press conference informing the public that Carlos had been found alive, and would be arriving to a Hospital in La Capital. With little legwork, it was not difficult for the reporters to find out which hospital he was going to be taken to. Word of mouth also got around and the entrance to the hospital looked like a circus.

Brenda was called and given the name of the hospital where Carlos was going to be taken to. She could not see herself visiting him at the hospital. She shared her feelings with her friends.

"I believed we were a family. Our lives were ideal. I don't want to judge, but I have no objectivity. I'm bleeding inside and I just can't make myself go to the hospital."

At times she said things that made no sense at all.

As soon as Carlos' ambulance arrived at the hospital, several television cameras were turned on him. The television station he worked at was given priority to reach him as long as they did not interfere with the medical attention he deserved.

It was a very emotional encounter when his mother hugged and kissed him. Then Carmen and the children arrived. They all hugged and kissed each other as a father and his children do when they have not seen the family in several days.

Teresa walked into her mother's rooms and asked her: "Mama, who where those children that were kissing my daddy on television?" It was a second blow for Brenda. She turned off the TV. She went over to her friends and repeated several times "This is cruel, unmerciful, and I feel miserable and enraged."

She did not see the panic in Carlos eyes when he started calling for his wife and Teresa; he thought they had been kidnapped. He was told that they were doing well and had been informed of his arrival. Then he looked at Carmen and asked her if Brenda knew. Carmen was very embarrassed and began crying; she turned her face away from his and let him know it was not her fault that Brenda found out.

He remembered what he had promised God, and he knew Carmen had kept silent for all these years, living on the sidelines. She had done so much for him without ever asking for anything in return. He took her in his arms and let her know he heard somewhere that "truth will set you free", and it had been a terrible thing to have their children live in hiding. It was better she finally found out the truth.

Teresa became agitated and wanted to see her daddy. William picked her up and looking at Marie Terre, he said: "You need to intervene with Brenda now that Carlos' life is out of danger." Diana and Marie Terre decided to talk with Brenda and find out her state of mind concerning Carlos' infidelity.

When they finally confronted her, she began crying and in between sobs she let them know.

"I had idolized him, raising him above reality, treating him as an object of pleasure. I have tried to face reality and see our life together as it really was."

She was talking to her friends, but it sounded as if she were talking to herself.

"He could be eloquent, but he is not intellectual. He has no imagination. My attraction for him is only physical. We never had a disagreement because most of the time he went along with my wishes. From sunrise to sunset I have meditated, and know I need to accept the idea of him having a family with the masseuse, but my own feelings keep interfering with my logic.

I don't think I have slept at all during the last three days. I have made plans in my mind, but these plans are all too shameful to discuss. The only solution that keeps coming to my mind is that I want to kill him."

Diana and Marie Terre provided consolation, comfort, and some relief, but Brenda had to take action and be in charge of her own life. She told her friends that if she saw him she would kill him; it was best for everyone if she left the country with her friends and stayed with Marie Terre in the UK for some days. There was no way she could confront Carlos or stay in this house any longer.

Her friends wanted her to think things over clearly, but she just wanted to run away and be with people that actually cared for her. She was in this ambivalent state of mind when the telephone rang. Diana picked up the receiver; it was Carlos.

"Carlos, are you doing well? Were you physically harmed in any way?"

He let her know he was doing fine and wanted to talk with Brenda. She insinuated it was not a good idea, but he insisted on talking with her. Diana looked at Brenda and let her know that Carlos wanted to talk with her.

Brenda hesitated for a few seconds, and then took the receiver and started screaming at him.

"You son of a bitch! You are a comedian, a charlatan, our entire marriage is a farce!"

He got very upset with her and for the first time in their marriage he did not comply. On the contrary, he yelled at her, stating the many ways in which she had neglected his feelings during their years together.

"You are cold and indifferent to my needs. I have pleased you in every way I could possibly think of and in return, sexually you just lay there expecting me to please you. You couldn't care less about pleasing me, never once have you given me a back rub when I was in pain from new exercises. You never confided in me with any of your innermost thoughts, or asked about how I felt. You would rather call your friends and confide in them."

Even at this point, she was thinking about herself.

"I couldn't care less if you were dead or alive."

He calmed down but continued to speak his mind.

"I did not want things to happen like this, but all those blank spaces in our marriage were filled by Carmen. When I was in pain, she would kindly rub my back. When I needed someone to talk to, she was there to listen, and when I was alone, because you were working or traveling, she was there to please me."

Brenda got even more agitated and screamed back at him.

"I can't believe that you are making things sound like it is my fault you have a family with Carmen. When I picked up the telephone, it was because I figured you would beg for my forgiveness, and what you are really trying to do is make me feel guilty for your sins."

At this point she was so enraged that she slammed the receiver. She went over to her friends.

"I have the extravagant notion of disappearing on him. My departure will make him realize how much he has lost. If he follows us to the UK we will move somewhere else."

Diana interrupted her. "So in your mind you see yourself going impetuously from one place to another, to prevent Carlos from seeing his beloved Teresa again, and you will change your life to that of a gypsy runaway?"

Tears rolled down Brenda's cheeks.

"He would probably be happier without me. I have been trying to remember when was the last time he told me he loved me, and I can't. Who will ever love me again? I know for sure no one in the world can make love to me the way he did, no one will pick out my wardrobe the way he does, or wake me up in the morning to make me do exercise every single day. I am sure that no one else will ever make me feel whole again. I feel I am worth nothing."

With a firm voice and a lot of attitude, Marie Terre said: "Stop feeling sorry for yourself. Pack your luggage, and you are coming with us until the waters reach their level. You are in no condition to stay alone."

Brenda agreed. She told them how Carlos had screamed at her, how he said she was cold and indifferent, and how he even tried to make her feel guilty, as if she were to blame for his second family situation. Then she became agitated again, repeating he did not love her. In between sobs, she let them know she was ready to pack her bags.

She asked Marie Terre to help her with the airline tickets, and asked Diana to help her with the luggage. Each and every one of them got busy with travel arrangements. They left that same night on an evening flight to San Juan. At the hotel in San Juan, Diana and Marie Terre stayed with Brenda; they did not leave her out of their sight for a moment. Her behavior had been so erratic they did not know what to expect. The next day Diana, George, and the twins took a flight to New York, and Brenda and Teresa flew to the UK with William and Marie Terre.

Carlos lay on his back, crying. He had damaged their relationship without hope of repair. He realized all his bottled up feelings rushed out as an attack on her. He had swallowed his own pride for so many years! He should have let her know how he felt little by little as married

people do, until they knew how the other one felt. But he
had kept his feelings locked up upside because he was
afraid of losing Brenda and his beloved Teresa, and out of
his own stupidity he had done just that.

He felt Brenda was his creation; she wore the dresses he
picked for her and accepted the vigorous exercise program
he had developed for her. He felt like the proudest man
alive whenever they walked into a place. He was the envy
of most men in a crowd. He knew he wanted to grow old
next to her and that Carmen was an excuse. She had been
a weakness, a fault in his moral behavior. He kept on going
to her because of the first child, and then came the second
and the third. He had sinned, and now he was going to pay
for it for the rest of his life.

20 A CHANGE OF DESTINY

On the flight to the UK Brenda could not sleep. She was trying to figure out what went wrong in her marriage. She remembered Carlos yelling at her and telling her it was her fault. Guilty feelings built in her soul. She wished it was a nightmare and that Carlos would run to her side and tell her it was all a lie he had made up to make her feel jealous.

In her daydreaming, she promised to be more affectionate and share her thoughts and worries with him; she would be the wife he wanted her to be. But reality crept in, and she realized she had to face whatever it was that awaited her in the future, without her man.

As soon as they arrived in the UK they all went to Bath. The children were delighted to have Teresa play with them and share the storybooks that Marie Terre would read for them. The family room had many toys, but what they liked the most was playing and listening to music.

Teresa was teaching the boys how to dance. Her father had taught her many useful steps, and he was going to present her on television as the baby cyclone of the Caribbean. The boys laughed and ran to their mother to find out what was a cyclone. Marie Terre had to get a dictionary to explain what a cyclone was, and then they got paper and crayons to draw it on paper.

Teresa made loud woo sounds to give them an idea what a cyclone sounded like. The boys were fascinated with her knowledge of dancing and hurricanes, and she was definitely the most beautiful little girl they had seen.

William went back to London to attend to his business. The business had more expenses than profits, but William had continued spending money as he did before the split with his brothers and the downfall of the franchises.

The franchises had started to lose money faster than he had anticipated. It had been some time since anyone had called him for a merger or acquisition. He found out that, as rumors had it, he had lost his edge for the fight, and deep inside his soul he knew it was true.

For several months now he had told himself he needed to develop some kind of business that would guarantee a steady income, but had not figured out what. His broker had been calling him during the holidays to give him the bad news; he had lost more than half of his portfolio in the stock market.

After that terrible blow, he made a conference call with his accountant. For some time now the accountant had been very worried about the lack of cash flow. He explained that if business continued the way it was he would be ruined within months.

He could not keep on waiting, he had tried to get rid of the franchises, but no one would buy them. He called his attorneys and they started the paperwork to declare the franchises bankrupt.

The accountant called William to let him know the first thing to go would be the jet airplane, then the apartment in Marbella, Spain, and before he even mentioned it William said, with pain in his voice; "The Tudor house in Bath." His place in London would become the family home.

It had taken him years of total commitment to build his fortune, and it seemed to be slipping away in no time. He had always been on top of things, finding out what was going on all over the world, but he had disconnected from that hectic world and dedicated his time and energy to his wife and children, abandoning the business.

It was not his style, but he asked Camille to investigate with her acquaintances in different industries what the latest venture was. After several hours of phone calls, she came up with two small airline companies in Latin America who were trying to work out a merger. Camille called the owners; they were pleased to talk with Mr. Burgess. He made an appointment to see them in two days.

William took Marie Terre in a loving embrace. "I am so pleased to have Brenda and Teresa staying with the family. I have to go to Latin America on business in a couple of days, but I will be back as soon as possible."

He did not want to give Marie Terre the bad news about the franchises, or that they would have to move out of their house in Bath, until he got back from the trip.

When the time came to leave for the airport, he kissed both of his sons.

"Take good care of Mommy, Teresa, and your aunt Brenda."

He went over to Brenda and told her she could stay in the house as long as she pleased; she was family. Then he walked with Marie Terre to the front door and lovingly kissed her.

"Thank you for making me so happy and giving me two wonderful sons. I'll see you soon."

As he was walking towards the car he turned his head back to look at his beloved wife, staring at him from the door's threshold. He couldn't help but smile.

"Everything is going to be fine."

Brenda was exhausted. She felt worn out and pathetic. Her behavior was affecting Teresa, who started to worry about her mother. Every time she asked about her father, Brenda would ignore her and not give her a reply. Even Marie Terre told her she had to spend more time with Teresa, and eventually give her some kind of explanation. But Brenda would get upset and reply: "I can't explain the unexplainable."

Twenty-four hours after William had left, Brenda was sitting on the love seat brooding, and the boys were playing with Teresa, when the telephone started to ring. Marie Terre answered it. It was a police officer from Santiago in Chile.

"I would like to speak to Mrs. Burgess."

"This is she."

"I called to sadly inform you: your husband was traveling on an airplane that crashed in the Andes Mountain. Rescuers were searching for survivors, but the mountains are the longest and range among some of the highest in the world. They have not found survivors or bodies. The airplane crashed on the southern region, near the Antarctic, where it is not very populated and is much cooler even though it is summer. We will call you back as soon as we have some definite information..."

Marie Terre fainted. Brenda saw her fall to the floor, but had no idea what had happened. As she approached Marie Terre's unconscious body she screamed for help. The housekeeper came running into the room and picked up the telephone receiver to find out who had called, but the communication had gotten disconnected. The housekeeper called an ambulance. Between the two of them, they lifted Marie Terre up and gently placed her on the love seat.

She woke up and started crying. She did not want to repeat what she had been told over the receiver, and just kept saying; "It can't be true, it's a lie, a bad joke." The ambulance arrived and Brenda explained what happened; the attendant examined Marie Terre and asked her if she had been given bad news. She began to cry and nodded. The attendant had her smell a small amount of ammonia that made her turn her face away. He told her he was going to give her an injection to tranquilize her.

This is when she reacted violently; she pushed the attendant away and said she would present a judicial lawsuit if he touched her. He backed off and said she would be fine, then he packed his equipment and left.

Brenda asked the housekeeper to take care of the children until she found out what was going on. Then the telephone rang again, and Brenda answered it. The police officer from Chile told her the line had gotten disconnected when he had been talking with Mrs. Burgess.

He gave Brenda the details of the airplane crash, and all Brenda could say was "Oh no!" The housekeeper started crying as soon as Brenda told her about the accident. Marie Terre looked at the two of them and realized that for the children's benefit they had to be brave. The bodies had not been found, and they were still working on the rescue.

Brenda called Diana in New York and told her what had happened. Diana let her know she would arrive as soon as possible; Marie Terre needed all the moral support she could get. That night the news media informed about the airplane crash and gave the names of the missing passengers.

William's brothers called Marie Terre, and Brenda answered; she did not let them talk to her. They were furious with Marie Terre for not having informed them of what happened to their brother and promised never to forgive her for this. They sent their own rescue team to find their brother, but it was all in vain.

As soon as Diana arrived from New York, she ran to Brenda and Marie Terre and the three of them hugged each other in a very long embrace, like three pillars supporting one another. They cried together, sharing each other's pain and protecting each other.

A certain kind of relief came to them by just knowing they could always count on each other. Their friendship would provide the strength to confront any affliction or misfortune; they would be there to pick each other up.

Ralph and Marie Terre's parents called her to find out if what they heard on the news about the airplane crash was true. She said there was still hope they would find him alive. The next day they were at her house in Bath to console her.

TV reporters and paparazzi surrounded the house; the telephone would not stop ringing. Her friends and family took care of the commotion, and the iron gates had to be kept closed at all times.

Diana stayed a week, and then returned to her own family in New York. Marie Terre kept on talking about hope and fortitude. Ralph also left, but her parents stayed to provide love and understanding as well as a shoulder to cry on.

Brenda's nightmare felt like nothing compared to what Marie Terre was going through. One morning she left Marie Terre with her parents and took the children to a museum and then to the park. She observed them playing with so much joy, not knowing, innocent of the tragedy that surrounded them.

Back at the house she left the children with the grandparents and went casually walking around the estate. The wind was very cold, but she felt the need to walk faster and faster. The faster she walked, the more invigorated she felt. She kept on walking, soaring, elevating to something sublime. It was as if she was walking into a new life with a different adventure, and she felt free.

As a child, she had felt prisoner in those cold boarding schools. As a young woman she had felt prisoner of her appearance, totally oppressed. Now she was free of all those oppressions. Her life was going to change, she would get up in the morning and not have to make love to Carlos, or do exercise. She would pick her own dresses, would walk, talk, or go anywhere she pleased.

She had allowed Carlos to take control of her life, and now she was going to take it back. Just the thought made her feel strong and capable. She was her own woman.

Ever since she found out about Carmen she had felt as if a big powerful stone had been placed on her chest, not letting her breathe. The more she walked, the more liberated her spirit became. The rock had been lifted from her chest and she could move on and do other things.

At work she had requested a one-month leave of absence. She walked back to the house and called the bank requesting a transfer, to wherever there would be an international staff position. She would stay with Marie Terre for the remaining of her leave, and start a new life wherever destiny provided. And destiny was providing even another challenge; she was expecting her second child.

Marie Terre's parents were very helpful with the children, keeping the reporters at a proper distance, as well as screening all telephone calls, but they were getting on her nerves.

They talked a little too loud, and were constantly speculating about the situation. They tried to decide what Marie Terre should do, and they were acting as if William was never coming back.

She kept on talking about hope, and wanted to get to the office to work with the franchises, but she also wanted to stay in the house just in case the telephone call arrived letting her know William was safe and sound.

She called Camille and requested information on the franchises. Camille had to inform her William's attorney had prepared the bankruptcy papers; she needed to talk to him right away. He had been waiting for her to return his telephone calls. He would take the papers to Bath as soon as she gave him her approval.

She knew the franchises were in bad shape, but William had not confided in her regarding the bankruptcy. She could not imagine why he had not informed her about his intentions. It made her very upset to say the least, but she wanted to meet with the counselor as soon as possible.

William's attorney arrived at Bath that afternoon. He treated her with plenty of sympathy, and this aggravated her, but she tried to stay rational. He explained ever since

William divided the company between the brothers in three equal shares, it had stopped producing revenue.

He had been paying the franchises' operating cost with his own money. He had kept everyone on the payroll, when he should have cut down on expenses. He also kept on living as if he were producing the amount of income he had produced before.

It was to her advantage he had filed for bankruptcy when he did. The lawyer needed her signature to present it in court as soon as possible. If they waited any longer, he would have to declare her and the children as William's sole heirs, but without a death certificate he could not do that, and it usually took months. In the meantime, the franchises would continue to drain the estate.

When he explained the formalities prescribed by law, her body started to tremble. He noticed it and recommended she talk with William's accountant, to find out the state of her finances.

Very sadly, and with a lump in his throat, he said Williams' life insurance policy would not pay without a body, or until he was declared legally dead, which could take about seven years. After signing the proper documents she thanked him for keeping her informed and solemnly walked him to the door.

When Marie Terre was working with the franchises, she never liked looking at the budget. She would ask William if she could do something, and he always gave her his approval.

Before she met William, she had worked for little over a year and she let Diana administer the budget. Diana would let her know how much she could spend, and she would not spend more than she was told.

William seemed to have so much money she always figured it would never end. She liked art, and they had collected an impressive amount of artwork from little-know artists. Some had made it big and others had not. Now she had to talk with the accountant and she was dreading it.

The accountant let her know William had finally given up the jet airplane; it was consuming lots of money in maintenance fees. William had planned on selling the Tudor house and the property in Marbella, Spain. She could not sell these properties without his signature unless they declared her and the children as full heirs.

The payroll was also consuming a big chunk of their estate; she had to do something about her financial situation, because she had sufficient money to last her about four or five months.

In her entire life she had never felt as confused as she did after talking with the accountant. She had two boys to take care of, and if she fired all the employees, William would be devastated. Guilt paralyzed her.

She felt it was all her fault William had divided the company with his brothers. It was her fault he kept the franchises when they were no longer profitable. It was her fault he stopped working hard. And it was her fault that he had that horrible airplane crash in the Andes. She finally started crying inconsolably and felt totally defeated.

Brenda found Marie Terre crying and took her for a long walk around the estate. During the walk she gave Brenda the details of her financial situation. Talking to Brenda gave her a clearer picture of what was happening.

She realized if she did nothing and left things as they were, in a matter of months she and her children would have nothing left. She had to take responsibility for herself and the children, and it could not wait. But first she needed Diana's financial expertise. She called her friend that night and informed her of the situation.

Diana called William's accountant and requested a complete financial statement. She studied the situation, and then returned to Bath to help her friend.

Diana sat down with Marie Terre and very carefully explained she had to close down the business as soon as possible. Marie Terre insisted they give the employees at least one-month notice. Bluntly, Diana told her William's attorney needed to handle the situation according to the law.

Her recommendation was to take as much cash as possible, and move in with her parents until the situation got stabilized. Marie Terre vehemently refused such a notion; she and the children needed to be in their own home when William returned.

With Brenda's help, Diana explained the situation over and over to Marie Terre. They finally convinced her by saying it would be very dangerous for her and the children to stay.

When fired, many people become impetuous and extremely angry towards the person they believe is to blame. In this case they would blame her for their misfortune.

The next day they sat with the attorneys at the law firm requesting to liquidate the business. The attorneys explained they would do their very best to save at least William's place in London. They would manage the tax and mortgage payments, but the other properties would be lost. The estate did not have sufficient working capital to keep up with the costs.

More than anything, Diana insisted Marie Terre and the children should be free of debt. After the accountant had figured out how much money they needed for the payroll and the counselor fees, they went to the bank and with Brenda's help transferred a little over half a million pounds to an account in New York. She would no longer be a millionaire, but she had sufficient money to give her a head start for the children.

21 LIFE GOES ON

George and Diana were in the limelight; it was more than they could have ever dreamed of. They loved living in New York City. Their reputation had skyrocketed and they had several managers, performing projects under different umbrella corporations. If something went wrong, only that corporation would go under. After realizing what had happened to William's capital, Diana and George had their attorneys figure out every legal precaution that could protect them against major losses.

They had nannies for the twins, and sent them to the most prestigious schools in the city. They worked every single day, but it did not seem like hard work because they were having a ball at it. It was something they enjoyed doing and it gave them a wonderful feeling of accomplishment.

Due to their social status, they were invited to many parties and social events. Most of the people treated them as royalty, and it felt good. Time with the children was given sparingly, and they justified it thinking the children were getting the best care and education money could buy, and they needed to work and socialize to provide for the children's needs.

One thing remained constant: the once-a-month conference call amongst the three friends. Updates were provided about children's health, accomplishments, schoolwork, or mischief.

Sometimes the anecdotes were hilarious, like when Marie Terre's youngest boy, Philip, was expelled from pre-kinder because he took off his socks to cool off his feet. He would not put them back on, refusing to obey the teacher, and they could not have that kind of rebellion in that school.

Talking with each other, sharing their innermost thoughts and daily experiences as well as any conflict they encountered, was more than therapy. It helped purged the negative stuff from their lives, making them dependent on each other for strength and support. Their bonds grew stronger as time went by.

Marie Terre still called the police department in Santiago de Chile once a month, to find out if something had showed up. But they just treated her as a friend in grief. As soon as that first winter arrived, they had discontinued the search party. She was told no one could ever survive the winter.

During the next summer some rescuers tried to find the remains, with no luck whatsoever. However, month after month and year after year, Marie Terre kept on calling. She could not give up; she had nightmares where William would visit her in her dreams and tell her it had all been a bad joke played on her.

During the first year after William's airplane accident, Marie Terre had been so grief-stricken that she stayed at her parent's house. Her parents had purchased a big old house near Lillian's sister's home in Puerto Rico. They fixed a room for Marie Terre and another one for the boys.

When the children were at school Marie Terre did house work, and as soon as she was finished she would lock herself in her room and cry.

Ralph purchased a two-bedroom apartment with a gorgeous ocean view in the posh section of the capital. The children enjoyed visiting their uncle during the weekends, where they swam and became excellent surfers.

Little by little, Marie Terre's children started to lift off some of her grief, with all their day-to-day talk and adventures. They gave her hope for the future. As boys they were audacious, daring, and fearless.

Their adventurous spirit sometimes worried her. On the other hand their boldness and confidence in themselves filled her with pride and joy. In her mind they were just like their father.

Her entire life revolved around her children's activities. Every single night before putting them to bed, Marie Terre would read a story to her boys. In the morning, she would help them get ready for school, fix them breakfast, and drive them to and from school.

In the afternoons she would take them to the park, and back at home she helped them with their homework. At their school, she volunteered to take the children's classmates on field trips and baked cookies for them.

One year she decided to bake a cake and celebrate Philip's birthday at the school. When she put the cake mixture trays inside the oven, they tilted a little. She was going to stack the cake in layers, but they came out of the oven with a big bump to the side. She had no time to bake another cake.

Her imagination began to work and she got a big box, which she wrapped in aluminum foil. Then she put the three mountain-looking cakes on top of the foil and frosted the cakes. On one mountain she placed lots of miniature trees, simulating a forest. On the second mountain she placed toy soldiers, and miniature Indians on the third. In between the mountains was a fake river.

When the children at school saw the big box with the three mountains of cake and the toy soldiers and Indians they started screaming with excitement. They said it was the most beautiful cake they had ever seen. Philip felt like the proudest birthday boy ever, filling Marie Terre with joy. She realized it was the highest point in her life for the past year or so, since Williams' disappearance.

After that first year Claudia insisted Marie Terre needed to do something with her life, like getting a job or going back to school. Marie Terre debated that looking after two boys was more than sufficient. However, Claudia would not take no for an answer.

One afternoon she just grabbed Marie Terre by the hand and they went to the University for her enrollment in a Masters Degree in Arts.

Marie Terre had her diploma from the UK and an old transcript of her courses. At the University, she was told she could pre-enroll in the program pending they received an official transcript direct form the UK. Claudia helped her organize a course load during the same hours the boys were at school; she also took it upon herself to request a transcript from the UK for her cousin.

Going to the University took her mind off the sadness of not knowing what had become of her beloved husband. She only took courses that would not interfere with her children's after-school daily activities.

The boys had obtained their diving license, and she took them to their Spanish guitar lessons, as well as photography classes, and they both enrolled in American Football. After picking the boys up from schools she had to take them to their different hobbies.

Football practices were Monday to Friday from four to six in the afternoon, and on Saturday mornings they played against other teams. If their team won the game, they would celebrate on Sunday with a pool party that would include hamburgers and hot-dogs.

Most of the other mothers were at the practices cheering for their boys, but eventually they became acquainted with one another and started socializing.

Marie Terre enjoyed talking with the other mothers and listening to their different stories. There was one mother that impressed her the most. She had four lovely children, two boys and two girls. Philip was infatuated with her youngest daughter, but she was older and taller than him and acted as if it was sweet of him to be interested in her.

One day this mother told the group that four years before, her husband had been diagnosed with cancer, and this had completely changed her life. She had stopped worrying about trivial things, such as climbing the social ladder or how many material objects she could obtain to impress others.

Ever since her husband's diagnosis, they focused on creating a happy and loving family life. His cancer was now in remission, and these last four years had been filled with caring and understanding.

Every morning when she woke up she would kiss her husband and thank God for having him for one more day. They had never been happier.

Marie Terre realized how everyday commitments could make people consumed with having things, and forgetful about the values that make our lives worthwhile. She thought about how William would have treated his nephews if one of his brothers had disappeared. She knew for a fact he would call them, send them a birthday card and gifts for Christmas, and serve as the male figure in their life.

But his brothers never called or sent her children cards, or had anything to do with them. She felt very sad her sons had no contact with their uncaring, cold, selfish, empty-hearted uncles and their forever vain and social climbing wives.

The one thing that consoled her was to know her family provided the boys with the support they needed to keep on going. She knew no matter what happened they would always be there for one another. And, of course, she had her two friends.

They had been the pillars of her resilience. Her family worried too much about her, and she worried about her children, but her friends gave her the balance she needed to keep in touch with her inner self. They understood her and were always there for her.

The football coach was a tall handsome American man in his early thirties. The other mothers insinuated he liked Marie Terre, but she would pay no attention to their hints and did not even slightly touch the subject. However, one day she was talking with one of the other mothers and the coach tossed a ball at her hitting her in the head.

He was furious at her because she was talking and had missed Phillips' touchdown. This absolutely convinced the other mothers about his interest in her and told her she should do something about it, but Marie Terre acted with total indifference.

The boys won every single game of the season, so almost every Sunday they had a pool party at one of the parent's houses. At their first party, the coach was openly flirting with Marie Terre, but as usual she paid no attention to him.

He knew he was a good-looking man, but could not figure her out. The fathers in the group told him he needed to do something drastic to get her attention.

He went over to her and tried to have a civilized conversation, but she cut him off politely and started to walk away. In order to get a reaction he grabbed her by the waist and, fully dressed, tossed her into the pool.

The adults started to applaud, but her sons did not like what the coach did to their mother. In a playful mood the couch gave her his hand to help her out of the swimming pool, but she used it to pull him inside the pool and everyone started laughing.

He, as well as the others there, believed this incident had finally broken the ice between the two of them, but it did not. As soon as she got out of the water she refused to get into swim wear, and politely asked the boys if they would like to leave.

By the expression on their faces, Marie Terre could tell that both boys were very jealous of their mother and saw her as their own property. Having another man touch her was not seen with good eyes, even if they liked the coach. The boys agreed without further comment.

After the incident at the pool, the coach came to every other Sunday celebration with a beautiful twenty seven-year old girlfriend. She was the typically attractive Puerto Rican girl, with a cascade of lovely brown hair and a sweet smile. The other parents kept on insisting he had just met this girl and he preferred Marie Terre, but she was not interested and it showed.

After the football season was over, none of the mothers called her or invited her to their activities. They were all married couples and she was an odd number. However, she was looking forward to the next football season and seeing the other mothers again. She liked feeling she was part of their group.

With lots of enthusiasm and cheerfulness she told the boys it was time to enroll in the next football season. Without even looking at her they told her they were not going to continue in football. When she asked why, they told her they were more interested in surfing. She never saw any of the people from that group again.

After her brake with Carlos, Brenda had been offered her choice of a job in Costa Rica or Puerto Rico. She took the position that kept her near her friend. Marie Terre stayed at the hospital with Brenda during the delivery of her daughter Mary. Marie Terre's parents also helped taking care of Teresa and the boys.

As soon as Marie Terre called Carlos, he arrived to meet his new daughter. He had been very generous with his beloved Teresa filling her with love, affection, gifts and lots of visits. As usual, he was very attentive to Brenda's emotional and physical needs. Brenda had mentioned the divorce was pending on the birth of their second child, but this subject was not brought up again.

Brenda's behavior towards Carlos was cold and indifferent, but she knew Teresa needed her father and all the attention he profusely lavished over her. She felt so content with the support of Marie Terre and her family that she purchased a two bedroom apartment where Ralph lived, making it easier for the families to collaborate with the care of the children and share precious time with one another. After all, they had become her extended family.

Several years after William's disappearance, Marie Terre received the benefits from his life insurance policy. Marie Terre cried as if she had just been informed her husband had passed away, and that is exactly what it felt like. Her friends and family went to church together for the special masses she had ordered for her husband. It was time to get closure.

Philip had asked her once where his daddy was, and she had told him on a trip, but that he would be coming back. Today she told her children their father had gone to heaven. Philip asked her when he would be coming back from heaven, and she told him that some day they would all go to heaven and he would be waiting for them there. Diana and George also came for the special mass held for William. It was a sad reunion, but it was a new beginning for Marie Terre.

To her own amazement, going back to college revived Marie Terre; she had no time for crying episodes. She completed her Masters Degree in Art in less than two years.

The many museums she had visited around the world had given her such a vast knowledge of the subject that the university offered her a position as a part-time college professor. She accepted the position with enthusiasm, and was looking forward to working again.

Meticulously, she prepared her curriculum. She even practiced what she would say in front of a mirror. One of the first things she included was visiting different museums around the island.

Two visits were to the famous art museum in Ponce, known worldwide because of its collection of over 3,000 pieces, including pieces from the art schools of Europe and the Americas from the XIV to the XXI centuries. One of the reasons for these visits was to get a feel of her students' art appreciation before they started the course, and again after they completed it.

She also took her students to the art galleries in Old San Juan at night. On the first Tuesday of every month the art galleries in Old San Juan were open to the public. This once-a-month event was very lively and enjoyed by people of all ages. The event was called "gallery nights," and the streets in Old San Juan filled with people going from one gallery to another.

At the street cafés, musicians played music with their guitars and many would join them by singing the songs they were playing. They found "gallery nights" the best part in the course. She enjoyed seeing their reactions towards the different art collections and listening to their witty off-hand comments.

These field trips had brightened up her spirit as well as that of the students. Marie Terre's own cheerful personality started to resurface; she began making jokes out of the silly nothings she observed in the environment.

Her reputation around the university students was spreading fast. She was the kind of professor that let students express their own individuality and proved to have a true understanding of the subject she was teaching.

Each semester her classes were booked to the max. Some students even asked permission to attend her courses without receiving the proper credit for their graduation: they just wanted the knowledge in art appreciation she provided.

With the money she received from the insurance company she could return and live in the UK, but her children and relatives were here, as well as her friend Brenda, and Diana was only three hours away on an airplane.

22 MOVING ON

Diana and George had told Brenda and Marie Terre they would pay for the children's college education when the time came. They had been donating money into a college fund designated for all of their children.

Every summer Diana and George sent Brenda, Marie Terre, and the children their airline tickets and had them stay with them in New York. The brownstone they lived in had a lovely backyard with three walls covered in roses; one had white roses, the other had pink roses, and the third wall had red roses. The aroma in their yard was exquisite.

The adults enjoyed having iced tea in the warm summer evenings. They also talked about their children and their future. Little by little Marie Terre started expressing her sense of humor.

She would make her silly little jokes about anything that was in her surroundings, such as when Teresa wanted a cube. In Spanish "cubo" is a bucket. Marie Terre knew what the child wanted, but she said: "Yes, I will calculate the cubic root and elevate it to the third power."

Her wittiness and the tone of voice she used made the
adults laugh out loud, even though the children stared at
her with total bewilderment.

When they were in New York, and after Diana and George
left for work, Brenda and Marie Terre would take all six
children out. One day they went to the Bronx Zoo. The
children were delighted with the giraffes, the lions and,
above all, the big elephants.

One of the first places they had taken the children was to
the Metropolitan Museum. But against their will, they took
them again, because Mary Terre had read in the newspaper
about a new exhibit.

She explained to the children they should feel privileged to
go and see the exhibit called the "Dresden Collection". It
had taken the Museum a big amount of work to have
private collectors from all around the world lending their
precious porcelains and artwork for the general public to
admire. The children were not interested in seeing the
collection, but Marie Terre was so excited there was no way
around it.

She kept on telling them to look at the fabulous details of
the paintings, the silk dresses that looked so real, and the
hands and toes of the porcelain figurines that were just
perfect. The children looked at everything she pointed out
to them with the condition that after seeing the exhibit
they would go row boating in Central Park.

Brenda and Marie Terre had never rowed a boat on their
own, but they had seen how it was done and did not think
it would be a difficult task to accomplish. Most of all, they
had promised the children and a promise was a promise.

After seeing the exhibit they went to Central Park to comply with the children's wishes.

They had to rent two rowboats and each one had three children with them. The children wanted them to row faster, but it was not an easy task for the ladies. In fact, their arms started to ache.

Mary, John and Manuel were in Brenda's boat. Both boys wanted to take turns rowing the boat and they got into an argument over the paddle. When Brenda told them to stop it, they got into a fistfight, throwing blows at each other.

As the struggle got more intense, the boat started to rock. It was very frightening for the mothers to see that the situation could easily get out of control. Very diplomatically, Brenda gave each child a paddle and she sat in the middle of the two boys.

When Marie Terre heard the commotion she approached with her boat, but not being an expert she crashed into it and her boat flipped. When they tried to get into Brenda's boat, they also flipped that one. They were very fortunate to have flipped where the water was not so high and that all the children knew how to swim.

The beautiful part about the incident was that most of the children were worried about each other, especially Mary, because she was the baby. After they had been rescued and made sure that everyone was fine, they started laughing.

They could not help it; people would walk by and laugh at their wet bodies. Brenda wanted the boys to apologize for having started the fight, and she asked them: "what did the two of you learn from this incident?" The boys stated that it was all Marie Terre's fault because she does not know how to row a boat.

The mothers were in no condition to argue, all they wanted was to get home and dry up. Getting a taxi in Manhattan in wet clothes was not an easy task. The taxi drivers would not even stop when they saw two women and six children dripping in water. Both mothers where worried that if they did not get the children dried up soon they could end up with a cold.

Brenda called Diana and explained what had happened. Diana's first reaction was to start laughing; she pictured them in her mind and thought it was very funny. But when she heard the worry in Brenda's voice she took the task seriously and immediately sent them a private car.

Once they were back at the house, and all six children were dried, dressed in their pajamas, fed, and put to bed early, the two friends opened a bottle of wine and sat in the romantic back yard.

They admitted to each other the need of having a man around, not only as a husband for them and a male figure for their children, but as part of the natural structure of things. Even Marie Terre admitted that in addition to sharing her life, thoughts, and opinions with a man, she also missed the sex.

They accepted the fact that they were lonely and wanted a male companion. Then Brenda acknowledged one of the facts of life is that most men know how to row a boat, and they did not. They never blamed anyone for what had happened, it just did, and they both laughed about it and enjoyed each other's company.

After the incident at the park, Diana and George decided to stay home with their friends and children. George had learned how to barbecue and made fabulous T-bone steaks, Brenda made a delicious potato salad, Marie Terre made rice with vegetables, and Diana purchased an original New York cheese cake for dessert. It was a splendid summer day for eating in the backyard. The food was delightful but the company was even more.

The original structure of the brownstone included a lovely fishpond situated on the corner opposite to the entrance of the backyard. George had it demolished because it presented a danger for the children. In its place he built a children's swimming pool.

All six children could barely swim in the small pool, but they had a ball being together. They played, laughed, and sometimes argued amongst each other, but at the end of each summer they had connected as true friends do at that age, ending the summer with sadness and with the desire to share more time with each other.

At one of the parties that Diana and George took their friends to, Brenda met an American-Italian descendant called Peter. He was somewhat shorter than Brenda, but their conversation flowed smoothly.

During dinner she was enjoying a Veal Parmesan with so much gusto that Peter could not help himself, and told her he could make her a Veal Parmesan that would make her lick her fingers. Then he invited her to his Italian restaurant in Queens, which she was delighted to accept.

During their conversation, she discovered he owned an ocean-view apartment in Isla Verde, Puerto Rico, a few miles away from where she had her own apartment. He explained several years ago he entered into a venture capital with two American friends in the island of Puerto Rico, were they started a window company.

It made more sense to have an apartment than to pay hotel accommodations. Eventually he sold his portion of the business to one of the other partners. But he had fallen in love with the island so he kept the apartment for vacation purposes. He also told her he had a fifteen-year-old son, and was separated from his wife.

The next day Brenda told her friends she had a date with Peter. He was taking her to his restaurant. Diana told Brenda to be careful with Peter.

He made big money selling fine Italian jewelry to the best jewelry shops in New York City. He had started that restaurant only as a hobby, because he enjoyed cooking so much, plus the restaurant provided him with a cozy place to eat and drink with his Italian friends.

He also owned the building where he had the restaurant, and had his bachelor's apartment above it. His wife and son lived in the east side. What he lacks in height and the good looks department he more than made up for with his charm.

Brenda knew very well where charm had gotten her to with Carlos. If there was ever a trophy offered for a charming man in this world he would definitely win it.

Peter was very punctual picking her up. She had forgotten how punctual people on the main land are, compared to island time. In Puerto Rico, you have to specify and say "American time" if you want things to happen at a specific time. If you don't say that, you could easily find people arriving two hours after the time you had told them.

With great pride Peter, walked Brenda into his restaurant and with exaggerated Latin gestures extended his arms to introduce her to his "domain".

The restaurant had about ten small tables. The walls were decorated with replicas of famous Italian paintings, and at a far end corner a small statue stood with an indoor fountain. The atmosphere was very inviting. It made you feel as if you were in some Italian corner.

Peter was attentive and introduced her to many of his friends. He was not expecting his son to come to the restaurant, but there he was, so he introduced her to his son, Peter junior.

The teenager was a polite, slim, and attractive young man that looked her over like trying to memorize every detail about her. She could not help but wonder if he was comparing her to his mother. He made her feel very self-couscous about the fact that Peter was still married, as was she. It was not the proper situation to be in and less of all to meet his son.

She thought about her own daughters, and how they would feel meeting another man. The only thing that really annoyed her was the fact that she and Carlos were still legally married.

Her mind drifted and she kept on thinking why she had not divorced Carlos, but it was impossible to explain. The only excuse she could think of was that she wanted him to make the first move.

A divorce in the Dominican Republic only takes about three days. That is why many famous people get divorced in Santo Domingo. She had to concentrate on where she was and tell herself she was not having an affair with Peter. These kinds of thought or feelings were like crossing the bridge before she even got to the river.

Some of Peter's friends entertained Brenda while he took care of some business. Before leaving, the somewhat shy teenager came over to her table and with impeccable manners Peter Junior said: "It was a pleasure to meet you, and I hope to see you again. Now I must leave."

Brenda was so impressed with his politeness that all she could say was "likewise". A few minutes after he left, Peter Junior's father approached the table with two plates of Veal Parmesan in his hands. He asked his friends to leave them alone. He was beaming with pride.

"The veal is so tender you can cut it with a fork. I made the sauce with the most exquisite and fresh spices you could find in today's market, and the cheese is, of course, imported from Italy."

With their meal they had two bottles of Chianti. The wine had made Peter somewhat melancholic, and he started telling Brenda the story of his life.

In his early twenties he married his childhood sweetheart. She had also been his next-door neighbor when he was growing up. As a teenager, he started working as a cleaning boy in a jewelry store. The owner was an old man that took a liking to him, and little by little taught him all about the business.

He got so good at it he would look at a piece of jewelry and could determine its weight in gold without even touching it. One of the things that amazed him was that most clients had a preference for the jewelry that was made in Italy. He saved the necessary amount of money to buy some jewelry, and for a trip to Italy.

In less than a week he had sold all the merchandise he brought back with him. With that money he returned to Italy and brought more. On this second trip he had a good idea of how much he needed to invest in order to open a shop of his own. A couple of months after his return from that second trip, he opened a small shop and started to make his own Italian style pieces.

By the time he got married he had expanded his shop into a mega discount jewelry store that was making very good money. His wife was a tall blond bombshell. She loved partying, making love, went to the gym every day, and kept her body looking fantastic. He wanted to start a family with lots of children, but she insisted on being too young to lose her figure.

After twelve years of marriage she told him that she did not want a divorce, but she did want to take a year off from their marriage to date and live the single life she had never had. His good Italian temper got the best of him and he insisted on an annulment, on the grounds that she did not want to have children.

She got herself a very good attorney, and gave him the annulment with some conditions: she kept their one-million-dollar apartment with a view of Central Park, all the jewelry he had given her, and what made him the most upset, he had to pay her ten thousand dollars per month for seven years.

It broke his heart and his pocket but he promised himself he would get a wife from the old country and build a family. His finances kept on improving very favorably, and he went back to Italy where he found a nice Italian girl from the old country and married her. The first thing they did was to have Peter Junior.

His new wife never adapted to the city and to the social life he had gotten accustomed to. She went to church every single day and had communion. Her entire life was dedicated to Peter Junior. The house was immaculately clean, and she refused to have a housekeeper, or a nanny when junior was a baby.

She never got pregnant again, and now she felt she was too old to have more children, and having sex is only to procreate, so she does not want to have sex. They have nothing in common except for Peter junior, and he feels very tense around her.

He looked over his jewelry shop as needed, but he tried not to interfere with the good work his managers were doing. He enjoyed cooking; it was like therapy for him. It was his way of relaxing. He opened the restaurant for him to cook and enjoy the company of his friends. It also gave him the excuse to avoid listening to his wife's reproaches every time any of his friends had too much to drink.

He also explained about the apartment he had above the restaurant. "I had dreamed of having a family and the only family life I have is in this restaurant. My wife is a good woman and a devout Catholic; she will never give me a divorce. My only son is devoted to her, and if I ever left her, he would never talk to me again." After a long pause, he added: "My son is my pride and joy, I would never do anything to compromise our relationship."

Listening to Peter's life story only made her wonder what Carlos was saying about the reason they had separated. He made love to her practically every single day, and she enjoyed sex, but every day was too much for her.

Could this possibly be Peter's wife problem? Or were all Latin males so hot blooded? Then she thought about Marie Terre. She was Hispanic, and she missed sex, but she had done without it for several years now.

Diana had told them she and George made love about twice a month. With all their work and social life, they barely had time for more than that. Marie Terre had admitted she and William made love about two or three times a week.

Brenda felt confused. She liked Peter, but his problems reminded her of her own life and its complications. She had not made love in such a long time; this conversation revolving around the subject increased her sexual desire.

With a smile, Peter got up from the table and brought some after-dinner drinks. He handed Brenda a lovely green Créme de Menthe on the rocks. It was this sweet and cool drink that erased their inhibitions. He started kissing her and slowly told her she should see his upstairs apartment.

He took her hands in his and walked to the apartment. As he was opening the door, he slowly started kissing her until they were both on the bed. He undressed her and they made love. She had been so lacking in this department, that as soon as he penetrated her she had an orgasm. This excited Peter, and gave him the impression she liked him a lot. It also accelerated his own orgasm.

Brenda was somewhat intoxicated, and thought that this quickie had not been bad. Peter could see the signs of satisfaction and sexual release in her face, and he wanted to make love to her again, but he had been drinking and he was no longer a young man. He knew he had to wait, so he asked her to spend the night with him.

Using her children as an excuse, very politely Brenda declined as she straightened up and got dressed. She wanted to get out of there; she was not ready to spend the night with another man. But more than anything she had a bitter taste in her mouth that felt dreadful.

It was a frightful feeling. She could not stop thinking that she was still legally married to Carlos and this made her feel like a traitor.

During the drive back to the brownstone Peter held her hand and told her how wonderful she was and how happy he felt to have met her. His words only made her try to think of how she ever found herself in this mess.

The next day Brenda sat with her two friends and without missing any details told them everything that happened the night before.

"What worried me the most is this immense feeling of disloyalty toward Carlos. Him of all people, who had three children with another woman."

Marie Terre thought about it. "It seems the disloyalty feelings are there because you are not in love with Peter. And to repeat what you said, you must see it for what it was; a quickie."

Diana was more pragmatic. "The feelings of disloyalty could be towards the marriage vows and the legal implications they entailed or represent."

"Both explanations are feasible, but I am the one who needs to figure out how I feel and why. I just can't make myself ask Carlos for a divorce. He has told me in the Dominican Republic you can get a divorce in 24 hours, but he did not want to get a divorce.

As usual, I think he exaggerated as far as the amount of time it takes. But he did seem sincere when he said he wanted me to get over the shock of his indiscretion with Carmen. He kept on repeating I am his legal wife, and how he wanted to grow old with me at his side. I kept changing the subject and never replied one way or the other.

I admit that I do not want to be near him, but a divorce represents failure and I am looking for a way to end this situation as a winner. However, if I were to do the same thing he did it would only make me as big a traitor as he is. Then I also have to look out for our daughters. He adores Teresa, but he is distant and totally indifferent towards Mary. I still can't determine what I am going to do about this situation."

Both of her friends embraced her and told her she had all the time in the world to determine what she wanted.

Practically every day before leaving New York, Peter called Brenda to invite her out. Very politely, she declined. He was a nice man, but dating him did not feel right.

23 RESILIENCE

For several years now Marie Terre's family had been pressuring her and Brenda to remarry. They both felt that having a career and children was more than sufficient to live a fulfilling life, but the family would not let the pressure down until they started at least dating men.

To please the family, both ladies dressed up and went to a nice piano bar for cocktails. They were still on their first drink when a man walked over to their table and invited them for a drink. Brenda looked a Marie Terre.

"Do you want another drink?"

"If we accept a drink from him, do we have to ask him to sit at the table with us?"

"I don't think that is actually necessary."

The debate about accepting or not a drink took so much time that the man got fed up with them, said "forget it," and left.

The ladies started laughing; later on it became like their personal joke. Every time something silly happed they would say: "forget it," and then laughed. Meeting men had become like a burden, something they did not want to deal with.

At work Brenda had been promoted to executive vice president of marketing. She talked about it with Marie Terre.

"The job entails lots of hardworking hours. It is very lonely at the top; many of the other employees envy my position, making my work environment a treacherous one. I have to juggle different tasks in order to spend some quality time with my two daughters, which are my biggest priority.

However, this job makes me feel accomplished, specially when I sit at a round table with other top managers with the power to take major steps and decisions."

At the university, Marie Terre had reached a full-professor's position. "I cannot say I understand how all that corporate power feels, but I can relate to the hard working part. My professorship means preparing for classes, going to staff meetings, extracurricular activities such as writing articles for the university paper and the local newspaper, as well as searching for places where local artists could show their art exhibits. But what I enjoy the most is going to the art exhibits and discovering the young and upcoming artists whose work I appreciate and admire."

Included in her schedule was driving the boys to their own activities as well as Teresa and Mary. Getting married was not in her agenda. She knew she had already married the great love of her life, and no one in the world would compare to her beloved William. She did not even want to try finding someone else. She would remember him until the day she died.

John, Marie Terrie's oldest child, and Diana's twins were ready to go to college. Diana and George sent all the children and mother's airline tickets for a big celebration party at their brownstone in Manhattan. The students had been accepted at a university in England and that was something to celebrate.

Without anyone's knowledge except George, Philip, Marie Terre's youngest son, had taken extra credits and had completed his High School and his college prep in less time than expected. He had applied and been accepted at the same University with his brother and friends. He had worked this out in total secrecy as a big surprise for his mother.

Just before sitting at the dining room table George uncorked a bottle of champagne, calling for everyone's attention.

"We are gathered here today to celebrate the beginning of a new challenge for the young adults in our lives; our children." The teenagers interrupted George's speech with screams and all kinds of silly noises.

"OK. I won't make a speech, but Philip and I have a big surprise for you all; he will be living, rooming and studying with all of you."

This came as a complete shock to Marie Terre; she had mixed feelings about letting John leave. She figured that at the age of 18 a person is still not sufficiently mature to be on his own. Philip was her baby, and he was the one closest to her. He had that special innate ability to look at her and provide love and comfort when she needed it the most.

When John had turned 16 years old she gave him a car. She no longer had to drive them back and forth to their different activities and teenage parties, and this left her feeling a big hole in the pit of her stomach. However, she still had to cook for them, and the family dinners at the table were something that she looked forward to every single day.

The fact that Philip was also going to college was not by any means a pleasant surprise for her. Very much the contrary, she felt ill and almost fainted. She turned pale when Philip hugged and kissed her and begged her to be happy for him and his accomplishment. She decided to be strong for her children, even though she felt as if a dagger had pierced her heart.

When the teenagers were all dancing, very solemnly Brenda told her friends that it was eminent for her to sell her share of the flat in the UK. She was very embarrassed.

"You want us to sell the London flat? But it is the absolute worst time to sell!"

Diana was fuming.

Brenda explained how Teresa's antics had gotten her in such a bind, so worried about her promiscuity and manipulative schemes that she wanted to send her to a finishing school in London. George went off to talk to his comptroller to see if he could help her out, after suggesting they take the discussion inside closed doors.

The three friends looked at each other, and slowly made their way into the house as Diana had promised.

After a long silence, they all looked at each other again, and all of the sudden just embraced in a heartfelt, tight three-sided hug. It was totally unexpected, but then again, so right for them.

Diana reassured Brenda. "We will figure it out. Let's leave it in destiny's hands. If the flat sells quickly, we will know it was meant to be. But even if it doesn't, we will make sure Teresa gets the direction she needs to stop making a fool of herself."

Marie Terre decided to change the mood. "Listen to her! I know I will! Once again I will take Diana's advice and look towards the future. The University has offered me a sabbatical in Spain or France for me to complete my PhD. Now that Philip is also going to the UK, I will be looking into it. This way I could visit with them on long weekends. And there is this history professor that is also going to do a sabbatical in Spain. He is a good friend, intelligent, a widower, and somewhat good looking."

It sounded so good that it lifted all three friends' spirit; they congratulated her for her determination on doing something for herself. Diana was specially relieved.

"You must tell us more about this widower." And then, in a more somber note: "Marie Terre, you were lucky not to follow my advice when you met William."

Marie Terre could not agree more. "So I count my blessings for my past, which you are all part of, for my present, and for my future, because it's looking pretty good!"

Brenda's mood was somewhat better. "Let's take advantage of the fact that we are young women in the prime of our life. Let's join the kids, enjoy the party, and toast for new beginnings."

The three of them hugged one final time and joined the others. All six teens and George were dancing. The ladies joined them, trying to imitate their moves.

Diana's children danced and shared with her friends, and not with her. She knew she would have to work very hard to get to know her children and have them accept her. She hoped some day they would open up to her, but tonight she would enjoy herself watching how her children enjoyed themselves with her own friends.

Brenda knew her daughters were caring people that needed to be lead in the proper direction. She just knew she had to find the correct place to help her oldest daughter. She always thought being beautiful was the answer for a happy and successful life. How blinded she had been. She put herself through so many vain efforts because of this misconception. Carlos and she had not been the best example for her daughter to follow.

Now Brenda wished for her daughters to have moral values, and a true code of ethics. She knew Teresa was a kind person, but she was doing things that were just wrong.

So with the support of her friends, she started the difficult and painful process of finding the place where her daughter would hopefully thrive, away from her.

Marie Terre was proud of her friend. She thought Brenda was finally taking charge of her own life and that of her daughters. She could see how Diana was mellowing about the sale of the flat.

Diana felt the sale of the flat, while not something she looked forward to, would be a new beginning for their friendship. The flat brought them together. Life kept them close to each other. Their lives had become so intertwined that flat or no flat, they would never be apart.

They promised each other their friendship would always provide comfort and support. They would always give each other the courage needed, and be friends forever. They promised to look to the future, not only for their children, but also for themselves. Together, they were invincible.

Together, they were resilient.

ABOUT THE AUTHOR

Ingrid Borges knows first hand what it means to follow your dreams, change your life, travel the world as a successful career women, and start all over again.

An Organizational Developer and Trainer, Ms. Borges started her career in Texas, later moving back home to Puerto Rico.

After living the College professor's life at the Inter American University, she tried her hand at entrepreneurship founding Borges & Fitzpatrick, a management training firm.

She moved to Spain enticed by an offer from Citibank, where she became their Training Manager. She delved into Organizational Development with the startup of a branch of ICI, a British company, which led her to move back to Puerto Rico. She later became Training Manager for all Latin America and the Caribbean for AVIS Rent a Car.

Ms. Borges has one son and two gorgeous grandkids, and currently lives in San Juan, Puerto Rico with Scooby, her beautiful cocker spaniel.